I0674460

THEN, NOW, AND ALWAYS

AN OTTER BLUFF ROMANCE

LINDA SEED

This is a work of fiction. Any characters, organizations, places, or events portrayed in this novel are either products of the author's imagination or are used fictitiously.

THEN, NOW, AND ALWAYS
Copyright © 2021 by Linda Seed

All rights reserved. No part of this book may be reproduced in any form or by any means without the prior written consent of the author, excepting brief quotes used in reviews.

ISBN: 978-1-7343453-8-4

The author is available for book signings, book club discussions, conferences, and other appearances.
Linda Seed may be contacted via e-mail at linda@lindaseed.com or on Facebook at www.facebook.com/LindaSeedAuthor. Learn more about Linda Seed's novels at www.lindaseed.com.

❀ Created with Vellum

BY LINDA SEED

Otter Bluff
The Icing on the Cake
Christmas in Cambria
Love and Joy
Then, Now, and Always

SIGN UP TO GET A FREE LINDA SEED STARTER LIBRARY

Sign up for Linda's twice-monthly newsletter and get her free ebook starter library: three full-length romances and a bonus short story available only to newsletter subscribers. Your information will never be shared or sold, and you can unsubscribe at any time.

To subscribe and get your free ebooks, go to the following address:
https://claims.prolificworks.com/free/hDF1LvnI

CHAPTER 1

*E*van Bridges looked around his new home and reminded himself to think about the future rather than the past.

The future: small-town living, a cozy beach house, a slower pace. The past: well, that didn't bear thinking about, not when the wounds were still so fresh.

He sighed, scrubbed at his stubbled face with his hands, and poured a cup of coffee from the pot on the countertop. He carried the mug onto the back patio, settled into an Adirondack chair, and looked out at the morning sunlight on the ocean, the waves crashing into the bluffs below.

Only an asshole could find himself in a place like this and be bitter about it.

In fairness, though, Evan had never claimed he wasn't an asshole.

When his PR firm had failed, it had felt like he'd been dropped out of an airplane without a parachute. He'd had a soft place to land, but that didn't mean the fall wasn't scary as hell.

He pulled his cell phone out of his pocket and texted Nix.

The place looks great. Thanks again.

Nix had been the one to renovate Otter Bluff after Evan had bought it as an investment property. He'd done a good job, and now that Evan was living here full time, he was glad he'd put the money into the project.

I was thinking of tourists when I redid the place, Nix responded. *If I'd known it would be for you, I'd have changed a few things.*

Hell, no one had foreseen the chain of events that had led to Evan living in Cambria again, in this house, under these circumstances.

If I'd known my partner was going to go down for insider trading, I'd have changed a few things, too, he responded.

Evan had grown up in Cambria. The day he'd left, he'd congratulated himself on casting off the rural lifestyle in favor of something more sophisticated and worldly.

Now here he was, a full-time Cambria resident again, about to close escrow on a small local business to take the place of the large national one his partner had shattered.

He was trying to look at all of it as a fun new adventure. God, he was trying.

Someday he might actually see it that way, but that day was not today.

CANDACE WEAVER NEEDED A NEW JOB, and she needed it sooner rather than later if she was going to stay sane.

The restaurant on Main Street where she'd worked as assistant manager had closed three months ago, victim of a first-time owner who'd thought good food was enough.

It wasn't.

Since then, Candace had been looking tirelessly for a new position, but she hadn't found one—mostly because she didn't want to leave Cambria.

As her savings account had dwindled, she'd moved back in with her parents to save money.

That, of course, was where the sanity part came in.

"You know, honey, this might be a good time to go back to school," her mother said, as though she hadn't already suggested the same thing at least a dozen times since Candace had moved in.

"I don't want to go back to school, Mom. I'm thirty-two. That ship has sailed."

Melissa was making a big breakfast of eggs, bacon, and toast, as was her habit every morning, regardless of the day of the week. She put a plate laden with salt and cholesterol in front of Candace.

"I don't see what your age has to do with it," she said, scowling.

"My age has to do with the fact that I don't want to start over. I want to build on what I already know, what I've already done." She softened her expression. "Thanks for the breakfast, Mom."

"Oh, that." Melissa waved off her daughter's gratitude. "It's just what I do." Melissa, clad in a KISS THE COOK apron, her feet bare on the hardwood floor, loaded up another plate with food and put it at Candace's father's place, which was currently vacant.

"Ed! Breakfast!" Melissa bellowed.

A moment later Candace's father walked in wearing his usual khaki pants and V-neck sweater, holding a newspaper. Ed and Melissa Weaver had to be the only people left in the country who still got an actual newspaper delivered to their driveway every morning.

Melissa paused with her hand on her hip, holding her spatula in the other hand. "I'm not saying you haven't accomplished a lot, honey." She pointed the spatula for emphasis. "I'm just saying I think you could do so much more."

Candace's father picked up a piece of bacon, munched on it, and opened the paper.

"Mom." Candace put down her fork. "Most parents would be thrilled that their daughter wants to stay in her hometown. If I went back to school—which I'm not going to do—it would mean moving away! Is that what you want?"

"Well, of course not." Melissa slid into the chair across from Candace and folded her arms on the table, the spatula set aside. "It's just, I always wonder what would have happened if I'd gone to graduate school the way I'd planned. That's all. I don't want you to get to be my age and wonder."

"If you'd gone to graduate school, you wouldn't have met me. You'd be married to some mogul right now," Ed said without looking up from his paper.

"I would, wouldn't I?" Melissa said it as though that were an appealing prospect, but at the same time, she cast an affectionate look toward her husband. She got up, planted a kiss on the top of his head, and went back to the stove to put together her own meal.

"And you wouldn't have me," Candace put in. "Or, you might have kids, but they'd be your kids with the mogul, so it wouldn't be me. They'd be mogul kids."

"Well."

"And anyway," Candace went on, "you could do it now. You could go to grad school. What's stopping you?"

Melissa let out a guffaw. "Talk about the ship sailing. I think mine's probably sunk."

THE PLAN for Evan to buy Jitters, a coffeehouse on Main Street in Cambria, hadn't come out of nowhere. He'd had his eye on the place since long before Greg had bought the stock that had ended both his and Evan's careers.

Then, Evan had thought he might buy the place as a side investment—something he could use to build his wealth. Now, he needed it for something more important: he needed it to give him a reason to get out of bed every morning.

Evan had money—that wasn't the problem. He could retire now and spend the rest of his life lying around watching Netflix. But who wanted to live like that?

He couldn't face himself if he didn't have some sort of job. A goal. A purpose.

So when his firm had collapsed, he'd approached the couple who owned Jitters and made them an offer. They'd been planning to retire in the next five years; he'd simply persuaded them to move up that timeline.

Now, standing inside the coffeehouse after closing hours on a Thursday evening, he looked around at the café tables, the worn leather sofa, the hardwood floors, the exposed brick walls.

This place had been a restaurant when Evan was in high school—he'd come here for burgers and fries with his friends. It had been Jitters for the past fifteen years, and God willing, it would remain so for many years to come.

"I hope you'll consider keeping at least some of the baristas." Mrs. Hubbard, who would continue to own the place with her husband until escrow closed, wrung her hands and looked at him with concern. "They're good kids, and David just signed a lease on a new apartment. I don't know what he'll do if he's out of a job right now."

Evan rubbed at the stubble on his chin. "Well, the place will be closed for a bit after we change hands so I can regroup. But I don't see why I can't rehire everyone."

"Well, maybe not everyone." She grimaced theatrically. "We were about to let Curtis go. Chronically late."

"Noted."

Evan wanted to change a few things when he took over. He wanted to update the decor, create more of a funky urban feel. Maybe change some of the menu items. He'd need a little time to figure that out. But for the most part, he wanted Jitters to remain Jitters, including the employees its customers were used to seeing when they ordered their morning lattes.

Minus Curtis, of course.

Mrs. Hubbard had been kind enough to invite Evan over so she could discuss the details of how she and her husband ran the place. But now, seeing her in the shop that had been her life for fifteen years, Evan started to feel a little guilty for wresting it away from her.

"Are you sure you're okay with this?" he asked. "I mean, you love the place. I might have been a little pushy, so …"

She laughed, a merry guffaw that transformed her face and made her look ten years younger. "Oh, don't you worry about that. I've been trying to get Hugh to take a vacation for years. Now he won't have an excuse not to. We've already booked a flight to Venice."

MR. AND MRS. HUBBARD had run Jitters themselves, which meant Evan didn't have the option of keeping the previous manager. There wasn't one.

Of course he wanted to be involved in the day-to-day operation of the business, but he didn't want to be so involved that he couldn't enjoy his new, slower-paced lifestyle.

That meant he needed to hire someone to do the heavy lifting.

When he got back to Otter Bluff that evening, he sat at the kitchen table with his laptop and wrote an ad to post on Craigslist.

Main Street coffeehouse needs full-time manager. Must have experience in food service. Salary to be negotiated based on qualifications. Includes benefits.

He posted the ad and hoped he'd get somebody who knew what the hell they were doing. Evan had never run a coffeehouse before, and this thing would go better if somebody involved was competent.

CANDACE SAW the posting that night after dinner as she did her regular, obsessive scroll of the employment ads.

Food service experience? Check.

Full-time? Check.

Benefits? That sounded too good to be true. They probably meant free coffee.

Still, it was worth looking into. She responded to the ad and attached her resume, which she'd updated and polished after she'd lost her job at the restaurant.

"Did you find something, honey?" Candace's mother was looking over her shoulder as Candace worked at the kitchen table.

"Maybe. There's an ad for a coffeehouse manager."

"In Cambria? Which one?"

"Doesn't say."

Melissa's face compressed, the wrinkles next to her mouth deepening as she considered it. "I heard the Hubbards were selling Jitters. Maybe the new owner is assembling his team."

Candace felt a spark of hope. She loved Jitters. She'd been going there since it had opened when she was in high school.

"Do you know who bought it?" she asked her mother.

"I heard it's that Evan Bridges—he's back in town. Do you remember him, Candace?"

Candace's jaw fell and she gaped at her mother before regaining her composure. "I … yes. I remember him."

"Well, of course you do. I don't know why I asked. You go to school with someone in Cambria, there's no way you can fail to notice them."

Melissa was right about that. Candace's entire class had amounted to about thirty kids—and Evan Bridges had been one of them. She'd met him in kindergarten, and they'd gone to school together all the way through to high school graduation.

"I remember him very well," she said.

"Well, if he's the one who posted the ad, that'll give you an advantage, I'll bet," Melissa said. "It's going to be a lot less nerve-racking being interviewed by a friend."

The problem was, Evan had never been Candace's friend.

He'd been the guy she'd loved since the moment she knew what love was. He was the guy she'd longed for in her tender teenage fantasies.

He was also the guy who'd never, even once, taken a second look at her.

CHAPTER 2

andace Weaver?

Evan sat up straighter in his chair the next morning as he looked at his laptop and the response he'd received to his job ad. Was this the same Candace Weaver he'd known in school?

On the one hand, it wasn't an especially uncommon name. On the other, this was a small town, and it seemed unlikely there could be more than one of them here.

He scanned the resume and saw that she'd gone to Coast Union High School.

Yep. Same one, then.

The name sparked a flurry of memories and impressions: Candace in the third grade, in a high ponytail and clothes her mother had made for her. Evan's name second in roll call, after Tracy Avery, Candace's second to last, just before Bruce Young.

Then, Candace during senior year, too thin, with a sprinkle of pimples across her cheeks. Not the prettiest girl, not the least pretty. Not the most popular girl, but not the least, either. Candace, on the sidelines while Evan had been front and center.

She'd been smart, he remembered that. He scanned her resume

8

and saw that she'd been doing restaurant work—first as a waitress, then, later, in management.

The fact that she was a local was a plus. She knew everyone and was an established part of the community. When longtime Cambrians came into Jitters, they'd appreciate seeing a familiar face.

He checked the time, saw that it was after nine a.m.—usually an okay time to call someone. Evan was still on his first cup of coffee, sitting at the dining room table checking his emails, but he'd slept in. Most people would be up and around by now.

He found the phone number on her resume and called it.

CANDACE WAS IN HER PARENTS' kitchen baking a batch of muffins when her phone rang. She'd taken up baking in the time she'd been unemployed, and the results had been mostly positive. Her mother protested about the calories, but she always ate what Candace baked.

Candace poured chocolate chips into the batter, wiped her hands on a dish towel, and answered the phone.

An unidentified number with a San Francisco area code. Probably a spam call.

But it wasn't an automated voice—it was an actual human being. "Uh ... hi. Is this Candace?"

"Yes, it is. How can I help you?"

"Candace, this is Evan Bridges calling about your job application. I wondered if you could come in for an interview."

After that, her mind blanked out for a bit.

Her inner monologue was chaotic and manic, like a bird trapped inside a building, its wings beating madly at the walls and roof.

Evan Bridges. Evan Bridges. Oh my God. It really is him. And I'm talking to him. Or, I'm not talking. I'm listening. But I'm supposed to talk. I'm supposed to be talking right now! Oh, shit. I'm an imbecile. I'm ... Oh, jeez. He sounds the same. That voice. Oh, God, that voice.

"Candace? Are you there? Did I lose you?"

"Ah ... I'm here. I'm ... It's been a long time!"

"Yeah, it has. Anyway. An interview? I'd love it if you could come in."

Candace pulled herself together long enough to set up the interview. Jitters, two o'clock that afternoon. He hadn't taken over the place yet, but he wanted to hit the ground running when he did.

"I'm looking forward to it," he told her.

Evan Bridges is looking forward to seeing me.

Long after he'd hung up, she held the phone to her ear, frozen and shocked, her fingers and toes tingling.

"Evan Bridges? Sure, I remember him. I mean, you guys were a year ahead of me, but … yeah. Wasn't he on the football team?"

Candace was taking a power walk at Fiscalini Ranch with her best friend, the two of them talking while they walked. Brittany's dark ponytail bounced as they sped along the bluff trail, arms pumping, a light sheen of sweat on her skin.

"Yes, he was on the football team. Offensive lineman. They called him The Brick. Because that's what it felt like when he hit you. Like you'd been slammed in the face with a brick."

"Wait. Didn't you have a thing for him?" Brittany shot Candace a look.

"Yes! Yes, I had a thing for him. I *have* a thing. The thing never went away, as much as I wanted it to."

Their sneakers crunched on the path. To their right, tall green grass carpeted the hills. To their left, the Pacific Ocean beat relentlessly against the rocky coastline.

"I seem to remember he was kind of hot," Brittany said.

"Oh, yes. He sure was." Candace came to a stop, caught her breath, then went to sit on a driftwood bench facing the ocean. "Honestly? I don't know if I can do this. I'm going to go in there, and he's going to be so … so *Evan*, and I'm going to forget how to form words. Just the way I always did when I tried to talk to him in high school. And it's going to be horrifying, and I won't even get the job."

"You're like an ad for the power of positive thinking." Brittany detached the water bottle from a strap at her waist and took a long drink. They sat side by side, looking out at the vast ocean.

"Maybe he's not hot anymore," Brittany offered.

"God. That would be great. Then I could let go of my whole Evan obsession finally, after all these years."

"I didn't even know you still had an Evan obsession."

"That's because I've been trying to let it go. Hell, I've been trying to let it go since I was twelve, for all the good it did me."

Even though Candace and Brittany had gone to school together, they hadn't gotten to know each other until Candace came back to Cambria after college. If they'd been friends in high school, Brittany would have known how intense the Evan obsession had been. After all, his name had been written all over Candace's folders, on endless sheets of notebook paper, and, for one memorable week, on her arm, which she'd hidden under a long-sleeved sweatshirt. Then there'd been the bad teenage poetry. Candace shuddered to think of it.

"Okay." Brittany nodded encouragingly. "I'm sure he's not hot anymore. Most guys who are hot in high school lose the hotness by the time they're thirty. You can see him and get over him, and get a much-needed job on top of that."

"Right." Candace wiped the sweat off her face with a hand towel she'd tucked into her waist pack. "Right. This is going to be good."

She didn't believe it, but maybe if she kept telling it to herself she'd at least be able to get through the interview.

THINKING about Candace Weaver made Evan think about high school, and he was still thinking about it as he hit the heavy bag at his gym in San Luis Obispo.

Gyms that offered boxing were hard to come by on the Central Coast, so Evan had to drive forty minutes from Otter Bluff to this one. He considered the inconvenience well worth it. He liked to hit things—and sometimes people—and boxing was a socially acceptable means of doing it. Without this, he doubted he would actually get into a bar fight or anything quite so low-class, but his stress would increase, and along with it, his general antipathy toward his fellow human beings.

Nobody wanted that, so here he was, pounding the bag with a series of combinations—jab-jab-cross, jab-cross–left hook, right cross–left hook–right cross—until his muscles were warm and loose and his body was covered in a glow of perspiration.

The thing about how he liked to hit people—that was how he'd gotten into football. Something in his primal, caveman brain found immense satisfaction in slamming into another male with the force of a freight train and putting him on the ground.

Football. High school. Candace.

His thoughts bounced around as he worked his muscles, modulated his breathing, paid attention to his feet.

He'd gone out with a lot of girls in high school, but he hadn't gone out with Candace. In retrospect, he could admit that his shallow boy-mind had gravitated toward the cheerleaders, the prom queens, the hot girls. Candace had been none of those. She'd been awkward, unsure of herself. Smart but nondescript. His simplified teenage classification system for the people he met hadn't even put her down in the category of *girl*. If his life had been a play, she'd have been a background character, Third Student From the Left, not even significant enough to have a named part.

That said more about him than it did about her, he was certain.

Still, the idea of hiring her—he'd have to think about it. The Candace he'd known had been smart but lacking in confidence, kind but unable to be assertive even when the situation direly called for it.

Probably not the right person for the job, then.

She had the experience, though, and so far, no one else had applied.

He finished up his workout with the jump rope and some time on the speed bag, then hit the showers. He felt loose and good, and at peace in a way he only did after a workout.

He'd missed it while he'd been in transition, and he also missed working.

Owning Jitters was going to be a significant change from running a PR firm. A significant step down.

Oddly, he was starting to look forward to it.

CHAPTER 3

*C*andace had just about convinced herself that Evan wouldn't be hot anymore. Sure, she'd Googled him, and there had been pictures, and he'd been hot in the pictures.

So hot.

But pictures didn't tell the whole story. In pictures, you made an effort to look your best. It was all a facade. In real life, surely, he'd be a disappointment.

She was counting on it.

But when she walked into Jitters that afternoon, scanned the room, and saw him sitting at a café table waiting for her, she knew she'd been horribly wrong.

If she'd thought the Evan Bridges of today would pale in comparison to the one she'd grown up with, her folly was both glaring and alarming.

He looked even better than she remembered, if such a thing was possible.

"Evan?" She approached his table, trying to keep her voice from wobbling.

He looked up from his laptop, stood up to greet her, and smiled.

And just like that, her palms started to sweat and her knees went weak.

"Candace. Hi. Thanks for coming in." He extended his hand to shake, and she took it, swallowing hard and hoping her palm sweat wouldn't be obvious.

He was just as tall and broad as he'd ever been, just as physically imposing, but the extra years had added an element of maturity and character to his face that only made him more attractive. It was so damned unfair that men got better looking as they aged while women just became ... well ... older.

Somehow, he looked more like himself now, as though he hadn't been completed yet when she'd known him, and now all of the extra pieces were in place.

"Thank you ... um ... for seeing me."

Damn it, Candace, get your shit together.

He motioned toward the chair across from him, and they both sat down.

"Can I get you a coffee?" he asked.

She accepted, both to indicate her love of coffee—certainly a plus in this business—and because having a drink in front of her would give her something to do with her hands.

When her beverage arrived, they began the interview. They discussed his plans for the business, her experience, what he was looking for in a manager, and what he considered to be his own weaknesses as he moved from one type of business to another that was so completely different.

Candace started off shaky—muttering a lot of *umms* and *uhs*—but gained confidence as she went on. She actually managed to sound composed and competent as she told him about her work at the restaurant and what had led to her departure.

"Most restaurants close in the first couple of years," she told him, maybe as an apology, considering that she'd failed to save her former employer. "It's about more than just the food, but ..."

"But the owners wouldn't listen to you, and you're trying not to trash-talk them right now because it would be bad form," he finished for her.

Yes. Exactly that. She stayed silent because she still didn't want to trash-talk her former employers, even if they deserved it and even if he was giving her permission.

Then they got around to the topic of salary. He told her what he had in mind.

"Oh."

"What does *oh* mean?" he asked.

"It means … It's just … It's very expensive to live in Cambria, as I'm sure you know. I'm not saying that what you're offering isn't competitive for the market. It is. But it's still not enough for me to live here in town, and I'd hate to have to get a place in Morro Bay and commute if I can avoid it."

I'd hate to have to keep living with my parents, too. She didn't mention that part.

"Ah. Right. Well, that's where the benefits come in."

"A health care package would be wonderful, but it still—"

"Not just a health care package," he said. "I mean, yes, I'm offering that. But I'm also offering you a low-cost apartment."

That was so surprising she simply gaped at him for a moment before she composed herself. "Really?"

"My purchase of the business includes the apartment upstairs. I don't need it, because I've already got a place. I can give it to you at a reduced rate to keep your living expenses down."

"What kind of reduced rate are we talking about?"

He told her.

"You want to go up and take a look? It's vacant right now, and Mrs. Hubbard said I could let you see it."

"I DON'T WANT this job. I *do not* want this job. I absolutely … no. I don't want the job."

Brittany gave Candace a skeptical side-eye. "So what you're saying is, you don't want the job."

They were hanging out at Brittany's place, lounging on the sofa with a pizza box and a bottle of wine open on the coffee table. Brittany, clad in fuzzy slippers, had her feet up after a long day cutting hair at a salon a block up from Main Street. In a while they'd be starting their girls' movie night, but right now, they were sorting out Candace's employment prospects.

"I don't," Candace said. "I really don't."

"Well, if you don't want it, I do." Brittany pulled a slice of pepperoni pizza out of the box and slid it onto her plate. "Health benefits *and* a cheap apartment? Do you know how rare that is? Here in Cambria, it's practically unheard of. I mean, I like cutting hair, but it's not my passion. I can learn to make lattes."

"Yes, okay. But—"

"And was the apartment nice?"

One bedroom, a small but tidy kitchen, hardwood floors, high ceilings. And a fireplace. A fireplace!

"Yes. It was very nice. But—"

"Do you have any idea how much I pay for this place? And it's only a studio!" Brittany went on.

"Living above the shop probably means I'll be expected to put in ridiculous hours," Candace said.

"Or it could mean you'll have time for a life outside of work because your commute will consist of one flight of stairs."

"But—"

"Candace. You're shooting yourself in the foot for no reason. This is a good job."

"I know. But it's Evan Bridges!"

"Candace, I think we've established that."

How could she make her friend understand? Candace couldn't work with him every day. Couldn't look at him every day. Couldn't feel what she'd always felt for him day after day for months or years on end. She was stupid in his presence, and she didn't want to be stupid. She couldn't think around him, and sometimes a person just needed to think.

"I just … Okay. Imagine you're on a diet. Not because you want to lose weight, but because … because you're diabetic. It's beyond your control. Would you want to take a job at a candy store? I mean, really. Would you?"

Brittany took a bite of her pizza and considered that. Then she pointed the pizza slice at Candace. "You're not diabetic. And he's not candy. Which is to say, if you ended up eating the candy, it wouldn't be the end of the world. It might even be pretty damned tasty."

The problem was, she'd never been offered a bite of that candy in high school, so what made her think she could eat it now? More likely, she'd have to watch while a stream of other women came into the shop and … ate the candy. Just like in high school. She was still scarred by that, and she couldn't bear to go through it again.

"It's not my candy," she said. "It's other people's candy."

"It could be your candy," Brittany said.

EVAN HADN'T OFFERED Candace the job, but more and more, he was thinking he would.

She had the experience he was looking for, and she'd come off in the interview as bright and competent—after a weird initial period of painful awkwardness.

The awkwardness jibed with what he remembered about her, but the more they'd talked, the more it had dissolved and she'd morphed into a more self-assured, more mature version of that girl he'd known.

Besides, the other two applicants he'd talked to had been crap, so there was that.

"Do you remember Candace Weaver?" he asked Nix one morning as they were eating pancakes at the Redwood Cafe. "From school?"

"Sure I do. She sat behind me in AP English. Why?"

Evan stirred some cream into his coffee and added a packet of sugar. "She applied to be the manager of Jitters."

Nix, his long hair up in a man bun and his chin darkened with stubble, let out a guffaw.

"What?" Evan asked.

"Oh, just the fact that she was in love with you. That'll be awkward as your fingers brush over the coffee mugs."

Evan squinted at him. "What are you talking about?"

"Don't tell me you didn't know that."

"Dude. I have absolutely no idea what you're saying to me right now."

Nix pointed his fork—already loaded up with pancake—at his friend. "Candace Weaver was so in love with you all through school that she practically had cartoon hearts where her eyes should be every time she looked at you. You seriously had no idea?"

Evan gaped at him. "You're full of shit."

"I'm not. Everybody knew it. Everybody but you. You were too busy screwing Janie McMaster and Carrie Lawson, and God knows who else."

Could that be true? The part about Janie and Carrie was true, but the rest? Had Candace really been mooning over him all that time?

"Was I ever ... I mean ... I wasn't a dick to her, was I?" Thinking back on his teenage self, it was entirely possible.

"No, man. You were never mean to her or anything. You just didn't see her."

"I saw her."

"Nah." Nix shook his head mournfully. "The Candaces of the world were just sort of invisible to you. They were background scenery. Like wallpaper."

Evan felt a flush of shame at the truth of it. He didn't think he could be held fully responsible for whatever assholery he'd done when his brain hadn't been fully formed yet, but he still wished that what Nix had said didn't feel so ... accurate.

He ate a bite of pancake, then took a sip of his coffee, thinking about the unfeeling kid he'd been.

"She's gotten prettier since high school," he said after a while.

"I know. She comes into the market during my shift sometimes. I see her around."

Where Candace had been too thin in high school, now she was pleasingly filled out, with hips and breasts and other things he shouldn't have noticed during a job interview. Where her skin had been marred with acne, it was now smooth and clear. Where her hair had been a nondescript shade of medium brown, now it was glossy and sparkling with streaks of blond.

She was probably good girlfriend material for someone—someone other than him.

"So, are you going to go there?" Nix asked.

"With the job, maybe. Probably. But personally? Hell, no. I'm with Anna."

Anna was a woman he'd met in the Bay Area when his partner had been dating her. When Greg had gone to prison, Anna had been devastated—but not so devastated that she hadn't jumped into Evan's bed within the week.

"You going to keep that up long-distance?" Nix asked.

"Sure. Why not?"

Nix shrugged. "No reason."

"You don't like her." It wasn't a question.

Again, the shrug. "I just think she's your usual type, for what it's worth. You might want to consider changing things up if you want different results."

A COUPLE of days after the interview, Candace was puttering around in her mother's kitchen, baking a batch of oatmeal cookies and trying not to wait by the phone for a call from Evan Bridges.

Her mother could tell she was preoccupied, though, and she poked at it while Candace worked.

"Is there something on your mind, honey?" Melissa, who was sitting at the kitchen table with her laptop, scrolling Facebook and answering emails, eyed her daughter.

"Just … you know. Cookies." She gestured toward her dough.

"*Mmm.*" Melissa pretended to be focusing on Facebook. A moment later, she tried again. "How's the job hunt coming?"

"Pretty good. I interviewed for that coffeehouse job. You were right, it's Jitters. And it went well, I think."

"That's good, then."

"Yeah. I guess. Except … that was a couple of days ago, and I haven't heard anything yet."

"Oh, well." Melissa waved a hand to dismiss her daughter's concern. "That doesn't mean anything. I'm sure they wanted to interview a few people before making a decision. It's standard procedure."

Candace supposed it was. But it wasn't standard procedure to work for someone you'd nursed a painful, all-consuming crush on since before you'd hit puberty.

"I'm not sure I want it." She stirred her dough. "I mean, I want it, but … maybe I don't. You know?"

Melissa closed her laptop and folded her forearms on the table. "No, honey. I can't say that I do."

Candace had never told her mother about the all-consuming crush on Evan Bridges, and she wasn't sure she wanted to get into it now. Instead, she said, "I just want to choose my next move carefully, that's all."

"Sensible," Melissa said.

Candace formed balls of dough, placed them on a baking sheet, then slid the pan into the oven.

"They're offering a health plan," she said. "And a low-cost apartment above the shop."

"Oh, well. You should consider it for the health plan alone."

Candace knew her mother was right. She should take the job if it was offered to her. She just hoped she hadn't made such a fool of herself during the first part of the interview that Evan wouldn't call.

◞

Nix's revelation about Candace Weaver made Evan hesitate to call her to offer her the job.

For one thing, he felt like a dick for ignoring her all through high school when, according to Nix, she'd had feelings for him the entire time. For another, if she still had feelings, that might make things awkward.

But why would she still have feelings? High school had been a long time ago. Surely she'd moved on.

He told himself he was being stupid and called to offer her the job.

She was the best of the candidates he'd interviewed. Wasn't that all that mattered?

CHAPTER 4

*C*andace told herself that while she was still attracted to Evan, those feelings would fade the more time she spent with him, the more she saw him as a real, flawed person rather than an impossible ideal.

By the time the coffeehouse changed hands and she'd both started work and moved into the apartment above the shop, she knew she'd been kidding herself.

Thank God he didn't spend all day at the shop, or she'd never have been able to focus enough to get anything done.

And there was a lot to do.

In the first days after Evan had taken possession of the property, he and Candace had worked together to choose new furniture, update the menu, spruce up the interior design, and negotiate employment with all of the former baristas—except Curtis.

Then they'd reopened, to the generally positive response of the community.

Candace had moved her furniture and other belongings out of her parents' garage and into the apartment, and she'd hung pictures, laid down area rugs, and bought new bath linens and bedding to make the place feel like home.

Candace went home every day after work feeling exhausted but satisfied with what she'd accomplished. It was probably unusual for a business owner to rely on his manager to shape the place as much as Evan was relying on Candace, and that made her feel useful and valued.

Everything would have been perfect if it weren't for the fact that at the end of every workday, when she said goodbye to Evan, it felt as though all of the air, all of the essential energy that made her feel like herself, went out the door with him.

"So? Can you make a perfect latte yet?" Brittany asked her when the two of them were on their way to San Luis Obispo to go to a sushi restaurant Brittany liked. It was a Friday evening—the end of a long, hard work week—and they'd decided to treat themselves.

"You bet your ass I can. The Hubbards were super helpful with the transition. Mrs. Hubbard taught me everything before the place switched over. I can make lattes, cappuccinos, macchiatos, mochas. Oh! And my cold brew is out of this world."

Candace had known quite a bit about coffee before this, partly because of her restaurant experience and partly because she just liked coffee, but the Hubbards had taught her more than she'd realized there was to know: how to get the perfect grind, pull the perfect espresso shot. The key to foaming milk into soft clouds of dairy goodness.

Candace wouldn't be making the drinks on a daily basis—the baristas would do that—but she could hardly manage a staff of people without fully understanding what they did and how. Not to mention the fact that she would certainly have to fill in on occasion.

"And how's Evan?" Brittany asked.

Candace glanced at her friend from the driver's seat as they made their way south on Highway 1. "He's … oh, God. He's Evan. I really wish your not-hot-anymore theory had been true. But it's not, Brittany. It's not."

"I know." Brittany shifted in the passenger seat to face her friend more fully. "I saw him the other day at the bank. You know how some guys who are super good-looking in high school just kind of look sad and defeated ten or fifteen years after graduation?"

"Yeah."

"Well, that didn't happen."

"No. It didn't."

"But, he's single, though?" Brittany asked.

"No! There's a girlfriend, apparently, but I haven't seen her. I've only heard about her. Anna. Every now and then I hear him talking on the phone to her, but she still lives in the Bay Area."

"*Hmm.* It can't be too serious if she didn't move here to be with him."

"What difference does it make?" Candace threw one hand into the air for emphasis, keeping the other on the wheel. "Even if he was single, he wouldn't want me. Even if I were the last woman on a ruined and desolate planet, he'd probably turn to a life of celibacy before he'd consider being with me."

That was quite a speech, and Candace wasn't quite sure where it had come from. Years of longing and sexual frustration, probably.

"Oh, jeez," Brittany said. "Is he being a jerk to you, then?"

"No. No. Not at all. He's ... he's lovely." And he was. He treated her with respect. He was friendly. He listened to her input, acted as though she were an equal partner in his business, and deferred to her opinions whenever she was right.

He was as close as she'd ever had to an ideal boss.

Damn him.

Why couldn't he be an asshole to her? Why couldn't he treat her like crap? It would be so much easier to get her mind off of him and let go of this Evan crush if he weren't so ... so perfect.

"If he's so lovely to you, then what makes you think you don't have a chance?" Brittany asked.

"Because he's lovely in a thoroughly professional, respectful, above-board kind of way. He's lovely the way you would be to your eighty-five-year-old aunt."

"Oh. Crap."

"Yeah."

Stop thinking about him, she told herself. *Just ... stop it.*

"You know what?" she said. "After dinner, let's go to a club. We can have a few drinks and flirt with people."

Maybe she'd find someone who could, at least for a while, make her forget about Evan Bridges.

EVAN HAD BEEN in Cambria for a couple of months now, and he still hadn't been able to persuade Anna to visit.

He went to see her, of course, whenever he could get away. A four-hour drive to the Bay Area, followed by a nice dinner at an expensive restaurant. Some sex that was, quite frankly, subpar these days. An argument about when and if he was going to return to San Francisco or she was going to move to Cambria. Then a four-hour drive home the following day or the day after that.

He was getting tired of doing that dance with her, and on top of that, he was getting lonely.

He knew it was unprofessional to talk about things like that to his coffeehouse manager, but he found himself doing it anyway during the hour after closing on Sunday evening.

It came up because he was moping around, and she asked about it. He'd meant to put her off with some kind of polite but vague response, but before he knew it, he was giving her an honest answer.

"Rough weekend." He shrugged. "Got into another fight with my girlfriend."

The baristas had gone home. Candace was checking the shop to make sure everything was ready for the next day, and Evan was sitting at a cafe table with his laptop looking over the schedule Candace had written, getting ready to give it his okay.

"I'm sorry." She looked at him with sympathy from where she stood behind the counter.

"Yeah, well. Seems like we do more fighting than anything else these days. We're getting good at it."

Why had he told her that? She probably didn't want to know. She probably was just being polite. And here he was, venting. But having started, he couldn't seem to stop.

"Anna acts like me moving down here and buying this place was some sort of attack on her. You know? Like I only did it to annoy her. Never mind that my business went under in a huge scandal and there was no way I could work in San Francisco again. No way I could work in PR again. I'm trying to rebuild a life, and it's all about her, apparently. Ah ... shit."

He rubbed his forehead with both hands. "I'm sorry. You don't need to hear all of this."

~

OH ... jeez. Evan Bridges was talking to Candace about his personal life, and she had no idea what to do with that.

Up until now, all they'd talked about was coffee: how to brew it, how to sell it, what to charge for it, what kind of atmosphere to create for the people who bought it.

But now he was talking about his girlfriend troubles, and that was both good and bad. Good, because it meant he was starting to see Candace as more than just an employee. But bad, because he clearly didn't think of her as a romantic prospect if he was talking to her about his love life so he could get the perspective of an outsider.

She was an outsider, all right—she couldn't be more outside if she were orbiting in space.

Candace walked around the counter, pulled out the chair across from him, and sat down. This seemed like the kind of conversation that required her to be close to him.

"I ... ah ... I'm sorry you're having a hard time." That seemed like a safe thing to say. "Are you and she serious?"

He ran a hand through his hair. That dark, wavy hair she loved so much.

"You know, I'd have said so before. But now? Ah, hell. I don't know."

"Is it just that she doesn't want to move to Cambria, or ...?"

27

"She likes the lifestyle we had before. Before … everything happened. But I can't give her that anymore, can I?"

She didn't have to ask him what happened, because she read the papers. She knew how to use Google. She already knew the story.

Evan's PR firm had focused on a clientele of tech companies—companies with names well known by anyone who owned either a computer or a smartphone. One of his clients had come to him seeking PR advice regarding the company's upcoming—but so far unrevealed—acquisition of a prominent rival.

Evan's partner, Greg Alcott, had bought stock in the client's company in anticipation of the acquisition—a clear violation of insider trading laws.

When the story had broken, Greg had gone to jail and Evan's clients had started fleeing as though there were a giant asteroid screaming out of the sky toward them. Evan hadn't done anything wrong—he testified in court, under oath, that he'd known nothing about his partner's personal financial activities—but that hadn't saved his business, and it hadn't saved his reputation.

"What about you?" she asked him. "Do you miss that lifestyle?"

He sat back in his chair, rubbed his hand over the stubble on his chin, and considered it. "Sometimes, sure. But other times? It's kind of a relief to be out of all that. Part of me is really glad to be home."

"He talked to me about his girlfriend troubles," she told Brittany on the phone later that night after she'd showered and changed into sweatpants and a T-shirt and was installed on her sofa with a mug of tea. "Which, I mean, was good, because it means he doesn't just think of me as an employee. But it's bad, too, because—"

"Because he's talking to you like a bro."

"Yes!"

"Candace. You need to meet a guy, go out with him, and have outrageous sex to get Evan off of your mind. Listen to me. I know what I'm talking about."

"But ..."

"You said you wanted to flirt with guys at the bar the other night, but you didn't. It was a good idea! What happened?"

The truth was, Candace's heart hadn't been in it. She'd had a beer, looked around, and saw a room full of men who weren't Evan. She and Brittany had gone home early.

"I don't know," she lied. "I just ... I didn't feel like it."

Brittany sighed. "You know, you might have been right when you said it was a mistake to take this job. How are you supposed to move on from your crush if he's just ... just *there*? Right in front of you? Every day?"

"Talking about his girlfriend," Candace added glumly.

"Yes. Talking about his girlfriend. Ugh. That can't be fun for you."

"It's not."

On the other hand, he wasn't just talking about his girlfriend, was he? He was complaining about her. Which meant he might not have a girlfriend for much longer.

CHAPTER 5

*B*y the time Candace had worked at Jitters for a couple of months, she'd fallen into an agreeable rhythm.

She liked the coffeehouse with its funky vibe and its comfortable spaces where customers could sit with a friend or relax with a complicated coffee drink. She liked the baristas, who had been working together for a long time and who all got along with each other better than any group of employees Candace had ever worked with. She liked her little apartment with its view of Main Street.

The one flaw in the arrangement was her pathetic, unrequited longing for Evan, but she'd managed to keep that under control. She'd managed to tamp it down into some secret place in her heart where it wouldn't be able to do much damage.

That was, until he invited her to the National Coffee Conference.

CANDACE KNEW ABOUT THE NCC. The restaurant where she'd worked had sent a couple of people there the year before, and Candace had come across it when she'd begun researching coffee for her job at Jitters.

It seemed like there was a national convention for pretty much everything, so why not coffee?

NCC would be held in the spring in Seattle. Thousands of coffee-house owners and managers, baristas, suppliers, roasters, and others would gather in a huge downtown hotel to discuss all things related to coffee and coffeehouse management.

She'd been thinking of asking Evan if she could go at Jitters' expense—as manager, it seemed like she should learn as much about the coffee business as she could—but before she got around to asking him, he brought it up himself.

Only, his plan was for the two of them to go together.

"I'm still learning about this business," he told her late one afternoon after closing, when Candace was in her office going through a stack of invoices from suppliers. "And so are you. We really can't afford not to go."

"Both of us? Together?" Candace knew she sounded like an idiot, but she couldn't seem to help it. The idea of traveling with him, staying in a hotel with him ...

"Sure. Why not? I can get David to fill in for you while we're gone. He used to manage the place for the Hubbards when they were on a cruise or whatever they did when they weren't working. I already asked him. He's good with it."

"I ... oh."

Apparently, he took her flustered response as uncertainty about David.

"What? You think he can't handle it?"

"No." She shook her head. "No, not at all. He'll be fine." David was competent, responsible, smart, and experienced. She was sure that end of things would go seamlessly. "It's just ..."

"What?" Evan stood in the doorway to her office, his hands on his hips and his eyebrows raised.

She had to think of something to cover for her ridiculous reaction. "I'll have to check with my mother, that's all. She's having surgery on her hip in the spring, and I need to make sure the dates don't conflict."

The part about the surgery was true. Melissa had been suffering from hip pain for a while, and she was finally going to do something about it.

"Ah. Sure. Check with her and let me know."

He accepted that without hesitation. Thank God for her mother's hip. There was no way Candace could tell him the truth: that being in close proximity to him for five days in an upscale hotel, probably eating and drinking together and doing God knew what else, might be more than she could handle.

That longing she'd forced down into a tight little box in her heart might just break out and go on a rampage, leaving untold damage in its wake.

ANNA WAS on one of her rare visits to Cambria when the topic of the coffee conference came up.

"You're planning to take a woman with you? A woman whom your friend says had a crush on you for years?"

Evan and Anna were at Otter Bluff on a Sunday morning, drinking their first cups of coffee out on the back patio with the roar of the ocean in their ears, when he told her about it.

"She's not *a woman*. She's my manager."

"Did she somehow lose her gender when she took the job?"

"Well … no." The fact was, he didn't think of Candace that way. He thought of her as a hard worker, someone whose intelligence and dedication made it possible for him to hand her the reins with confidence when he didn't want to oversee things himself.

That's what he'd been looking for when he'd hired her, and it was working out well.

Why wouldn't he want her to learn more about coffee?

"Candace's background is in restaurant work and mine's in PR. We both need to learn the business. We both need to be there," he said.

Anna shifted in her chair to face him. Her long hair was up in a messy bun, and she was wearing a fluffy bathrobe, her pale feet bare. "Fine. You're right. You both should go."

That seemed easier than it should have been. A moment later, he discovered why.

"I'll just come along, too," she said.

"Why?" He blurted it out without thinking, and she narrowed her eyes at him.

"I love Seattle," she said. "And it's been ages since you and I had a getaway. Two birds, one stone."

With another woman, he might have thought it was a good idea. With another woman, he might have welcomed it. But Anna was, in essence, a female-shaped black hole that sucked up all of the male attention from entire galaxies.

He could see how it would go: *Evan, can't you just skip today's sessions so we can go shopping? Evan, honey, can't you spend the day with me? It's just one day. You can attend the conference tomorrow. Why do you always put your work ahead of me? Why is everything else always more important than what I want?*

This was supposed to be a business trip so he could educate himself on his new line of work. He didn't need it to become a showcase for Anna's insecurities and manipulation.

"Ah ... I really don't think that's a good idea."

"Why not?" She raised those sculpted eyebrows in question and rebuke.

"Because I'll be busy. It won't be fun for you, sitting in the hotel room while I'm in sessions all day."

She laughed, as though the idea were ridiculous. "I won't sit in the hotel room all day, silly. I'll be exploring the city."

"By yourself."

"Of course. Why not?"

The *why not* was that Anna loathed doing anything without an attentive man at her side to ease the way—to open the doors, arrange the cars, carry the bags, and, of course, pay the checks.

Right now, she was saying she'd be content to spend the day alone in the city, but that would change once they were there. Suddenly the nagging and wheedling would begin, and before he knew it, he'd be leading Anna on a tour of the spas and boutiques and upscale restaurants of Seattle, and he wouldn't learn shit about coffee.

"Anna, babe, I just don't think that's going to work," he said.

"Of course it will."

"No, it won't. This is business, not pleasure. I need to do this alone."

"Except, you won't be doing it alone, will you? You'll be with your manager," she said.

He didn't like the way she said it.

Not at all.

"I don't know what to pack. Oh, God. There's going to be a banquet on the last night and it's dressy, but it's still work, so …"

Candace was freaking out. She'd managed to keep calm in the days and weeks leading up to NCC, but now, when it came down to getting herself and her belongings ready to go, she was overcome by anxiety.

That's why she'd called Brittany over to help.

"Okay, take a breath." Brittany surveyed the clothes that were scattered across Candace's bed, her hands on her hips. "Let's deal with the banquet thing first."

"Okay. All right." Candace took a breath, as instructed, and closed her eyes for a moment, trying to find her calm center.

"First of all, it's not work," Brittany said. "I mean, yes, it is, but those kinds of events—conference banquets—are supposed to be fun, too. They're supposed to be a chance to get glammed up in clothes that don't smell like espresso."

Candace frowned. "My regular clothes don't smell like espresso."

"They kind of do."

Okay, well, there were worse things she could smell like.

"So, if I'm going for glammed-up girl who doesn't smell like espresso, what do I pick?" Unspoken was the fact that she needed to look sexy enough to make Evan want her, but not so sexy that she seemed unprofessional.

Brittany picked up one dress, then another. "Jeez. You don't really have anything."

"I live in Cambria! I don't need a cocktail dress to go to a fundraiser spaghetti feed at the veterans' hall! When would I have bought one?"

"Good point." Brittany's eyebrows rose. "We could go shopping."

"But I'm leaving tomorrow."

"It's still early, and it's your day off. That gives us plenty of time."

BRITTANY HAD WANTED to go to the nearest Nordstrom—even though it was a three-hour drive from Cambria—but Candace didn't want to spend a full day driving back and forth, and anyway, she couldn't afford Nordstrom prices. Instead, they opted for the Macy's in Santa Maria.

Not only was it considerably closer, but Candace also figured the store would have a wider variety of prices, some of which might even fit her budget.

They got into Brittany's car and headed south, and the drive gave Candace a chance to vent about her various Evan-related anxieties.

"I mean, it's work, but it's social, with meals and drinking and everything. And there I'll be, in some fancy dress at the banquet with Evan pretty much ignoring me, and it's going to give me flashbacks to the senior prom."

"Evan ignored you at the senior prom?"

"Evan probably doesn't even remember that I was at the senior prom. Which I was. With Joseph Laramore, who was the only guy to ask me, and I didn't even like him. I just went with him so I could get a look at Evan in a tux."

"Poor Joseph," Brittany said. "We were in ASB together, and we talked sometimes. He really liked you."

"No, he didn't."

"He did." Brittany gave her a look that was almost like a wince. "He really did."

Candace tried to remember, and she couldn't. Apparently, she wasn't the only person to have her dreams shattered by an indifferent love object.

"You know," Brittany said after a while, as they drove through Morro Bay with the ocean at their right. "Worshipping Evan didn't work very well back in high school."

"No. It didn't."

"So maybe at the conference, and at the banquet, you might try … you know. Not doing that."

"Are you saying I should ignore him?"

"No. Of course not. Be gracious and sociable and all that. But maybe try focusing on other people. Even flirting with other people, if the mood strikes."

"Are you saying I should try to make him jealous?"

"No. No, no. Just maybe … broaden your scope a little, that's all."

CANDACE DIDN'T EXPECT to fall in love with a dress—much less with one she could actually afford. But she found the perfect thing in the Macy's special occasion section. A knee-length, A-line, crepe cocktail dress in plum. It was sleeveless, with a cowl neck, beading at the waist, and a back that was low enough to be sexy but high enough to be respectable.

It was perfect.

"You look amazing," Brittany said as Candace spun around in the dress under the harsh fluorescent lights of the dressing room.

"I do, don't I?" Candace let out a giggle of joy. "All of this Evan angst might actually be worth it if I get to wear this."

"I don't know that I'd go that far," Brittany said.

CHAPTER 6

The National Coffee Conference was being held in a large downtown hotel that had all the facilities one would expect of a convention venue: business center, meeting rooms, ballroom, two bars, and three restaurants—one upscale, one casual, and one poolside.

When Evan and Candace came into the lobby rolling their suitcases behind them, the place was already buzzing with all things coffee. A big banner over the reception desk declared, WELCOME NCC! People with NCC lanyards around their necks milled around holding—what else?—cups of coffee in their hands.

"Well, I'll just get us checked in." Evan left Candace to wait in an upholstered fireside chair while he took care of business.

When he came back to where she was sitting, he offered her a key card. "We're in room 783."

"We?" She looked up at him, certain she must have misunderstood. Surely he couldn't have meant they were sharing a room.

"I got us a two-bedroom suite," he said. "It costs less than two separate rooms, plus we get access to the Club Level lounge and concierge."

"Why do we need the Club Level lounge and concierge?"

"You're kidding, right? The lounge has free food all day long, plus a hosted cocktail hour. And the concierge? You never know. One time in Paris, I got mugged and lost my bag with my wallet and passport in it. Jean-Pierre was a lifesaver."

Candace tried to process the fact that Evan was the kind of guy who traveled to Paris and was on a first-name basis with the VIP concierge at some five-star hotel. To her, he was still the boy she'd known in school. But he'd changed—maybe more than she'd realized.

She didn't know whether she was excited that she would be sharing a room with him during the conference or alarmed by it.

"Well. Let's go up and check it out," he said.

FOR THE REST of the day, Candace was too busy with conference activities to worry about the hotel room situation and how close she'd be to Evan.

She got registered for the conference, collected her name tag lanyard and her bag of swag—which included an insulated coffee mug, a pound of coffee beans provided by one of the conference's sponsors, a neat little travel kit you could use to make pour-over coffee in your hotel room, and a T-shirt—and perused the schedule of events.

The sessions were separated into three tracks: one geared toward coffeehouse owners and managers, one for coffee roasters, and one for baristas.

Candace wanted to focus on the sessions for managers, of course, but she also planned to attend some of the barista training so she could improve her skills in that area. Evan would focus mostly on material for coffeehouse owners, but he also wanted to learn about roasting, since he was considering expanding into that area if things went well at Jitters.

Of course, a coffee bar was set up at the back of the room at each session, so Candace's free insulated mug was full as she took notes on customer service, store design and layout, and inventory management.

By the time they broke for lunch, Candace had chatted with several fellow managers, exchanged business cards with a few of them, and had several pages of notes on things she wanted to try at Jitters.

She was standing in the hotel lobby awkwardly, trying to decide whether to grab an unsuspecting stranger with a lanyard and persuade them to eat lunch with her, when Evan came striding across the polished floor, his mug in his hand and his messenger bag slung over his shoulder.

"Lunch?" he asked, eyebrows raised in question.

THEY MADE the ten-minute walk to Pike Place Market in a light rain that was really more of a heavy mist. The sky was gray and foreboding, and they both pulled their jackets around themselves to fend off the spring chill.

They went to a casual seafood place and sat in a booth at a window overlooking Elliott Bay. The place was buzzing with noise and customers as they ordered Dungeness crab cakes and fish and chips.

At first, Candace tried to keep the talk professional.

"Did you go to any good sessions this morning?" She picked up a french fry and dipped it in ketchup.

"Yeah, I did." He nodded while he cut off a piece of crab cake with his fork. "I'm really interested in getting into the roasting end of things—there's a lot of money in selling coffee beans to local restaurants and bakeries—and the morning speaker gave me a lot to think about. You?"

They talked about that for a while, including some tips she'd learned for how to make the morning rush go more smoothly. Then, the conversation moved toward Evan's memories of high school.

"You were smart," he said, pointing one finger at her. "I remember that."

"You were, too, you were just too busy with football and dating to study."

He gave her an endearing half grin that made her insides go soft and squishy. "That's what my mom always said."

"Well, your mom was right. Last semester of junior year, you got a D in algebra when everyone knew you could have aced the final if you'd wanted to. But you were really into Cindy D'Amico that semester, and you and she were sneaking out at night when your mother thought you were doing homework. So. The D."

He was staring at her, and only now did she realize she'd said far more than she should have.

"How do you know all of that?"

"Oh." She felt herself blushing, and she looked down at her plate instead of at him. "Just ... people talk, that's all."

"They do," he agreed. "Plus ..."

"Plus?"

"Plus ... I might have heard something about ... you know. You having a crush. On me."

Now her cheeks were burning. She had two choices: deny it or come clean. She opted to come clean, but to downplay it.

"Oh, well." She made a dismissive gesture with her hand. "Sure. I did. I had crushes on a lot of people."

There. If she could play it off as typical teen girl stuff, then maybe her humiliation might be brought under some sort of control.

"Right. Of course. So did I," he said.

"Including Cindy D'Amico."

"Yeah. Including her." He smiled wistfully, as though he were having fond memories of Cindy D'Amico, who'd worn a D cup at seventeen and who had dressed to emphasize her pride in that fact.

Candace, herself, had never progressed past a modest B. She glanced down at her own chest ruefully, then caught herself doing it and abruptly stopped.

They chatted about college. Evan had gone to UCLA on a football scholarship, but everyone knew he wasn't good enough to go pro. He'd chosen a communications major because it didn't sound too challenging, but he'd ended up loving it. From there, he'd gotten a master's in PR from USC.

Candace had majored in English at Cal Poly San Luis Obispo, thinking she might teach it one day, and then, upon getting her bachelor's degree, learned how useless the degree had been in terms of immediate earning potential. A series of waitressing jobs had followed, and eventually the assistant manager gig she'd had before she'd gone to work at Jitters. She liked restaurant work, mostly because it allowed her to stay in Cambria.

"You never did wander very far from home, did you?" he asked. "Cal Poly's just down the road."

"Yeah. My parents couldn't afford to send me to college unless I lived at home. Which was fine with me, really. I love the Central Coast. I've always known I'd live there forever."

"Not me." He took a sip from his water glass, then folded his forearms on the table. "I wanted out. But now? After living in the Bay Area for more than a decade? I'm starting to appreciate small-town living."

EVAN HADN'T MEANT to bring up the thing about Candace's crush on him. The *plus* had just slipped out, and once it did, he had to finish his thought. Now, though, it was good to have it out there. Cards on the table. She'd said he was just one crush among many, and that certainly rang true with his own high school experience. He'd changed crushes more often than he changed his socks.

Whatever feelings she'd had for him, she must be over them now. And that was good, since they were working together.

Still, it seemed to him that if he'd gotten to know her better back in school, he might have been interested in seeing where things went. Had she been this nice to talk to in eleventh grade? If he were being honest, he'd have to admit he didn't know because he'd rarely talked to her.

41

He'd known very little about her back then, but apparently, she knew everything about him.

And that made him wonder if her crush had maybe been a little more than she was letting on.

"Your family's still in Cambria, right?" he asked. "Seems like I've seen your folks around."

"Yeah." Candace broke off a small piece of a fried fish fillet and popped it into her mouth. "My parents will never leave. That's one of the reasons I stayed. What about yours? Your mother must be glad you're back."

He waggled his head: maybe yes, maybe no. "She's glad I'm closer, sure. But the circumstances …" He didn't need to elaborate.

"She blames you for your partner's insider trading?" Her eyebrows drew together in an expression of concern, and her sympathy made him feel better, somehow.

"Not as such."

"What does that mean?"

He sighed. "She knows I didn't have anything to do with that. She does believe me. But she blames me for choosing a partner who turned out to be shady as hell. And, you know, that's valid." He rubbed the back of his neck and glanced at her. "Also, she liked bragging about her successful son. She isn't bragging anymore."

Candace and Evan walked back to the hotel together after lunch. The rain had stopped, and the world smelled like wet asphalt and car exhaust.

As they walked, Candace was intensely aware of Evan's presence next to her, his long stride, his powerful build. She'd led him to believe she was over her crush. She'd told him there had been others.

There had never been others. There was only Evan.

Yes, she'd had boyfriends. She'd had relationships. But they'd all suffered because she'd spent the whole time thinking of someone else, and that was a hard thing to hide. Her boyfriends might not have known the particulars—might not have known she wanted another man instead of them—but they knew her mind was elsewhere, and that was enough to doom her relationships, one after another.

Just this, just walking beside him on a cool day on a sidewalk wet with rain, filled her heart in a way she wouldn't have thought possible. She tried not to look at him because she knew her feelings would be right there on her face. Still, she couldn't keep the smile from emerging—couldn't keep the joy from spilling out just because she was near him.

All of that happiness, all of that contentment ended when Anna showed up.

CHAPTER 7

*T*he first clue Candace had that something was wrong came right after the last session of the day. She texted Evan to ask if he wanted to meet for dinner, but he didn't answer.

Then, when she was walking through the lobby on her way to her room—she wanted to drop off her notebook and regroup after a long day—she saw Evan near the reception desk having a heated discussion with a leggy brunette.

From a distance, Candace couldn't tell if they were fighting or just talking. Then Evan put his hand on the brunette's arm and she jerked back out of his grasp.

Fighting, then.

Was he already seeing someone from the conference? That seemed impossible, given how short a time they'd been here. And from their body language, this wasn't someone he'd just met. This was someone with history.

She admonished herself for snooping and went to her room, the way she'd planned to do, a sick feeling of dread in her stomach.

Evan had told Anna not to come to Seattle during the conference. He should have known she wouldn't listen.

They'd been arguing via text message about it since he'd gotten here, and that was annoying, but he'd assumed that was all it would be —just arguing.

When he'd emerged from his last session of the day and saw her standing in the lobby, scanning the crowd for him, he'd felt a cold knot of tension in his chest.

And, really, that had to say something important about the relationship, didn't it?

"Anna. What are you doing here? I told you not to come. I told you I'd be too busy and—"

"Busy. Is that what you're calling it?"

The lobby was full of people making their way from the conference to dinner or their rooms, and Evan didn't want to have a fight right here, in front of everyone. He kept his tone neutral.

"Is that what I'm calling what? I *am* busy, Anna. The conference—"

"The conference is not what I'm talking about."

In that case, he didn't know what the hell they *were* talking about.

He pinched the bridge of his nose between his fingers, feeling a headache coming on. "Anna …"

"Would you like to tell me why you and your female manager are sharing one room?"

How could she possibly know that? He was considering that question when he noticed a man in his twenties behind the reception desk who was suspiciously red in the face and who was studiously trying not to look at them.

Okay, then. She'd either bribed him or flirted with him. Probably flirted.

"We're not in the same room," he said.

"Oh, now you're just lying. Because—"

"We're in a two-bedroom suite. We each have our own room, Anna."

She paused at that, then regrouped. "But you're sharing a suite, and isn't that cozy? Whose idea was that? Yours or hers?"

"It cost less than two separate rooms, and it has Club Level lounge access. It would have been stupid to turn that down."

"So now I'm stupid?"

Ah, here they were at the phase of the argument in which Anna twisted his words into unrecognizable shapes in order to put him on the defensive.

"I didn't say that, and you know it."

"What does she look like, Evan? Is she young? Is she pretty?"

He wasn't about to say that she was, even though it was true. He wasn't a complete idiot. He put his hand on Anna's bicep intending to lead her to a more quiet spot for the argument, but she yanked her arm out of his grasp.

"Don't touch me!"

He closed his eyes, took a deep breath, then opened them. "What do you want me to do, exactly, Anna? Tell me what you'd like to have happen next, because I really don't have a clue."

A thin, predatory smile formed. "I want you to take me to your room so I can confirm that you're in separate bedrooms. And then I want to meet this manager of yours."

CANDACE WAS up in the suite, thinking about where to go for dinner and trying not to wonder about the woman downstairs with Evan, when suddenly the woman was no longer downstairs with Evan.

She was here in the room with him.

When they walked in together, Candace froze in the center of the shared living area, her heart hammering.

Please God, don't let him go into his room with her. Please don't make me listen to their sex sounds through the wall.

"Oh. Hi," she said, a few beats too late for it to sound natural.

"Candace Weaver, this is Anna Devane. Anna, this is Candace, my manager at Jitters." He sounded tired in a way she'd never heard from him before.

Anna put out a manicured hand, the fingers stiff. Candace shook it.

"It's lovely to meet you," Candace said, even though it wasn't lovely. It wasn't lovely at all.

Anna narrowed her eyes at Candace. "How nice that you and Evan work so *closely* together." The way she emphasized the word *closely* left little doubt about what she meant.

"Well, I—"

"See?" Evan broke in. "Here's my room, and there's hers. You want to go in and perform an inspection to make sure we're really using both of them?"

"Yes," Anna said.

"Wait. What—" Candace, uncertain about what was going on, tried to interject. But Evan spoke over her.

"You are not going into Candace's room without her permission, Anna. But you can go over mine with a fine-tooth comb if you want. You're not going to find anything of hers in there. You're not going to find her panties on my floor."

Candace gasped—she couldn't help it.

At least now, the situation was clear.

Evan and Anna did go into his room—then promptly started yelling at each other. Candace grabbed her purse and slipped out the door while she had the chance.

HE'D TOLD Anna she could inspect his room, but now that she was actually doing it, Evan was getting increasingly pissed off.

She went through the dresser drawers, sorting through his things. She examined the closet, his suitcase. She looked under the bed. Then she moved to the bathroom—he and Candace each had their own—and checked the countertops, the shower, the cabinet under the sink.

She even smelled the pillows, expecting what? A hint of a woman's perfume?

"Are you happy now?" He stood with his arms crossed, watching

47

her as she checked one of the water glasses, probably for lipstick. "There's nothing. There couldn't be anything, because she's in her room, and I'm in mine."

Anna spun around, her dark hair shining under the fluorescent lighting in the bathroom. "That doesn't change the fact that it's inappropriate for the two of you to be sharing a suite."

"I told you, the cost—"

"The cost, the cost." She mocked him, doing a vicious impersonation of his voice. "What do you care about the cost? You could certainly afford two rooms."

"I could have, but it wouldn't have made sense."

"So it was just a business decision."

"Yes."

"If that's true, why didn't you want me to come with you? Why did you keep putting me off when I offered to come up and see you? Why, if it wasn't so you could have your fling with your manager in private?"

He squeezed his eyes shut, trying to keep his temper under control, but he couldn't seem to keep himself from yelling.

"Goddamn it, Anna, I told you, I'm not having a fling with my manager!"

And Candace was right in the next room, wasn't she? Surely she was hearing all of this. How humiliating—for himself and also for her, probably.

"If you're not, then you want to," Anna said.

He opened his mouth to deny it, then wondered what the point of that would be. He and Anna rarely saw each other anymore, and when they did, she was either manipulating him or fighting with him.

Why was he trying to save the relationship?

What was there to save?

He scrubbed at his face with both hands, then ran his fingers through his hair, feeling exhausted and defeated. "You know what, Anna? You're not happy in this relationship, and neither am I. Maybe it's time to call it."

She froze, and her mouth fell open in shock. "You want to break up with me? *You* want to break up with *me*?"

The way she said it indicated that she found the idea ludicrous. Obviously, *she* should be the one doing the breaking up, because obviously, *he* was the one at fault. Or, alternatively, because she was so much better than he deserved.

Either interpretation was pure bullshit.

"Yeah. That's what I'm saying. We're breaking up. I would think that would be a relief to you, given how unhappy you've been."

To his horror, her eyes grew red and filled with tears. "Evan ..."

Ah, shit. He hated this. He hated the emotional messiness of relationships, hated the raw pain of their inevitable demise.

"Look, I don't want to hurt you. I never wanted that. But—"

"I came all the way here to see you. And now ... this?"

"You came all the way here to catch me cheating on you, which I'm not doing, but which you insist on accusing me of anyway. Doesn't that tell you something? Doesn't that tell you it's time for this thing to be over?"

She pressed her lips together into a tight line, muttered something that included the words *bastard* and *dick*, and stomped out the door.

CHAPTER 8

*C*andace didn't feel like going out for dinner, given everything that had happened, but she couldn't order room service because she couldn't go back to her room. Still, she did have to eat.

She walked toward the elevator, thinking to go to the bar downstairs to grab something quick. Then she remembered the Club Level lounge.

Instead of going down, she went to the top floor, where she showed her key and was ushered into a large, plush room with dining tables, seating areas with comfortable chairs where guests could enjoy conversation or sit with a book, buffet tables along one wall, and a full bar staffed by a young man in a starched shirt, a plastic name tag affixed to his chest. Floor-to-ceiling windows looked out onto the city.

A handful of people were enjoying the VIP perks—some eating in small groups, others with cocktails in the sitting area.

Feeling a little unsure of herself—she'd never been in a Club Level lounge in her life, nor had she ever expected to—she went to the buffet, picked up a plate, and helped herself to an array of hors d'oeuvres that were substantial enough to be a meal. She found a table, sat down, then decided that if she was going to take advantage of all the lounge had to offer, she might as well have a cocktail, too.

She was just enjoying a mini quiche and sipping a mojito, beginning to feel better as the alcohol relaxed her, when Evan walked in.

Anna wasn't with him.

EVAN NEEDED A DRINK. He was headed straight for the Club Level bar, thinking of the sweet release that might be offered by a glass of bourbon, when he saw Candace at a table near the windows.

He gave her a wave, went to the bar, got his bourbon, then took it to her table.

It would have been great not to have to talk about any of this—to be able to just drink and maybe get drunk and wake up hungover in the morning with all of it behind him—but Candace had been a witness to the whole thing, so he could hardly pretend it hadn't happened.

"You mind if I sit?" he asked.

"No! Of course not." Candace wasn't looking at him, and she was blushing a little.

Clearly, she was as embarrassed by Anna's drama as he was.

He sat, settled into his chair, took a slug of his drink, and said, "So. What did you think of Anna?"

Candace burst into helpless laughter, and he couldn't help smiling himself, despite everything.

"I'm sorry. I know it isn't funny. I know it isn't." She gasped for breath, dabbing tears of mirth from her eyes with the corner of her napkin. "I just …" She gulped some water, trying to compose herself.

He supposed he should be offended, but the whole situation was so ridiculous that laughter wasn't an unreasonable response. He was relieved that Candace was being a good sport about the way his girlfriend had treated her, and he could also admit he felt a weight lifted from his chest now that it was over between himself and Anna.

"Oh, God. I really am sorry I reacted that way." Candace took in a shuddering breath. "That wasn't nice. You're probably upset and hurt and I—"

"I'm fine," he said, and realized it was true.

"You don't have to say that just to put me at ease. You don't have to pretend."

"I'm not pretending. I'm really fine. Stressed as hell after all that, but fine."

"Did you and she … Are the two of you okay?"

"The two of us are no longer the two of us. There's just her, and there's just me."

"I'm so sorry. You broke up because of me? Oh, no. That's—"

"We broke up because of her. I mean, you saw how she acts. I should have done it a long time ago. I should have been running away from her like my hair was on fire." He downed the rest of his drink. "I need another. Can I get you a refill?"

CANDACE WAS STARTING to feel lightheaded—from the alcohol and from knowing that Evan was no longer in a relationship and was, therefore, a free man.

She finished her second mojito, and he finished his second bourbon, and they both ate the free hors d'oeuvres and watched the sunset out the big bank of windows.

"I knew it wasn't working," he said, relaxing into the story of himself and Anna. "She had absolutely no interest in coming to Cambria to see me, and I was becoming less and less interested in going to the Bay Area to see her. She didn't want me. She wanted a lifestyle that I was no longer providing. I guarantee she'll have someone else within a week, if she doesn't already."

Candace shifted in her seat to face him more fully. "Well, it's probably good that it's over, then. Still, it's got to be hard. Breakups suck, even when you know they're for the best."

I could comfort you, she thought. And, God, did she want to. She wanted to hold him to her breast and stroke his hair.

"I'll probably feel like shit tomorrow," he admitted. "But right now? I feel like I've been let out of prison."

MAYBE IT WAS THE ALCOHOL, but Evan looked at Candace and thought about how much he'd like to make himself feel better by taking a woman to bed.

It would be so good to celebrate his new freedom by having single-guy sex with someone attractive, someone who didn't yell at him.

Someone who actually liked him.

Here he was, and here Candace was, and they were sharing a suite, and Anna had been right about that—their room arrangement really did put them very close to each other.

What would be the harm in enjoying that closeness to its fullest potential?

But even as he asked himself the question, he knew the answer. What if Candace slept with him and then one or both of them regretted it? They still had to work together. They still had to run a business together, and that would be so much harder if in an atmosphere of post-coital awkwardness and contempt.

And then there was the other thing. The *Candace might still be in love with him* thing. If she was, then having casual sex with her would be cruel when he didn't expect things between them to go beyond that.

If he couldn't make himself feel better with Candace, that didn't mean he couldn't soothe himself with someone else—someone who might be up for a one-night conference fling.

Obviously, he couldn't tell her that's what he had in mind, so he finished what remained of his second drink and put his glass down on the table.

"Well, I should probably be downstairs networking. The real value of a conference like this is at the bar after the sessions. That's what people say."

He knew it was true—he'd spent enough time at hotel events as a PR man to consider himself something of an expert on the subject. The sessions gave you information, and that was good. But the bar talk gave you connections, and that was better.

But the connections he had in mind had nothing to do with business, and he felt like Candace could see the lie in his half-truth as clearly as she could see his face from across the table.

"Oh. Right. Of course." She looked down at her hands in either shyness or embarrassment, maybe because she really had read the lie, or maybe because she thought he was trying to get rid of her.

"What are you going to do for the rest of the evening?" he asked.

"I don't know. I might just read in the room for a while. It's been a long day."

CANDACE WENT BACK to the room, grateful to find that Anna really wasn't in it. She flopped on her bed and texted Brittany.

Evan broke up with his girlfriend tonight. Over me.

She answered seconds later: *Whaaat?!*

Candace: *She showed up unannounced, found out we were sharing a suite, and went ballistic. There's still an Anna-shaped hole in the ceiling.*

Brittany: *Oh, shit. So, is she right? Are you and he sharing more than the suite? *Wink, wink.**

Candace: *I wish.*

Brittany: *Well, at least he's single now, right? That's got to be a good thing.*

Candace thought it *was* a good thing, but not because it made him more likely to see her in a nonprofessional light. It was good because Anna made him miserable, and Evan did not deserve to be miserable.

He deserved a woman who really loved him, a woman who'd put his feelings first, a woman who would truly take the time to know him and fill his life with positivity and caring … and really great sex.…

She was so involved in her reverie that it took her a while to notice that Brittany had texted her again.

So, are you going to make your move now that he's on the market?

He's been on the market a half hour, Candace answered.

A half hour? What's the holdup? Brittany asked, then added a winky face emoji.

CHAPTER 9

*E*van went down to the hotel's main bar with his conference lanyard around his neck to advertise that he might be amenable to a little coffee-related conversation. He'd already had two bourbons and he didn't want to make an ass of himself, so he ordered a beer and nursed it as he sat at the gleaming oak bar.

The place was busy, and he'd been lucky to get a stool. Conference attendees stood in groups with drinks in their hands, talking and laughing more loudly than they probably had two drinks earlier.

Evan spotted a woman from one of the sessions he'd attended and made his way to her through the crowd. She was a tall brunette—not unlike Anna—but she was less polished and more funky with her eyebrow piercing and her T-shirt that read, I RUN ON COFFEE AND CHAOS.

Perfect.

"Evan Bridges," he said, extending his hand for her to shake. She took it in hers and held it for a period of time that would have been uncomfortable coming from someone he wasn't hoping to sleep with.

"Kiki Hodges." A smile curved her lips as she looked him up and down and apparently found him acceptable.

"Kiki? That's an interesting name."

"It's a nickname for Kayla."

She finally released his hand, and he gestured toward a table that had just opened up. "Care to sit, Kiki? I'd love to buy you a drink."

CANDACE DID READ FOR A WHILE, but then she started to wonder what Evan was doing—whether he was talking to anyone, whether he was having fun without her.

Also, he'd been right about networking. She wasn't making the most of the conference if she was here in the room, hiding out.

She'd had two mojitos so she certainly didn't need any more alcohol, but she could order a sparkling water. She didn't have to drink in order to be social, did she?

She checked herself in the mirror, touched up her makeup, put the shoes she'd discarded back on her feet, and went downstairs.

EVAN SHOULD HAVE LIKED KIKI. Objectively, he should have been attracted to her. But for some reason, the more he talked to her, the more they flirted, the more he realized it wasn't working.

Why not? She was pretty in a funky hip-girl sort of way. She was smart. She had some of the same interests he did—she liked coffee, good books, working out.

But his mind kept wandering, and even though he'd come down here thinking to have some mindless sex to get over his breakup, he found he couldn't generate enough lust to go ahead with it.

And if that didn't say something about the pathetic state of his heart, then nothing did.

He was just thinking about how to extricate himself when he saw Candace come in, glance at him, then go to the bar.

EVAN HAD SAID he was coming down here to network. Now, Candace suspected that the networking he was doing had nothing to do with business.

He liked brunettes, apparently. She thought of her own light brown hair with hopeless despair. She could dye it, sure. But that wouldn't make her the kind of woman Evan went for any more than changing her eyeliner had back in twelfth grade.

She'd planned to order something nonalcoholic, but now, seeing Evan chatting up some hot floozy, she thought, screw it. She ordered a gin and tonic and studiously avoided looking at Evan while she sat at the bar to drink it.

Was he really trying to get laid less than two hours after breaking up with his girlfriend? Or was she misreading the situation? Was he maybe just making professional connections like he'd said he was?

She sneaked a look at him and the woman. The brunette laughed at something he'd said, laid her hand on his arm, and left it there far too long.

Not just networking, then.

Shit. Shit.

Okay, so he wanted comfort sex, which was understandable. She wouldn't begrudge him that. But had he never considered Candace? Had he never considered his own suitemate?

She didn't really want that, of course. She didn't want to be someone he used to make himself feel better and then walked away from the next day. That would be worse than never having him at all.

Probably.

Still, the thought of that woman—she of the big breasts and the COFFEE AND CHAOS T-shirt—touching him, having her hands on his body ...

She was lost in her thoughts when she realized someone was talking to her.

" ... taken?"

"Um ... excuse me?"

A man, about forty years old and ruddy-faced, with a buzz cut and a black T-shirt tucked into camo pants, was looking at her expectantly.

"I was just asking if this seat's taken." He indicated the barstool next to Candace.

"Oh. Help yourself."

She put her focus back on watching Evan while trying not to look like she was watching Evan.

For some reason, the guy was still talking to her, though she hadn't been paying attention to anything he was saying.

"... coffee?"

"Ah ... what?" She blinked at him and sipped her drink.

"I said, are you part of this coffee thing?"

"Oh. Yes."

"I'm in town for a job interview. I get to the hotel, and it's all coffee, everywhere you look. Keeps the world running, though, am I right?"

"I ... ah ... yes. You're right."

She shot another look at Evan and saw that the brunette had scooted her chair closer to his.

"So, what do you do?" the guy asked. "I know it must have something to do with coffee."

She sighed and reminded herself not to be rude. "I manage a coffeehouse. I'm new at it, so I'm at the conference to learn about the business."

He launched into a monologue about what he did—computer programming—and how he was hoping to get a job at a tech giant with a reputation for treating its employees poorly.

"But just because I'm in town on business doesn't mean I can't have a little fun while I'm here. Right?"

She tuned back in to what he was saying just in time to notice that he was pressing his thigh against hers.

Enough of this.

"Well, good luck with your interview, and I hope you have a nice stay in Seattle." She picked up her drink and moved to the other end of the bar, where a seat had just opened up.

~

EVAN WAS TRYING to focus on whatever it was Kiki was saying, but he couldn't help noticing that some guy was making a move on Candace at the bar.

If she wanted the guy to make a move on her, well, Evan wasn't her father or her guardian or anyone else who had any right to say a damned thing about it.

But judging by her posture, that wasn't the case. She'd been angling her body away from the guy—some stiff in camo—and now she was picking up her drink and moving to a seat as far away from him as she could manage.

That should have been the end of it, but the stiff picked up his drink and followed her.

Candace was saying something to him, and Evan couldn't hear it, but the look on her face told him she was irritated and was probably telling him to fuck off. Knowing her, she was saying it much more nicely than that.

Now the asshole was putting his hand on her arm. She jerked it away, spilling some of her drink.

"Excuse me," he told Kiki, interrupting her in the middle of a sentence.

He pulled himself up to his full, considerable height, squared his shoulders, and walked over to where the asshole was pressing in closer to Candace, pinning her back against the bar.

"You got a problem?" Evan said to the guy.

The man, who was three inches shorter than Evan and about thirty pounds lighter, flinched slightly when he saw the size of the guy who was challenging him. Then he recovered and smirked.

"No, but you're going to if you don't back off."

Evan matched the smirk with his own. "I seriously doubt that."

"Okay. Hold on." Candace looked at first one of them, then the other. "This doesn't have to be a thing. I'm just going to walk away now."

But the asshole grabbed her arm again when she tried to go. "What's the hurry? We were having a nice conversation."

"Take your hand off her, or you're going to be having a nice conversation with the floor." Evan gave him the same look he'd used to intimidate opposing players back in his football days.

The guy might have been a dick, but he wasn't completely stupid. Evan could see him sizing up his chances and deciding that he liked having all of his teeth and bones intact. He took his hand off Candace's arm and showed the hand to Evan, palm out.

"Fine. Okay? Fine. You happy?"

"I'll be happy when you take your drink and go back over there." Evan pointed to the empty barstool where the guy had been sitting before he'd followed Candace.

CANDACE DIDN'T HANG out in bars often, and now she remembered why. The simple act of having a drink made a woman a target. It wasn't fair and it wasn't right, but it had probably been true since the ancient Babylonians had opened the first alehouses to serve watered-down beer.

As she processed what had happened—the guy and the way he'd followed her, the way he'd grabbed her arm—she began to absorb the fact that Evan, her Evan, had come to her rescue just as he had in any number of her teenage fantasies.

"Thank you." She looked up at him, at his face still dark with menace. "I just … thank you."

"You okay?"

"Yes. I'm fine. He was just annoying, that's all." But that wasn't all, because her hands were shaking. She shoved them into her pants pockets to hide her trembling.

It occurred to her that he'd been watching her since she came in. He must have been, or he wouldn't have known she was in need of rescue in the first place.

"I ... ah ... I'm sorry I interrupted your conversation with ..." She gestured toward the brunette at Evan's table.

"Kiki," he supplied.

"Oh."

"Don't be sorry. I was thinking of ways to excuse myself without being rude, and you helped with that."

She felt a little hum of happiness in her chest at the thought that he didn't like the brunette and would not be going to her room.

"I think I'll just go upstairs and turn in," she said.

Evan glanced at the asshole, who was still sneaking looks at them and grumbling something under his breath.

"I'll go with you. Just give me a minute." He went to his table, said something to Kiki, then came back and joined her.

"What did you tell her?"

"The truth. That you're a colleague, and I want to make sure you get to your room safely. You ready?"

Candace blanched a little at the word *colleague*, but she tried not to show it. She slung her purse over her shoulder, and they left the bar together while the camo guy glared at them.

WHEN THEY GOT to the room, Candace half expected Evan to drop her off—having seen her safely in for the night—and go back downstairs to either continue things with the brunette or find someone else to make a move on.

Instead, he sighed, flopped down on the sofa in the sitting room, and kicked off his shoes.

"Thank you for rescuing me," she said. "Really. I appreciate it. If you want to go back down there and talk to that woman some more, I'll be fine here." She wouldn't be fine if he did that—she'd be a wreck, imagining what might happen between them—but she was trying to be gracious.

"Nah, I think I'm done. It's been a long day." He dragged his hands through his hair. "I'm kind of sorry that asshole didn't try me. I haven't punched anybody in the face in a while, and I miss it."

Candace found the comment so unexpected that she had no reply at first. Then, upon recovering herself, she said, "You enjoy hitting people in the face?"

He gave her a wry smile. "I like boxing. I found a gym in San Luis Obispo, but I haven't worked with a sparring partner in a while. Hitting the heavy bag is fine, but it's not the same."

"I guess it wouldn't be."

Now that he'd brought it up, Candace remembered that Evan used to get in fights in school until he joined the football team. She supposed that had satisfied his need for male aggression. In light of all that, the boxing made sense.

She sat down on the sofa next to him, a good two feet of space between them. She wanted to scoot closer to him. Hell, she wanted to burrow into him, tuck herself into his arms and inhale his scent. She wanted to feel his heartbeat against her body. Instead, she stayed at her end of the sofa as though there were an invisible wall between them.

"I'm sorry about you and Anna," she said.

He rubbed his face with his hands. "Ah, hell. I'm not. You want to watch some TV?"

CHAPTER 10

*T*he next day, Candace began to enjoy the conference. She recognized some of her fellow attendees from earlier sessions, and she struck up conversations and exchanged business cards.

She attended a session on coffeehouse design that gave her ideas she wanted to share with Evan, and she popped into a latte art competition that was both entertaining and lively—maybe due to the caffeine surging through the competitors.

At lunchtime, she ate with a coffeehouse owner and a barista she'd met during the morning sessions, and she found herself so engaged that she almost didn't think about what Evan was doing.

When he happened to be in the same room with her, though, forgetting about him became impossible.

When Evan was nearby, Candace felt a light and warmth and comfort inside her that only he could inspire, and when he was gone, she felt the absence of that light and warmth and comfort like a shattering loss.

She knew all of these feelings were doing her no good. If he hadn't decided to love her by now, he probably never would. Obsessing about him meant she would never learn to love someone else, which meant she'd be alone for the rest of her life unless she could let him—or at least the idea of him—go.

But knowing all of that and acting on it were two different things.

She was sitting in a folding chair before a session talking to Robin, a woman who was about to take over her family's coffeehouse, when Evan walked in and Candace's eyes went straight to him.

Robin continued what she was saying—something about the desperate task of competing with Starbucks—but Candace didn't hear it.

Finally, the woman gave up on making her point and said, "He's very handsome, isn't he?"

That, at least, got through.

"What? Oh. Who's very handsome?"

Robin smirked. "The man you've been watching since the moment he came in. Don't tell me you aren't interested, because you'd be lying."

Candace's shoulders fell. "Is it that obvious?"

"If you were wearing a neon sign that said I LOVE YOU, it would be slightly more obvious. But not much."

"Oh … God. That's mortifying."

"It doesn't have to be." She bumped her shoulder into Candace's in a friendly, just-girls-here fashion. "You want me to figure out some way for you to meet him?"

Candace let out a breathy laugh. "I've known him since we were both five years old. And now we work together. He owns a coffeehouse and I manage it."

"Oh."

Candace could see her mentally rearranging her perceptions. "But the look you were giving him was an unfulfilled-longing kind of look, so I guess you two haven't …"

"No. We haven't."

"Have you been carrying a torch all this time?"

"I … no, not the whole time. I don't think I noticed him much in kindergarten."

Robin guffawed. "Have you made a move? Any kind of move?"

"Other than hanging around him as much as possible feeling desperate, humiliating love and hoping he'll suddenly see me? No."

"Well, that's just sad."

"I couldn't agree more."

At some point, she was either going to have to make that move—a real one that could not be misinterpreted—or she'd have to forget him and move on.

Neither option seemed particularly appealing.

THAT EVENING AFTER DINNER, a big-name coffee distributor held a cocktail party for conference participants, with all of the cocktails coffee-themed: Irish coffee, coffee with Baileys Irish Cream, coffee and Kahlúa, espresso martinis, and more.

Candace and Evan decided to pop in before settling down for the night.

The idea had been to have one drink, do a little networking, and make it an early night. But the drinks were delicious, the crowd was lively, and the snacks laid out on a long table at one end of the room were appealing, so they stayed much longer than either one of them had planned.

"What have you got?" Candace peered into Evan's highball glass, which was topped with a white cloud of whipped cream.

"I don't know what it's called, but it has rum and ginger in it." Evan took a sip. "Pretty good, actually. Tastes like a ginger snap, but with coffee and booze."

He offered it to her, and she took a sip. "Oh, my God. That's amazing."

"You want me to grab one for you?"

"No." Candace had already finished her second drink. But then she thought, why the hell not? "Actually, yes."

He went to get the drink, and she struck up a pleasant conversation with an older man who was thinking of expanding his coffeehouse offerings to include lunch items and wanted to know if Candace and Evan had tried it.

All in all, she was having a wonderful time.

~

THE THEORY—OR, at least, Evan's theory—had been that the coffee and the alcohol would counteract each other, resulting in him and Candace getting neither too drunk nor too wired.

In practice, that didn't turn out to be true. By the time he and Candace got back to their suite, they were both swaying on their feet at the same time as they were buzzing with caffeine-driven energy.

"Oh, my God. I'm so drunk, and I want to sleep it off, but I may never close my eyes again." Candace dropped her purse onto a chair, sank onto the sofa, then promptly jumped up from the sofa and started pacing the room.

"Damn. Whose idea was that?" Evan's eyes felt gritty, his hands were tingling, and his mind was fogged with alcohol.

"I don't know! It seemed like a good idea. Right? Fancy adult coffee drinks—who doesn't want that? I shouldn't have wanted that! I shouldn't have!"

She was gesticulating wildly with her arms as she talked, and Evan found something about that damned cute.

"Maybe we should watch a movie or something," he suggested.

"I couldn't sit still long enough to watch a movie. Not with this much caffeine in my system."

"Well, we could take a walk, then. See the city by night. It's only, what? Midnight?"

She considered that, then nodded a little more vigorously than the situation warranted. "Good. A walk. That's good. Let me get my coat."

~

CANDACE, as a woman, never would have walked alone in a big city at midnight. The threats were too real, the intimidation too stark. But being in the company of a very large man who liked to hit people changed the dynamic considerably.

They walked past Pike Place Market and the aquarium, turned inland past the Seattle Art Museum, wandered past the public library, then made their way back toward the water and the Bainbridge Island ferry terminal.

The night was clear, and the streets were still wet and shining from a rain earlier in the evening. A good number of cars still whooshed along the roads—a city like Seattle was never entirely quiet —but they mostly had the sidewalks to themselves.

Candace's thoughts were still fuzzy from the alcohol, and her body was still humming with caffeine. But another sensation was joining those two: she felt simple contentment being here in this place with Evan.

She was so conscious of his nearness as they walked that she longed to reach out and take his hand, but she didn't dare. Occasionally they bumped hips, having drifted too close to one another, and Candace felt the contact like a jolt of electricity.

"So. Tell me about Anna," she said.

AT FIRST, Evan didn't want to talk about Anna. But he did it anyway, and the more he said, the more he realized that talking about her was just what he needed to get her out of his system.

"She was my partner's girlfriend." He shoved his hands into his pockets for warmth as they walked.

"Your partner? The one who ..."

"The one who destroyed my business? Yeah, that one. When he went to prison, she jumped right over to me."

He realized that made it sound as though he had nothing to do with it, so he walked it back a little. "I mean, of course I had a part in that. I could have brushed her off. But ..."

"But maybe you were interested in getting back at him?"

He shrugged. "Maybe. Hell, probably. He'd been treating her like shit, and she was hurt, and I was hurt. So we decided to be hurt together."

"Did that help? Having someone to be hurt with?"

"At first it did, yeah. But that's not the kind of thing you can build a long-term relationship on. At some point you have to stop being hurt, and then what do you have?"

She stopped walking and turned to face him. They stood in front of a cafe, its windows dark.

"Have you, then?" she asked.

"Have I what?"

"Have you stopped being hurt?"

It was a good question. Had he?

"Mostly, yeah. I think so."

He liked living in his hometown again. He'd missed it. He liked having a new challenge in the coffeehouse. He liked the slower pace, the lower percentage of assholes in his life. And he liked being here, right now, talking and walking with Candace.

"I'm glad," she said. "I'm sorry you went through everything you did, and if you're feeling better about things ... well, I'm really happy for you."

THEY WALKED SOME MORE, then ended up sitting on a concrete bench overlooking Elliott Bay. The lights from the nearby buildings shone on the water, the reflections bobbing and dancing lazily.

"What about you?" Evan asked. "No boyfriend?"

She felt her face burn with a blush and was happy that the darkness hid it. "Oh, you know. I date."

"But nobody in particular?"

She was silent.

"Okay. I get the sense you don't want to talk about it," he said.

"It's not that."

"What is it, then?"

She couldn't say what she was really thinking. She couldn't tell him the truth. How could she, when the truth was that nobody she'd ever dated had matched up to him? Every man she flirted with, every man she went out with, every man she'd ever slept with had been a pale imitation of Evan, so nothing had lasted. She was beginning to think nothing ever would.

"It's just … I guess I'm waiting for my dream man to ask me out."

"And who's that?" His voice was soft, rough, intimate.

Now is the time. If you're going to tell him, this is the moment.

She was just about to open her mouth to say, *you, you are,* when two cars on the street behind them nearly collided, both drivers leaned on their horns, and Candace, in her caffeine-fueled state, jumped and squealed in surprise.

The moment was over.

"We should probably head back," she said.

CHAPTER 11

Once they were back in the room, Candace knew she still wouldn't be able to sleep. That wired, overcharged feeling she'd gotten from too much caffeine had lessened somewhat, but certainly not enough for her to settle down and drift off—especially in an unfamiliar bed.

She opened one of the complimentary bottles of water the hotel had provided, took a deep drink to stave off the inevitable hangover, and plopped onto the sofa.

"I think I'll go for that movie now."

Evan seemed to be considering his own chances with sleep as he stood with his hands on his hips, looking at her.

"You want to join me?" she asked.

"I guess so, but it had better not be a chick flick."

THEY PICKED a movie they both could agree on from the pay-per-view options. She'd wanted some girly rom-com and he'd wanted a martial arts movie, so they compromised and settled on a World War II film that had fighting for him and some romantic elements for her.

He was on his side of the sofa and she was on hers, the space between them large enough to fit another person comfortably or two uncomfortably.

It seemed to him that if you were on a sofa watching a movie with a woman late at night, you really ought to be making some kind of move on her—unless the woman was your sister.

Candace wasn't his sister.

The idea of making a move was appealing, but it presented a number of problems, starting with the fact that they worked together and ending with the fact that he'd be using her because she was female and she was here, and that would make him a real dick.

He didn't want to be a dick, so he stayed on his part of the sofa while they watched the Allies invade Normandy.

He stretched his legs out and propped his feet on the coffee table, getting comfortable.

He'd have thought it would be impossible to fall asleep, but about halfway through the movie, his eyes began to drift closed.

SITTING in the dark with the TV playing was just the thing Candace needed to relax.

They'd kept the volume low in an effort not to disturb the neighbors, and the murmur of sound lulled Candace into a half-waking daze by the time they were an hour into it.

Evan was here with her, and even if they weren't touching—even if he was over there and she was over here—his presence gave her a sense of comfort, of things being right.

She slumped down into her seat, closed her eyes, and let herself sleep.

WHEN CANDACE OPENED HER EYES, daylight flooded the room through the big bank of windows. She was stretched out across the length of the sofa, comfortable and warm.

It took her a few seconds to realize that the reason she was so comfortable and warm was that she was sprawled across Evan's body, her head resting against his chest, her legs entangled with his.

How? When? Had she passed out in an alcoholic stupor?

As she rose to full wakefulness, she assessed the situation. They were both fully dressed, so clearly nothing had happened. But *something* had happened, or they wouldn't be … cuddling. That was the only word she could come up with for what they were doing.

She had so many questions: Who had initiated the cuddling? And when? And how? Was Evan fully aware of it, or would he wake up to find it a surprise as she had?

She needed to move before he woke up. If he opened his eyes and found her on top of him and was visibly unhappy about it, Candace would be mortified and her feelings would be crushed, and she didn't think she could take that on top of all of this unrequited longing.

But the last thing she wanted to do was leave this spot. He was warm and comforting, she could smell the scent of his body, and she could feel his heartbeat beneath her cheek.

How many times had she yearned to hold him? How many times had she wanted this?

She would get up. She would. But for now, she wrapped her arms around him and nuzzled her face into his chest, just breathing him in, and felt her heart hum with happiness.

EVAN FELT Candace moving around on top of him—felt her put her arms around him—but he didn't open his eyes.

If he did, they'd have an awkward moment of polite demurrals, each of them claiming they hadn't meant anything by all of this nocturnal nuzzling.

Also, he didn't want it to end quite yet. It felt good to have a woman holding him, even if the woman was someone with whom he wasn't enjoying an intimate relationship.

So he lay there and kept his eyes closed and his breathing steady, thinking he could stretch things out a bit and just enjoy the physical closeness of someone sweet and lovely.

He hadn't even realized he thought of Candace as sweet and lovely until this moment. But she was both of those things. She had a beauty he'd failed to recognize, not just physically—though there was that— but as a person.

Maybe she hadn't yet blossomed in high school, or maybe she had and he'd been too self-absorbed to notice.

But he was noticing now, especially with the weight of her sprawled across him.

And, okay, his body was noticing, too. If she didn't get up soon, it would become readily apparent to her that he was awake and knew she was there.

At least, certain parts of him were wide awake.

CANDACE ABSOLUTELY DID NOT WANT Evan to wake up and catch her smelling him, so she got up carefully, slowly, trying not to jostle him.

Standing next to the sofa, she took a moment to watch him sleep, to watch the beautiful, manly grace of him.

The TV was still on from the night before, playing an ad for the hotel chain, and she turned it off, then crept silently into her room and closed the door behind her.

THANKFULLY, Evan didn't seem to know what had happened the night before. Candace was grateful for that when she emerged from her room, showered and dressed for the day, and found him looking fresh and professional with his messenger bag over his shoulder and his hair still wet from the shower.

"Hey. I'm about to head down. You want me to wait for you?" He raised his eyebrows in question.

Obviously, he didn't know about the cuddling. He couldn't know, because there was no trace of awkwardness, no hint of any change in the status of their relationship.

Candace was grateful for that because, while she did very much want a change in the status of their relationship, she didn't want it this way—through covert snuggling.

Feeling better about things, she gave him a winning smile. "I'm not quite ready. You go ahead, and I'll be down in a bit."

When he was gone, she lay on the sofa where he'd been the night before, closed her eyes, and remembered the feel of his body.

Then she got up, smoothed her hair back into place, gathered her things, and got ready for the conference.

Evan was pretty sure he'd pulled it off and Candace didn't know what had happened between them.

He reflected on that as he got into the elevator to go downstairs. If she'd known, he'd have had to make some kind of decision on whether he wanted to pursue things with her.

He wasn't opposed to it—he was becoming less and less opposed as time went on—but he wasn't exactly ready to pull the trigger, either, not with things between him and Anna so fresh, and not with all of the possible emotional ramifications for both of himself and Candace if they got involved.

Not to mention the professional ramifications.

He'd enjoyed holding her in his arms, but that had to be it for now. Leaving it there was the only responsible thing to do.

If she'd been aware of their closeness the night before, they'd have had to air the whole thing out, but she wasn't, so they could both forget it ever happened.

Even if he didn't want to completely forget.

He was sure he would bring it to mind fondly on many happy occasions.

CHAPTER 12

*C*andace kept her distance from Evan the rest of the day. It wasn't because she didn't want to be with him—God, no—but because after last night, it was too tempting to press things further, with results that might be disastrous.

So, even though she wanted to stay close to him, she made an effort to meet new people, focus on learning, and remember that she was here to become a more valuable coffeehouse manager, not to make moves on her boss.

At lunchtime, she grabbed a sandwich at the poolside cafe and texted Brittany about what had happened.

Oh my God, Brittany answered. *You both got roaring drunk, and instead of using each other for fabulous sex, you cuddled! That's either sad or adorable. I don't know which.*

Candace wasn't entirely sure which it was, either.

I don't want us to use each other for fabulous sex, she wrote back. *Well, I do want the fabulous sex, but I don't want him to use me, and I don't want to use him. I want him to love me. I want it all.*

So, he didn't make a move on you at all?

No. And he's been chatting up other women. Candace scowled, thinking of Kiki.

Three dots bounced on Candace's screen, indicating that Brittany was composing her answer.

Finally, it came.

You know, Candace, you might consider moving on. Seeing other guys. You've been pining for Evan for decades. If it hasn't happened by now ...

She left the thought open, though it wasn't as if Candace hadn't considered it before.

I can't see someone else. There isn't anyone else. There will never be anyone else.

Even as she wrote it, Candace had to acknowledge that Brittany had a point. She couldn't keep wanting and wanting and never getting what she needed. She couldn't keep needing something she would never have.

If she did, she would end up sad and alone.

Maybe it was time she came to terms with that.

CANDACE HAD a chance to practice letting go of Evan that evening after the conference wrapped up for the day.

During her last session, she'd been seated next to a man in his mid-thirties who was setting up his own coffee roasting business. He and Candace chatted a bit before the speaker began and again during a break in the middle of the lecture.

When they broke for dinner, he turned to Candace and put a hand lightly on her forearm.

"You want to grab some dinner? With me, I mean? I want to hear more about Jitters."

The way he'd said it—all cutely awkward and shy—suggested that he didn't really want to hear more about Jitters. He just wanted to go out with Candace.

She was on the verge of politely declining when she remembered what Brittany had said about moving on. If things hadn't progressed with Evan by now, they never would.

She couldn't keep chasing a fantasy.

"I'd love to," she said.

EVAN HAD it in mind that he would linger in the lobby after his session, find Candace when she came out of hers, and ask her to have dinner with him.

Why wouldn't he? It was reasonable to think they'd eat together since they had come to the conference together. Since they worked together.

It had nothing at all to do with the nighttime snuggling and anything he may or may not have felt about it.

Except, he waited until the crowd thinned out, and she never came. Had she already gone up to the room?

He texted her to find out.

Dinner?

She responded a few minutes later.

Oh, I'm sorry. I've already got plans to eat with a coffee roaster who wants to know more about Jitters.

It made sense that she would invite him to join them, since he was, after all, the owner of Jitters. He expected that invitation any second.

It never came.

Finally, he decided to take matters into his own hands.

Mind if I join you? I can tell them about Jitters, and I'd like to ask them about the roasting business.

This time, the response took longer.

That would be great, except we're already seated, and it's a table for two. This place is packed, so we can't really ask for a bigger table.

He felt let down in a way that went beyond the simple need to have someone to share a meal with to avoid awkwardly eating alone.

Okay, no sweat, he wrote. *I'll see you later.*

THE COFFEE ROASTER, whose name was Rob, seemed nice enough, but he didn't cause Candace's hot guy meter to so much as move the needle. That was okay. She wasn't looking to fall in love with a man from Minnesota, marry him, move across the country, and have his kids. This was practice. This was Candace getting into a frame of mind that was post-Evan.

They ordered dinner and drinks and they talked—about coffee, about what each of them thought of the conference, and about their personal lives. It was ... fine.

She was telling Rob about Cambria, her parents, and her siblings when Evan walked in with a tall blonde, his hand on the small of her back, and Candace forgot what she'd been saying.

EVAN HADN'T INTENDED to end up in the same place as Candace, but he hadn't been trying to avoid her, either. When an attractive barista he'd met in the fitness center the day before spotted him in the lobby and asked him if he wanted to eat with her, he'd simply chosen the hotel restaurant for convenience.

That's what Candace had done, too, it seemed, because there she was at a table in the corner with some guy in a polo shirt and sport jacket. The guy had red hair and a pale complexion, like he might burst into flames in the sun. He was leaning toward Candace and saying something, and Evan would have bet his ass it had nothing to do with coffee.

"Something wrong?" The barista, whose name was Stephanie, looked at him with either concern or irritation—it was hard to tell.

"Ah ... no. I just saw someone I know, that's all."

"Oh. Well, let's get a table. I'm starving."

REALLY, what did Evan care if Candace ate dinner with some guy she'd met at the conference? And what did he care if the guy kept touching her—a brush of his fingers on hers here, an emphatic hand on her shoulder there—when she didn't seem to mind it?

The thing was, though, he *did* care. He just couldn't figure out why.

Had she ditched him to have dinner with this guy? Did her interest in the guy go beyond professional networking? Was this redheaded bastard going to end up in the suite later tonight, going into Candace's room and locking the door behind them to do God knew what in privacy?

Or, worse, would she go to the guy's room and not show up in the suite at all, leaving Evan to wonder about her safety?

"Evan?"

He'd just have to keep an eye on them, that's all. He would just have to monitor the situation for her well-being. It was only gentlemanly. It was only—

"*Evan.*"

He emerged from his thoughts to find Stephanie glaring at him.

"Uh ... sorry. What were you saying?"

"I wasn't saying anything in particular, I was just trying to get your attention. You're staring pretty hard at that woman over there."

"Oh." He picked up his menu and made a show of studying it. "Right. I was just ... It's nothing. She's my colleague, and I want to make sure she's okay, that's all."

Stephanie craned her neck to get a better view of Candace. "She looks okay to me."

"Yeah. That's ... I think I'll get the scampi."

Stephanie wasn't fooled by his scampi diversion.

"You're into her, right? Is that what this is? You're into her and you're jealous? I mean, it's fine if that's the case. I'll just eat and get out of your hair. But I was kind of thinking dinner might lead to more, if you're up for it. So I'd like to know the lay of the land."

He wasn't an idiot. An attractive blonde was telling him she wanted him, and he wasn't about to squander the opportunity.

"The land is fine. I'm not into her, and I'm not jealous. She got harassed at the bar the other night by some asshole, and I want to make sure she's okay. That's all."

"All right. Well, the guy she's with looks like he wouldn't hurt a baby chick if it was attacking his mother. I'd say she's fine."

"Yeah." He picked up the wine menu and studied that. "Yeah. Okay. You want red or white?"

CANDACE STOPPED in the middle of a sentence when she noticed Evan at a nearby table with an attractive woman.

"Candace? Is everything all right?"

Rob was talking to her, but she barely heard him.

"Which is it, him or her?"

That, she heard.

"What do you mean?"

"That couple." He pointed toward Evan and the blonde. "Which one are you staring at? Him or her?"

"Oh." She was tempted to say neither, but he wouldn't believe it, and what was the point in lying? "Him."

"Ah. So, I'm wasting my time."

"How do you mean?" She knew exactly how he meant it, but she had to say something to bide her time while she composed herself.

He fidgeted with his cloth napkin, picking it up from his lap, scrunching it between his hands, and putting it back down. "Well, you realize I didn't ask you to dinner to talk about coffee, right? I mean, I like talking about coffee, and that's fine, but ..." He was blushing. With his fair coloring, that probably happened often.

"No, I knew that."

"Right. And if you're staring at him and not her ..." He left the thought unfinished.

She shook her head and didn't look at him. "He's my boss, that's all."

Rob let out a soft guffaw. "That's not all."

She thought of lying, but again, what was the point? "You're right. That's not all."

She could have sat there having dinner with Rob, trying to make conversation, trying to convince herself that she could move on by practice-dating someone else, but she didn't have it in her. Not when Evan was across the dining room with someone younger, prettier, and blonder than she was.

"Look. I'm sorry, but I think I'm just going to go." She picked up her purse and put her napkin on the table.

"You don't have to. We can just ... you know. Talk about coffee."

Even that would be beyond her with Evan right there. Him and the blonde.

"Thank you, but ... I have to go."

EVAN'S CANDACE RADAR sent off warning alarms when she got up from the table abruptly and walked out.

She and the stiff she was with had only had wine so far—their dinner hadn't come yet—so something had upset her and made her leave early.

Was it the guy? Had he said something? Done something?

"Evan, I swear to God ..."

He hadn't heard what Stephanie said, but he'd heard the tone, and that was universally understood by men everywhere. Pissed women didn't require translation.

"Sorry. Sorry." He turned to face her and picked up his wineglass.

"So, I was *trying* to tell you about my sister and her husband," Stephanie went on. "Last Christmas—"

"I'm sorry. If you could just ..." He held up a finger to stop her, then got up and went over to where the guy was sitting alone across from the chair Candace had vacated.

As Evan crossed the restaurant, he became more and more convinced that this asshole had done something to drive her away. So by the time he arrived at the asshole's table, he was on the offensive, ready to hit somebody if need be.

"Hey." He stood over the guy, straightened to his full height, his broad shoulders squared.

"Oh. Hi." The redhead peered up at him, blinking.

"What did you say to her?"

"What?"

"You heard me. She left in a hurry, and she looked upset. So I want to know what you did or said to upset her. And I want to know now."

The guy blanched, probably fearing for the integrity of his face. Good. That's exactly what Evan wanted him to feel.

"I didn't upset her. You did."

Evan opened his mouth to say something then closed it again. "What?"

"Would you sit down, please? I don't want to have to bend my neck to talk to you."

If Evan sat, he'd lose his considerable height and size advantage and the natural intimidation that came with them. But he was curious, and people at other tables were starting to look at him, so he sat.

"Okay. What do you mean, I did?"

The guy picked up his wineglass and took a gulp, then patted his lips with his napkin and folded his arms on the table. "I mean, she was upset because she saw you with another woman. That's why she left. I didn't do anything. You're the one who got her all worked up."

Evan's eyebrows shot up. Could that be true? *Well, shit.*

He picked up Candace's wineglass, which was still half full, and drained it.

"Are you sure?"

"Yes. I'm sure. She was distracted from the minute she saw you, and when I asked her what was going on, she told me."

"She told you she was upset that I was with a woman?"

"More or less."

Well, this was an interesting development. He had gone back and forth on the question of whether Candace's teenage crush on him was still going on. Sometimes he thought yes, but other times, he convinced himself she'd moved on.

Apparently, she hadn't.

"Okay. Okay, then."

"Are you done trying to intimidate me?" the guy asked. "Because I promise I didn't do anything except ask her to dinner and buy her a glass of wine."

Evan ducked his head, embarrassed. "Yeah, about that. Sorry. I thought—"

"I get it. But you misread the situation. She's in love with you."

With that thought heavy on his mind, he got up and went back to his own table to find that Stephanie was gone.

The waiter arrived and asked to take his order.

"Let's wait a minute," Evan said. "I think my date is in the ladies' room."

"Sir, your date left a few minutes ago."

"She did?"

"Yes. And, to tell you the truth, she didn't look too happy."

CANDACE TOLD herself the night hadn't been a complete failure. She'd taken a step toward moving on. The fact that it hadn't worked didn't negate the fact that she'd taken the step. Next time, she would just have to make sure Evan wasn't anywhere nearby.

Except, he would always be nearby, wouldn't he? They lived in the same small town. They worked at the same coffeehouse. It was hard to stop yearning for someone when they were always there.

Her life was inextricably tangled with his. She worked for him. She lived in an apartment he owned. She relied on him for her livelihood.

The problem merited careful consideration.

CHAPTER 13

*E*van intended to ask Candace about the guy and about why
she'd left the restaurant so abruptly. He was only concerned
for her safety and well-being.

But when he got back to the suite, she was already in her bedroom
with the door closed. He lingered in the sitting room for a while,
thinking she might come out, but she didn't. He finally went to bed,
feeling uneasy about everything that had happened.

In the morning, he resolved to try again. But Candace put him off
as she bustled around the suite getting ready for her day.

"Good morning." He tried for a sunny tone of voice, a devil-may-
care casual note that would encourage her to let down her guard. He
wasn't sure he'd achieved it.

"Oh. Good morning." She fussed around with her bag, putting a
notebook and pens inside, then slipped into her shoes and checked
her makeup in the wall mirror.

"I saw you at the restaurant last night." Again, he tried to sound
jaunty and unconcerned.

"I saw you, too."

"Did you?" He nodded his head a few times.

"Yeah. How was your dinner?"

"Fine. It was fine." And they were getting nowhere with this.

He decided to dive into the subject he really wanted to explore.

"So. You left kind of suddenly," he said. "I was wondering ... That is, I hope the guy you were with didn't do anything to upset you."

"What?"

She looked surprised, and the surprise seemed genuine. So, the guy was fine, then.

"I just wondered. I mean, you stormed out of there before you'd even eaten, so ..."

Candace straightened from where she'd been bending over her bag. "You were watching when I left and whether I'd eaten?"

Well, it sounded bad when she said it like that. "No. No, no. I wasn't watching. I just kind of noticed, that's all. After the guy at the bar, I wanted to make sure you were okay."

"I was." She slung her bag over her shoulder. "I'll see you downstairs." She left the suite without another word to him.

CANDACE GOT into the elevator with her heart pounding. Evan had been watching her? Why? What did that mean?

She wanted to believe he was jealous seeing her with another man. But that was ridiculous. He'd been with another woman, after all. He'd come home alone, so that was something. But he'd taken a beautiful woman to dinner, and that didn't suggest that he was interested in pursuing a romantic relationship with Candace.

This whole thing was ridiculous. She was ridiculous. How much longer was she going to want him? Was she really going to waste her entire life dreaming about a man who could never love her?

As the elevator descended, Candace decided somewhere between the fourth and first floors that she'd had enough. Sometimes giving up was a way of moving forward.

It was time to do both.

Today was the last day of the conference, and she told herself to focus on coffee, the coffee business, her own skills in that area, and her own professional development.

That's why she was here, after all. Nothing else mattered. Not her feelings for Evan, and not that gnawing ache she felt whenever she was around him. She could rise above all of that.

She would just have to rise.

WHEN EVAN GOT DOWNSTAIRS, he tried to find a seat next to Candace, but she hadn't saved him one. She shrugged apologetically, indicating the lack of a space beside her.

He took a seat across the room with the uneasy feeling that something had shifted between them. Was she angry with him? What had he done?

He tried to focus on the material being presented—an overview of where the coffee business would be going over the next five years—taking careful notes and trying not to think about Candace.

It seemed like he was thinking about her more and more these days, whether he wanted to or not.

THAT NIGHT at the banquet that marked the finale of the conference, Candace wore the dress she and Brittany had picked out, and she chose a table with only one unoccupied seat, ensuring that Evan couldn't sit with her.

She hadn't responded to his text message asking if she wanted to attend the banquet together, and she ignored his questioning look when he came into the event hall and saw her at a table with no room for him.

Candace didn't want the dress to go to waste, so she flirted with a coffeehouse owner from Rhode Island, smiling and making small talk as though she were having a good time.

She wasn't.

When the banquet was over, she slipped into her room in their suite before Evan got back. She heard him come in about an hour later, and she turned on her television to try to get her mind off him.

~

IGNORING EVAN WAS RIDICULOUSLY DIFFICULT, and Candace wasn't sure she could do it.

She'd almost cracked when he texted her about the banquet, and she'd almost given in again when he came into the suite. It would be so easy to fall asleep on the sofa with him again, waking up in his arms.

Some travel show was playing on Netflix, and she tried to focus on it while Evan moved around in the sitting room just beyond her door. He hadn't brought anyone back with him, thankfully. But then again, what did she care? If she would never have him for herself, why did it matter who he did or did not sleep with?

It did matter, though. It mattered so much she worried it would burn her to ashes, leaving nothing but a charred and smoking wreck.

She wanted to call Brittany—wanted to hear her friend's voice—but Evan was on the other side of the wall, and she worried he would hear her talking about him. So she texted instead.

This is harder than I thought it would be.

What? Brittany texted back. *The coffee business?*

No. Sharing a suite with Evan. He's right there, but he might as well be on the other side of the world for all the good it does me.

Did you try flirting with someone else, like I told you?

Yes. I went out with someone, and Evan showed up before our entrees came. It kind of ruined things.

I'm guessing he didn't show up alone.

No. He didn't.

And that was the heart of it, really. If Evan were to stay single forever, Candace could probably go on like this, wanting him in silence indefinitely. Because the hope would always be alive. But he wasn't going to stay single forever, or even for much longer.

First he was with Anna, and then he wasn't, and his unattached state had lasted less than a day before he'd started flirting, drinking, and having dinner with women who weren't Candace.

He was casual with his relationships, which meant he would probably be casual with Candace—if they ever got past their strictly professional and occasionally friendly relationship.

This might not be the best work situation for you, given everything, Brittany texted.

That was probably true, but at this point, Evan had spent money on her professional training. He'd put time into her. She lived above the shop, for God's sake.

She couldn't just walk away—not without serious inconvenience, awkwardness, and hurt feelings.

Though, the hurt feelings seemed to be happening anyway. At least for her.

EVAN KNEW there was something wrong on the way home from the conference. He just didn't know what.

He and Candace shared an Uber to the airport early in the morning, then sat together on the flight not in silence, but in something worse than silence: awkward courtesy.

Candace was being cordial—but cordial in a way you'd be with your eighty-six-year-old neighbor. Not with someone you worked closely with and had known since kindergarten.

On the flight, she put in earbuds and stuck her face in a book, and he wasn't an idiot. He knew she was doing all of that to avoid talking to him.

Well, hell. Maybe she'd gotten some troubling news from home. Maybe she was deep in thought about coffee. Maybe her distant attitude had nothing to do with him.

Still, he couldn't help but think that was wrong. He was sure it did have something to do with him—something to do with what that redheaded guy at the restaurant had said to him.

She's in love with you.

Could she really still be, after all this time?

And if she was, how did that translate to her giving him the silent treatment?

He'd just have to wait it out, he guessed. He'd wait, and once she thawed, they would talk about it.

He put in his own earbuds and closed his eyes, trying to focus on the podcast he was listening to and not on the woman sitting beside him.

CHAPTER 14

*E*van held out throughout the flight, but once they were in his car heading from the San Jose airport to Cambria—a drive of more than three hours—his resolve broke.

"You want to tell me what's going on?" he said.

She'd been reading the book in the car—the same one she'd had on the plane—and he suspected the content wasn't nearly as interesting as she wanted him to think.

"What do you mean?" She looked at him with wide, innocent eyes.

"I mean, there's clearly something bothering you, and I would like to know the nature of it."

"There's nothing wrong. I'm fine. I've just really been looking forward to reading this book," she said.

He glanced at the title as he drove. "*The World Atlas of Coffee?*"

"I'm trying to improve my professional skills."

"Wasn't that on the giveaway table at the conference?"

"Your point?"

He didn't have one, he supposed, other than the fact that no one could be so engrossed in a coffee reference text that it would dominate their attention through a flight and a lengthy drive.

As they headed south through Gilroy, he exited the highway,

pulled into the parking lot of a store devoted to garlic, parked the car, then turned to her.

"This is stupid. Just tell me what's going on. If I did something, I want to know."

She stared through the windshield instead of looking at him. "You didn't do anything."

"Okay, then what? You've been avoiding me, and when you couldn't avoid me anymore, you went all ... civil and polite."

"Well, God forbid I should be civil and polite." She threw him a cold glare. "Would you rather I be rude and hostile?"

He opened his mouth to say no, of course not, then changed his mind. "You know, I would. At least that would be honest. When you were being rude and hostile, you'd probably be yelling at me, and the yelling would probably give me some indication of what the hell's wrong."

She threw the book onto the floor of the car. "You want to know what's wrong?"

"I said I do."

"You really want to know, Evan? Do you?"

"Yes!"

"What's wrong is that I'm in love with you! I'm in love with you, and I always have been, and I just spent five days watching you try to pick up other women. It's torture! All right? Are you happy? I love you, and you don't love me, and it's putting me through hell!"

CANDACE WAS HORRIFIED by the words coming out of her mouth. She wanted to stop them, but they just kept coming.

Oh, God. Had she really said that? Out loud?

Her eyes were wide, her mouth frozen in an O of horror, as she stared at him in the aftermath of what she'd said.

"Candace ..."

"No." She waved her hands frantically in front of her, stopping him. "No, don't say anything. This is humiliating enough without you trying to let me down easy. If you say something about how I'm a lovely girl and I'll find some nice guy someday, I'm going to wait until the car's moving at full speed and then throw myself out of it. So just … don't." A few tears leaked out of her eyes, and she swiped at them with her fingertips.

She turned with a jerk to face forward in her seat, crossed her arms over her chest, and looked out the windshield. "Can we just go now?"

"But Candace …"

"I swear to God, I need you to shut up. Can we just go?"

EVAN GOT BACK on the highway feeling uneasy and confused. Candace had just declared her love for him, but she was also yelling at him.

The mind of a woman was an eternal mystery.

Yes, he'd suspected that Candace still had feelings for him. But as long as she hadn't said anything about it, he could go on as though he didn't know, working with her and being friendly but not having to make any kind of decision about anything.

Now, he suspected that going about his business, basking in the glow of Candace's regard but never having to do anything about it, was no longer an option.

She would expect him, at some point when he was allowed to talk again, to say something indicating how he felt about her.

He'd either have to admit he had feelings or say he didn't.

The first meant he'd be plunging headlong into a relationship right after getting out of another one and before he felt ready. And the emotional stakes for Candace would be higher than he felt comfortable with. The second meant he'd have to hurt her, and he didn't want to do that.

Compounding all of this uncertainty was the fact that he didn't know how he felt about her.

If someone had asked him a month ago, he'd have said he thought of her as a friend and colleague.

But something had changed for him that night on the sofa when he'd held her sleeping body in his arms. He wasn't sure what had changed or how much it had changed. He only knew it had.

When he'd seen her in the restaurant with that guy, he hadn't liked it. He hadn't liked it at all.

But that meant he was ... intrigued. It didn't mean he wanted to start some big thing with her, and it didn't mean he was in love.

They drove the rest of the way to Cambria in silence, speaking only when they went through a Starbucks drive-through and Evan had to ask Candace for her order.

He dropped her off at Jitters and carried her suitcase upstairs to her apartment for her. He tried again then, when he was standing in her living room with her luggage on the floor beside him.

"Candace, what you said to me ..."

"No." She held up her hand like a traffic cop, palm out.

"But—"

"We'll talk about it if you want to, Evan. We will. But not now, okay? Please, not now." Her face was pink and her eyes were shiny and wet.

He left without saying another word.

SOMETHING about the whole thing made him feel keyed-up and edgy.

He went home, changed into his workout clothes, drove to the gym through the light traffic of late afternoon, and pounded the heavy bag for a while to get out his various frustrations.

Some, though not all, of the frustration was sexual in nature.

Okay, so he hadn't looked at Candace that way back in high school. He was looking now, and it had taken a lot of his personal reserves of character and restraint not to take advantage of her feelings for him.

If he didn't care about her, he might have. But he did care. Taking her to bed just because he could would be a dick move, and he hated guys like that.

He wasn't above using a woman for sex, but she had to know ahead of time what it was, and she had to be using him, too. Cards on the table. Mutual using.

This wouldn't be that, so it was out of the question. If he took Candace to bed, it would be because he thought they might have a future together. He wasn't there yet, but that didn't mean he hadn't imagined her naked all the way from Gilroy.

He hit the bag: jab, cross, hook, cross. His muscles were warm and loose, and a sheen of sweat dampened his skin.

"Hey, Evan."

He paused, looking up to see Avery Pierce in a similar state of recent exertion. He was wearing cutoff sweatpants and a tank top, his skin gleaming with perspiration.

"Avery. What's up?"

"Want to do some sparring?"

Just the thought of pounding the crap out of a willing opponent made him feel better.

"God, yes."

THE EVENTS of the past twelve hours had been so momentous that Candace decided to tell Brittany about them in person. She called first, then went to Brittany's place on Lodge Hill without bothering to shower, change the clothes she'd traveled in, or do any of the things she usually did at the end of a trip.

She just needed to see her friend.

At Brittany's place, a small cabin in a grove of Monterey pines, she plopped down on the sofa and buried her face in her hands.

"Oh, God, Brit. I told him. I can't believe I did that. I told him."

"You told Evan you love him? Hot damn." Brittany clapped her hands and bounced a little on her toes.

"Why? Why did I do that?" Candace moaned, feeling sick.

"So, what did he say?" Brittany perched her butt on the edge of the sofa, her body turned to face Candace.

"He didn't say anything. I wouldn't let him."

"What do you mean you wouldn't let him?" Brittany jumped to her feet, her voice raised.

Candace gave Brittany the rundown of what had happened: how she'd been distant with Evan after the incident at the restaurant, how he'd confronted her about it during the drive, and how she'd blurted out that she loved him. And then, how she'd refused to let him respond in any way to what she'd said.

"I couldn't let him say anything, Brit. I couldn't. Because he obviously doesn't love me back. Obviously. So, what would he have said? Some happy shit about what a great person I am and how I'll eventually find someone, and how he values my ... my ... *fruh-fruh*-friendship ..." She was starting to cry, and the crying had made it hard to get out that last part.

Brittany scooted next to Candace and rubbed her back in little circular motions. "Oh, Candace. You don't know he'll say that."

"He will. Or else he'll think, hey, why not give it a try? And we'll sleep together, and he'll decide he doesn't have those kinds of feelings for me, and I'll be crushed, Brittany. I'll be *cruh-cruh* ..." She gave up on saying the final word and sobbed into her hands.

Brittany stopped the rubbing, put her arm around Candace, and squeezed. Then she jumped up, grabbed a box of tissues from a side table, and brought it to Candace.

Candace pulled a wad of tissues out of the box and blew her nose into them. Then she took in a long, shuddering breath.

"I mean, am I wrong about any of that?"

Brittany sighed. "Probably not."

Candace blew her nose again into a fresh wad of tissues. "See? Even you think I'm right."

"Well ..."

"And now I have to work with him, after what I said. God. I'm an idiot. Why did I say that? Why couldn't I have just kept ... kept ..."

"Yearning in silence?"

"Yes!"

Brittany resumed the back rubbing. "Because yearning in silence was making you miserable."

"Well, I'm not any less miserable now, so."

Brittany went to the kitchen, poured a glass of water, and brought it to Candace. "When you think about it, this might be a good thing," she said.

"How?"

"Well, now you'll know for sure. Before, there was always the possibility that if he knew you loved him, he'd love you back. That's what you always thought, right? Now ..."

"Now I'll know he doesn't."

"If that's the case, it'll hurt, but you'll have closure. You'll be able to move on."

"But ... how can I move on if I'm working with him and living in an apartment he owns?"

"How indeed?" Brittany said.

EVAN WENT HOME after his workout feeling better. He always felt better when he'd pounded himself into happy exhaustion at the gym.

He took a long, hot shower, got dressed, and pulled a bottle of beer out of the refrigerator. He took it out on the back deck at Otter Bluff to drink it.

Settling into his Adirondack chair with a view of the ocean spread out before him, he called Nix.

"So, it turns out Candace really is in love with me," he said.

"I could have told you that. Oh, wait. I did."

"Yeah, well, earlier today *she* told me that. What am I supposed to do with it, man? She drops a bomb like that and I'm just supposed to, what? Stand there and let it explode?"

"You could try enjoying the blast," Nix suggested.

"I'd rather try to find a way to defuse it." Feeling that the metaphor had run its course, Evan let the bomb thing go and moved on. "I just

... I want to keep being colleagues and friends. Is that too much to ask?"

Nix made a humming sound as he considered it. "It is if it's too hard for her to be near you every day without any potential for more."

"I guess."

"So, *is* there potential for more?"

That was the question, wasn't it? The problem was, he didn't know. He'd been thinking about her more and more often, and he hadn't liked it when he'd seen her with that guy at the restaurant, and he *had* liked it—he'd liked it a lot—when she'd fallen asleep in his arms at the hotel. He might have considered taking things slowly and seeing where they went, but Candace's declaration had made going slowly impossible. It seemed to require an equivalent declaration: yes or no, in or out.

It was too much too soon.

Except it wasn't soon—not for her. If she'd really felt this way since they were kids, she'd been waiting a lifetime.

"I don't know," he said finally.

"*I don't know* isn't no."

"No, it isn't."

"For what it's worth, I like her," Nix said. "I liked her in school, and I still do. She comes into the market sometimes, and we chat. She's a nice person. And she's very attractive, even if it's not in the really obvious way you tend to go for."

"I don't go for that," Evan said.

Nix laughed. "Like hell you don't. When was the last time you dated a woman who didn't look like she could be a lost Kardashian sister?"

He opened his mouth to protest—to name some woman he'd dated who didn't fit that description. When he realized he'd have to go all the way back to his college years to find someone, he opted to stay silent.

"I'm just saying, you could do a lot worse," Nix said. "And you have. Many times."

CHAPTER 15

Candace had a lot to do at work the next day. She came downstairs at five thirty a.m.—a half hour before opening—and helped Molly and David fill the big air pots with fresh coffee, remove the chairs from atop the tables, fill the glass-front bakery case with pastries Cassie's Cakery had delivered that morning, refill the sugar and cream containers, stock the freshly cleaned restroom with paper towels, toilet paper, and soap, and do all of the many things they needed to do to get ready for an influx of customers seeking their morning caffeine fix.

"So, how was the conference?" David asked as he went through the process of signing into the electronic payment system.

"Oh … it was fine." Candace wanted to sound more enthusiastic than that, but she couldn't quite manage it.

She didn't want to talk about the conference, so she changed the subject, asking about how things had gone when she and Evan were away.

When they opened the doors at six, four customers were already waiting, and many more soon followed. After that, everyone was too busy to talk, and the topic of the conference didn't come up again.

Until Evan arrived.

HE BREEZED IN AT SEVEN, freshly showered and shaved and looking as delicious as Candace had ever seen him. He chatted a little with the baristas, greeted a few customers, then headed into Candace's office. She was checking the milk supply in the refrigerator, and he gave her a wave that suggested he wanted her to join him.

Candace steeled herself and went into the office, expecting to have to talk about what she'd said, how he felt about it, and what it all meant.

Evan was already in the visitor's chair, so she plopped down into the chair behind her desk.

"Look, Evan. We—"

"I was wondering about the layout of the shop," he said before she could go any further.

"You ... what?"

"The layout. That session about using layout to maximize productivity gave me a lot of ideas." He grabbed a pad of paper and a pen from her desk and dashed off a quick floor plan of the shop. "What do you think of moving the espresso station here and running the line through here?" He indicated the locations with his pen.

"Oh. I ... Well, I was kind of thinking the same thing."

"Great. We can maybe play with it a little after closing."

CANDACE HAD DINNER AT HER PARENTS' house that night. Her mother was still recovering from the hip surgery she'd had a couple of weeks before the coffee conference, so Candace brought takeout for herself and her parents.

"How are you feeling, Mom?" Candace put plates on the kitchen table, then placed a napkin beside each one.

"Oh, not bad." Melissa had a limp as she walked into the room and settled in at the table, but she seemed to be getting around okay. "I'm off the prescription pain medication—I can get by on ibuprofen now—which means my head's not foggy anymore. So that's good."

"That *is* good. You're not trying to do too much, are you?"

"Oh." She waved off Candace's question. "I know what I can handle."

Candace wasn't sure that was true. Melissa had always been busy with one project or another for as long as Candace could remember. Gardening, housework, club meetings, volunteer work—she was always doing something, always in motion with a to-do list and a limited number of hours in the day. Candace doubted she'd slowed down quite as much as she wanted her daughter to believe.

"You're not letting her do too much, are you, Dad?"

Ed was puttering around in the kitchen, looking for a can of soda in the refrigerator. He emerged with a Coke in his hand.

"Me? What makes you think I have any control over what your mother does?" He delivered the words with affection in his voice, and he kissed the top of his wife's head as he passed her to get to his place at the table.

"You don't have to worry," Melissa said. "I've taken up rock climbing and skydiving, but other than that, I'm taking it easy." She gave Candace a serene smile.

"Oh, Mom." Candace opened containers of pasta and salad she'd gotten from a local restaurant and spooned food onto her parents' plates.

"She's not actually rock climbing," Ed said. "But she is using her downtime to plan her future."

Candace stopped what she was doing at looked at her mom. "What does that mean?"

"It means, I'm thinking of applying to graduate school," Melissa said, looking a little embarrassed.

"You are?"

Melissa shrugged as though it were no big thing. "Cal Poly has a graduate program in history. You know I've always found the subject fascinating. I'll be able to commute to the school a couple of days a week. Then, once I get my degree, who knows? I can write a book. I can teach."

"Mom, that's fantastic." Impulsively, Candace leaned over and gave her mother a hard hug. "Really. I'm so excited for you."

"Well." Melissa waved it off. "I might not even get in. And if I do get in, I might flunk out once I get there."

"You'll get in. And you won't flunk out," Ed said mildly.

"Dad's right. You'll do great. But what brought this on?"

"I haven't had much to do but think these past few weeks, have I?" Melissa said. "And what I was thinking about, mostly, was what I want to do with the rest of my life. I don't want to spend it playing Bunco and gardening, Candace. Well, I do want to do those things. But that's not *all* I want to do."

CANDACE HOPED that with all of the talk about Melissa's college plans, maybe no one would ask how her job was going. It took all the way until dessert, but of course, her parents did get around to asking.

"How are things at Jitters?" Melissa inquired as she cut slices of Candace's favorite banana cake. "And how was the conference? Tell me everything."

Melissa set Candace's plate of cake in front of her, and Candace toyed with her fork. "Oh ... the conference was informative. I got a lot of good ideas for the shop. And work is ... fine."

The pause before the word *fine* tripped Melissa's radar.

"Oh, honey. What's wrong?"

"Nothing's wrong, Mom. I said it was fine. And it is. It's fine."

"I know that tone. There's something you're not saying." Melissa reached out to grasp Candace's forearm. "Just come out with it. You'll feel better."

Would she? Would she feel better? She could hardly feel worse. And anyway, once her mother got wind of some kind of discontent in her daughter, she would dig and dig until she unearthed it. Might as well get it over with.

Candace pressed her fingertips to her forehead, her elbows propped on the table, and avoided looking at her parents. "It's just ... I have feelings for Evan, okay? And I have to work with him, and he was right there during the whole conference, and I had to watch him go out to dinner with ... with women, and it's hard, that's all. It's just really hard."

"Oh, Candace." Melissa's tone softened. "I knew you had a thing for him back in high school, but still?"

"Then, now, and always." Candace threw her hands into the air in frustration. "And he sees me like a ... a coworker! And maybe a friend. But not the way I want him to see me. I don't think that will ever change."

Ed, who was growing visibly uncomfortable with the conversation, shifted in his chair and said, "Oh, jeez."

"I just don't know how much longer I can be this close to him, knowing he doesn't feel the same way about me as I do about him." Candace slumped in her seat. "But what choice do I have? I live above the shop. He's put time and money into training me. I'm too ..." She grasped for a word. "Enmeshed."

"Well, honey," Melissa said, "maybe if he knew how you felt ..."

"He knows."

"How can you be sure? If you—"

"I told him. That's how I'm sure. I told him I'm in love with him and always have been. I told him! And today at work, all he wanted to talk about was the layout of the store!" She plunked her forehead down onto the table.

"Then he's an idiot," her father said. "What do you want with an idiot?"

"I'm the idiot. Me. I am." Candace gently and repeatedly bumped her forehead against the table. *Thump. Thump. Thump.*

"Oh, Candace. It's never wrong to love someone." Melissa put her hand on Candace's shoulder.

"I can think of a few scenarios," Ed put in.

"If you're not going to be helpful, maybe you'd like to enjoy your dessert in the living room," Melissa told her husband.

"Don't have to tell me twice." He picked up his plate and left the room.

When he was gone, Melissa lowered her voice. "So, when you told him, what did he say?"

"I didn't let him say anything at the time because I was too mortified. Then, when I did expect to talk about it, he just went on about where we should put the espresso station."

"So he never actually said he doesn't feel the same way."

"He didn't have to say that. It's obvious."

"It's not obvious to me, and it might not be obvious to him, either. Sometimes you have to hit a man over the head with something before he realizes how he actually feels."

Candace wanted to hit Evan over the head with something. And not metaphorically.

EVAN THOUGHT things had gone pretty well. He'd pretended Candace hadn't said the thing she'd said, and she hadn't seemed to notice.

Best-case scenario.

Except, now that he was home after work, drinking a beer and waiting for a pizza to be delivered, he started to feel uneasy about it.

Why had it been so easy for him to avoid the subject? She claimed to be in love with him, but when he'd started rambling on about espresso station placement, she'd just gone with it. Surely her feelings couldn't be that strong, then.

What was he supposed to do now? Keep pretending she'd never said it? Hope that it all just went away?

He wasn't sure he wanted it to go away, though. He kept thinking about her—and more and more, it was in a way that was distinctly unprofessional. He remembered her smell at the oddest times—the scent of her as she'd slept in his arms in the hotel room. Some floral shampoo and her warm skin. Remembering it made him happy but also a little unsettled, as though there were something he'd forgotten to do.

He'd forgotten to kiss her when she said she loved him, for one thing.

The doorbell rang, and he took delivery of his pizza. He carried it into the kitchen, thinking about Candace.

He liked seeing her every day when he came to work. He liked knowing she'd be there. Any time she wasn't—if she was off at the bank on Jitters business, say, or picking up milk when they ran out—he felt a little rush of disappointment at her absence.

All of that meant something, but he wasn't sure it meant enough for him to jump into something it would be hard to get out of.

He'd always been able to walk away from relationships. Always. He'd never been with a woman who'd meant enough to him that he couldn't call things off any time he felt like it.

That wouldn't be the case with Candace—if only because she was so invested and he didn't want to hurt her.

The fact that he didn't want to get into any relationship he actually cared about probably bore some introspection, but not tonight.

He took a slice of pizza and his beer onto the patio to watch the ocean while he ate.

CHAPTER 16

*C*andace settled into a routine of throwing herself into her work and avoiding Evan for anything other than professional interactions.

She got up early and helped the morning crew open the shop. She did the bookkeeping, ensuring each day that the amount of cash in the register corresponded with the total cash sales for the day. She made bank runs, interviewed applicants for an open barista position, wrote work schedules, and fielded requests for days off. She and Evan moved the espresso station to the spot he'd suggested, and they repositioned the set of stanchions they used to control the line, routing their patrons toward the door instead of toward the back of the store.

In her spare time, Candace hung out with Brittany, visited her parents, did chores in her tiny apartment, and resolutely tried not to think about Evan.

All in all, it was going well. Yes, her heart still jumped and her palms still grew damp when Evan came into the room. But she wasn't letting it control her. She reminded herself that however strong her feelings might be, she wasn't required to act on them.

She was enjoying her work, and she liked all of the baristas. She had fun chatting with the regulars, and she took pride in Jitters.

Everything was going smoothly enough that she shelved the idea she'd had about finding new employment. She could do this. She could work with Evan without it breaking her heart. Things were good. She was fine.

And then she met Shane Brody.

CANDACE HAD HEARD from some of the locals that a big Victorian house on Bridge Street was being renovated as a medical practice. Everyone had heard. Cambria had so few doctors, forcing people to drive a half hour or more just to get a checkup, that the new practice had been a hot topic of conversation.

But no one had told her that one of the new doctors was sexy as hell.

She discovered that fact while she was filling in for a barista who was taking her fifteen-minute break.

His hair: deep chestnut. His eyes: a rich chocolate brown. His physique: tall, broad-shouldered, and deliciously fit. His voice: warm and deep and spine-melting. His order: vanilla latte, large, with an extra shot.

"Can I get a name for your order?" Candace asked. She didn't want his name for efficiency's sake so much as for her own.

"Shane." Even his name was sexy.

"Are you visiting for the weekend?" The question was standard—it was always nice to make small talk with the tourists—but in this case, it wasn't just courtesy. She really wanted to know.

"I just moved here, actually." He handed over his debit card to pay for his drink. "My family and I are setting up a medical practice on Bridge Street."

"That's you? Everyone's been talking about it."

"Saying good things, I hope. Yeah, that's me. Shane Brody." He held out his hand for her to shake.

"Candace Weaver. A pleasure." In the interests of professionalism, she tried not to think of what other pleasures he might be able to provide.

As much as she wanted to flirt, there were other customers in line behind him, so she finished the transaction, thanked him, and moved on.

When his drink was ready, his fingers brushed hers as she handed him the cup. She felt a little jolt of electricity, a frisson of desire she hadn't felt for anyone but Evan.

"Listen," he said. "I haven't been in town very long, and it might be nice to have a local friend who can show me around, point me in the right direction."

"I can see how that might be useful."

"Maybe you wouldn't mind helping me out? We could have coffee —or, wait, not coffee, you're probably sick of it—and you could ...you know. Orient me. If you're willing."

"Orient you," she said.

"Sure. Why not?"

Why not, indeed? She plucked one of her business cards from a holder on the counter, turned it over, and wrote her personal number on the back. She slid the card across the counter to him. "Call me. And, Shane?"

He raised his eyebrows in question.

"I hope you enjoy your latte."

I HOPE you enjoy your latte? That was her best flirtation gambit? Was her game really that inept?

"Ah, jeez. I sounded like some generic Starbucks employee. I don't know what I was thinking."

Brittany was upstairs at Candace's place, each of them with a glass of wine. They'd just finished a dinner of takeout burgers from the West End Bar and Grill, and they were about to begin the negotiations for what to watch on Netflix.

But before they did that, Candace had to air her mortification at how she'd handled the hot new doctor.

"*Enjoy your latte* is fine," Brittany said. "Really. I don't see the problem."

"I'd have said it to anyone! I do say it to everyone. Well, everyone who orders a latte, obviously."

"What were you supposed to say? *That latte would be tastier if you were licking it off my breasts?*"

"Of course not." She paused. "Although …"

"Does this mean you're moving on from Evan?" Brittany asked.

"I don't know." Candace leaned her head onto the back of the sofa and looked at the ceiling. "I don't know if I can. I want to, though. I'm going to try."

"That's good. It's good that you're going to try. And it sounds like the hot doctor is a great first step."

"I gave him my number. That's something, right? I gave him my number just like a confident, self-possessed woman instead of the awkward mess I am."

"That is something." Brittany reached out and gave Candace's forearm a squeeze. "Seriously. It's a step."

Candace didn't want to take a step away from Evan. She wanted to run toward him. But she couldn't keep chasing a man who didn't want to be caught. She couldn't keep wanting what she'd never have.

"So," she asked Brittany. "Do you think he'll call?"

He called two days later during her lunch break, when she was upstairs in her apartment heating up some frozen macaroni and cheese in the microwave.

"It's Shane Brody," he said.

"Large vanilla latte with an extra shot," she responded.

He laughed, and she liked the sound of his laugh. It was deep and resonant, as though it came from low in his belly. "That's right. Do you always identify people by their drink order?"

"It's an occupational hazard."

They chatted for a bit about how things were at Jitters, how the renovations on the Bridge Street building were coming, and how he was settling in. Then he got to the point of his call.

"I wondered if we could get together."

"Right. Sure we can. Where would you like to start?"

"What do you mean?"

"Well, you said you needed someone to show you around."

He laughed again, that sexy laugh. "That was a line. My parents have lived here for almost five years, so I know my way around. I just wanted to go out with you."

And, God, wasn't that cute as hell? He offered honesty, charm, and that tingling feeling that came when a guy who was way out of your league showed an interest in you.

"Still, same question," she said. "Where would you like to start?"

"How about we start with a drink and work our way up?"

"You're going out with one of those Brody boys? They're all so good-looking. And doctors!"

Candace had told her mother about Shane Brody's invitation, and now Melissa was practically incandescent with pleasure.

"Well ... it's just a drink. I'm not lined up to be Mrs. Doctor Brody."

"Oh, but you never know. When are you going? What are you going to wear?"

"Friday after work. And I haven't thought it out that far."

In truth, Candace didn't have much in her wardrobe that said *evening out with a handsome doctor.* Most of her clothes said *I'm likely to spill espresso on myself, and I hope it won't stain.* Surely she had something in the back of her closet that would do. Or, since she was going straight from work, she could claim she hadn't had time to change.

"Aren't you excited?" Melissa fussed around in her kitchen, making cups of herbal tea for the two of them. Candace had offered to make the tea, but Melissa insisted that doing things for herself was good for her recovery.

Candace knew she should be excited. By any measure, Shane Brody was a man who should rouse feelings of excitement in a woman he'd asked on a date. On paper, he was perfect: handsome, successful, and interested.

But he wasn't Evan.

"All right, what's wrong?" Melissa planted her fists on her hips and faced her daughter.

"Who says anything's wrong?"

"I'm your mother—I can read your facial expressions. You're dreading it. But why?"

"I wouldn't say I'm dreading it, exactly." Candace fidgeted with a napkin she'd grabbed from the table. "I really am excited. I'm just … skeptical that anything will come of it, that's all."

"Oh, honey." Melissa sat down in the chair next to Candace and grabbed her daughter's hand. "If this is about self-confidence—"

"It's not that."

"Then what?" Melissa's face changed as she realized what the problem was. Her motherly intuition might have taken a moment to kick in, but once it did, she had unerring accuracy. "It's Evan Bridges."

A tear leaked from Candace's eye and she wiped it away. "I know he's never going to love me. I know that. And I know I have to date people so I can move on. But … But …"

"Oh, sweetheart." Melissa leaned over and pulled Candace into a hug. I know you have feelings for him. I know you do. But if it hasn't happened by now …"

"I know. I know."

Melissa gave Candace a squeeze, then straightened up and moved a lock of hair out of her daughter's face with her fingers. "Take a deep breath, dry your eyes, and figure out something perfect to wear for your date," she said. "You're going to go out with Shane Brody, and you're going to have a great time, and it'll work out or it won't. But either way, you're putting yourself out there, and that's a good thing."

"Right. Okay." Candace took in a shuddering breath and told herself to pull it together. Her mother was right.

If she couldn't have a genuinely good time going out with someone who wasn't Evan, she could certainly do a hell of a job pretending.

And if she pretended hard enough, maybe it would turn out to be true.

CHAPTER 17

*C*andace decided that wearing her work clothes on her date would be a cop-out. Sure, it would give her an excuse not to have to make an effort, but screw that. She was going to make an effort if it killed her.

After Jitters closed on Friday evening, Candace went upstairs, showered, put on tight skinny jeans and a low-cut, close-fitting sweater, did her hair, and carefully applied her makeup. When she was done, she looked at herself in the mirror in satisfaction. She still wasn't the kind of woman she would expect someone like Shane Brody to go for, but she looked good. Her hair was full and bouncy, her boobs looked great, and she'd chosen her jeans for maximum ass-flattering.

She was ready to go.

She picked up her purse and headed downstairs, ready to walk down the street to meet Shane at a wine bar on Main Street.

She reached the bottom of the stairs just as Evan was locking the front door of the coffeehouse.

"Bye, Evan. Have a good evening," she said in what she hoped was a breezy, devil-may-care way.

He just stared at her, his keys in his hand.

~

EVAN KNEW he was supposed to say something: *Have a good one,* maybe, or *See you tomorrow.* But his mouth didn't seem to be forming words.

Candace looked ... Well. She looked hot as hell, and she was smiling, and all of that happy hotness was going somewhere without him.

"Ah ..." He cleared his throat. "Where you headed?"

"Oh, I'm just going down to De-Vine to meet a friend."

A friend? What kind of friend? He knew about her pal Brittany, but Candace had never dressed like this for Brittany, as far as he knew.

Her clothes, her hair, her general bearing—all of it had the aroma of a date, a certain romantic bouquet.

"You hanging out with Brittany?" he asked hopefully, though he knew she wasn't.

"No, not Brittany. It's a new friend. Well ... I'll see you." She walked past him with her purse slung over her shoulder, and he watched her go.

There was a bounce in her step that wasn't usually there. And did her ass usually look that good? How had he not noticed?

He finished locking up and walked to his car. Was Candace dating someone? If so, who was it? He needed to know whose teeth he'd be knocking loose.

But even as he thought it, he knew that wasn't fair. He and Candace weren't dating. They weren't thinking about dating. They were just ... colleagues. And maybe friends.

Why shouldn't she go out with someone? And why shouldn't he wish the best for her?

He went home feeling unsettled and grumpy as hell.

~

CANDACE FOUND Shane to be an interesting person, a lively conversationalist, a courteous and attentive date, and a hell of a lot of fun to look at.

She knew he was a catch, as far as dates went, and she should be thrilled to be here with him.

And she *was* thrilled. A little. If one could be said to feel just a hint of a thrill.

"Candace? Is everything okay?" He looked at her across the table at De-Vine with some concern.

"Yes. Yes! Of course. Why wouldn't it be?"

She was protesting too much. Even she could recognize that.

"It's just that you seem like you have something on your mind."

Not something. Someone.

How was she ever going to move beyond her feelings for Evan if she didn't give someone else a chance? And if she couldn't make the effort for someone like Shane Brody, then what hope did she have?

She picked up her wineglass, took a sip, and smiled at him, resolving to keep her mind here, with him, and off of Evan. She was going to have a good time, damn it, if it killed her.

EVAN GOT TO OTTER BLUFF, took a shower, put on a pair of sweatpants and a T-shirt, and went out to the patio with a bottle of beer.

Why couldn't he get his mind off of Candace's date? Why did he even care? The question baffled him. It wasn't as though he had feelings for her. Okay, yes, he cared about her—as a friend and colleague. But that was it. So why did he care who she was out with and what they might be doing?

He took a deep drink of his beer and looked out at the ocean, at the waves pounding the rocks as the sun lowered toward the horizon.

It wasn't that he wanted her for himself—obviously. The problem was that she was out having a nice evening and he wasn't. He was here, alone. Otter Bluff was, admittedly, a beautiful place to be lonely, but that didn't fully compensate for how pathetic he was.

So, that was why he couldn't stop thinking about her, certainly. It didn't have anything to do with her as a person. It had to do with being left behind while someone else did something positive with her life.

Or, maybe that wasn't it at all. Maybe he was just worried about Candace's safety. He'd had to rescue her from an asshole in Seattle. How could he be sure she didn't need rescuing now?

He thought about that while he finished his beer. He thought about it some more as he went inside, made a sandwich, and ate it. He continued to think about it while he settled in front of the TV for some Netflix.

His mom called, and he chatted with her for a while about Jitters, the conference, and whether he was seeing a nice girl.

The subtext was that Anna hadn't been a nice girl and that he really needed to find someone with whom he could settle down.

His mother would like Candace.

He shooed that thought away as soon as it came into his mind. So what if his mother would like her? What did his mother know about love? The woman was on her fourth marriage, so she wasn't the one to turn to for relationship advice.

Besides, nothing was going on between himself and Candace, and it was likely that nothing ever would.

So why was he still thinking about her?

It occurred to him, after a while, that he had some paperwork to do at Jitters. And then it occurred to him—strictly coincidentally— that if he went over there and did it, he would see Candace when she came in from wherever the hell she'd gone.

His only interest was her safety.

Obviously.

He'd feel better if he knew she was tucked in for the night. Preferably alone.

He cleaned up his sandwich mess, swapped the sweatpants for a pair of jeans, grabbed his keys, and went to Jitters.

WHEN CANDACE and Shane finished their wine at De-Vine, they decided to have dinner at Indigo Moon. By the time they were finishing their dessert, Candace had almost forgotten that Evan Bridges existed.

Dinner had been delicious, the chocolate lava cake they were sharing was decadent to a nearly orgasm-inducing degree, the conversation was interesting, and she was slightly buzzed on good wine.

He is going to make someone a terrific boyfriend.

Only once she'd thought it did she realize the implication: that he was going to make *someone*—not Candace—an excellent partner.

He told her about his family, all of whom were doctors—his parents, his four brothers, and him. He told her how his parents had retired to Cambria, then had grown bored out of their minds and decided to open a medical practice here. And he told her how his entire family was coming together to make it happen.

"That's wonderful," she said, meaning it. "My mother just had a hip replacement, and she had to drive to San Luis Obispo for everything. That's a lot of driving. I mean, I know she'd still have had to go down there for the surgery, even if there'd been a comprehensive medical practice in Cambria. But at least she would have been saved the trip for diagnosis, follow-ups, and that kind of thing."

"I think we can do a lot of good for a lot of people," he said. "Especially since we won't take insurance."

That part stopped her. "What?"

He leaned forward with his forearms on the table, warming to his topic. "We're going to be cash only, charged on a sliding scale, and no one will be turned away for lack of ability to pay. No HMOs, no insurance lackey on the phone in another state deciding what you can and can't do for your health. If you think you're sick of the insurance bureaucracy as a patient, you should see how much it sucks for the doctors."

"But ... can you afford to do that?"

"We're a nonprofit, and we've got some deep-pockets investors. We're going to do medicine a different way, a way that's patient-centered." He stopped, smiled, and sat back in his chair. "You probably don't want me to go on and on about it."

"I do," she said. "It sounds wonderful."

He looked so endearingly pleased that Candace impulsively reached out and put her hand on his forearm. He slid his arm backward slowly until his hand slipped into hers.

How had that happened? How had they started holding hands?

Her heart sped up, and she felt a little thrill of excitement. But beneath that, she felt something else—guilt. As though she were cheating on Evan.

He could be with me if he wanted to. But he doesn't want to.

The check came, and Shane paid it.

"Should we get out of here?" he said.

CANDACE WASN'T GOING to invite Shane up to her apartment. She absolutely was not. This was a first date, and it was only practice, and anyway, she didn't want to become intimate with anyone until she was sure she wouldn't be thinking about Evan the whole time.

Shane was a gentleman. He'd walked her to her door, but he didn't seem to want to push things any further, so that was okay.

Just because she didn't want to take him upstairs didn't mean she wouldn't enjoy a goodnight kiss. She wanted to try it, just to see how it would feel. Just to see if the touch of his lips to hers would banish thoughts of Evan Bridges from her mind.

The door leading up to her apartment was next to the front door of Jitters. She unlocked it, then turned to Shane beneath the light above her doorway.

"I had a really nice time," she said.

"So did I." His voice had that low, husky quality that told her he was ready to kiss her—and maybe, sometime in the future, do more.

He was handsome and interesting and they'd had a lovely date, and why shouldn't she kiss him? Kissing Shane wouldn't just be pleasant, it would be necessary. It was a key step in her quest to become a woman who was finally free of her hopeless need for a man who could never love her. It was an essential piece in the puzzle of her recovery.

He ran the fingertips of one hand along her cheek, and she closed her eyes, waiting.

She could feel him drawing closer to her, smell the scent of his skin, sense the warmth of him as she waited to feel his lips on hers.

"Oh. Hey, Candace. You just coming in?"

Candace's eyes flew open and she involuntarily lurched away from Shane at the sound of the deep voice behind her.

She spun around. "Evan."

It was almost as though she'd thought him into being with all of her musings about moving on and getting over him. As though she'd somehow summoned him with her mind.

"Evan Bridges. I'm the owner here at Jitters." He looked at Shane and extended his hand to shake.

"Shane Brody."

They shook, and the whole thing seemed amiable enough, but each of the men had a wariness about him that suggested there was more going on than simple courtesy.

"How do you know Candace?" Evan asked.

"We met when I came in for coffee. She made me a latte, and then she gave me her number."

Evan smiled without warmth and without humor. "That's not usually how we do business here."

"Oh. I ... Shane is new in town, and he doesn't know anyone—well, except his family—and I was just ... He wanted someone to show him around a little, so ..."

She was rambling. She told herself to shut her mouth and stop it.

"You were just being friendly," Evan observed.

"Yes. Yes, I—"

"I'm sure that's something you value in your team," Shane said. "Friendliness, I mean."

"Of course."

The way they were sizing each other up, Candace expected them to start butting chests. But why would they? Why should Evan care whom she dated? It wasn't as though he wanted her for himself. It wasn't as though he ever would.

"Ah ... What are you doing here this time of night?" Candace asked.

Evan shrugged. "Just finishing up some paperwork."

"Oh."

"And while I've got you," he went on, "I had a question about something on one of the spreadsheets. Could you maybe pop into the shop when you're done here?" He raised his eyebrows in question.

"Sure. Of course."

"Great. Nice to meet you, Shane." He gave a crisp nod and then went back into Jitters.

Candace was so rattled that all thoughts of kissing Shane had been forgotten. She offered him her hand instead.

"Thank you for a nice evening."

He looked at her, then looked in the window of Jitters to where Evan was sitting at a cafe table with his laptop, then back at Candace.

"If I'm getting in the middle of something ..."

"Oh. You're not."

"Are you sure? It seems like he's—"

"He's not."

"Because I'd like to do this again," he said. "I'd like to call you again, and go out, but if you're not available ..."

"I'm available. I'm completely available. I'm so available it's kind of stupid."

Still holding his hand, she went up onto her toes and kissed him quickly on the cheek. "Well, I'd better ..." She pointed toward Evan.

CHAPTER 18

*E*van saw Candace coming in the front door of Jitters and scrambled for some kind of question he could ask her to justify breaking up her date. And it had to be about a spreadsheet.

He pulled up the spreadsheet showing the shop's payroll, thinking that was a safe bet. He could ask about somebody's hours, or maybe about their tax withholding.

He wasn't sure why he'd gone out there and interrupted what was clearly about to be a kiss. He wasn't Candace's father. He wasn't her brother. And he sure as hell hadn't been tasked with protecting her celibacy.

Assuming she was currently celibate.

The idea that she might not be currently celibate nagged at him, and he pushed it away. Of course she was. If she was dating someone, he'd know about it.

Hell, she *was* dating someone, and he *did* know about it.

The guy's very existence irked him, but it irked him more that the man was tall and handsome. At least, Evan was certain that women would think of Shane as handsome. He had that obvious kind of attractiveness you saw in ads for men's clothing at Target.

He was still turning all of that over in his brain when Candace plopped down in the chair across from him and said, "Okay, what?"

Okay, what wasn't what you said when you were happy to have been rescued from a bad date. It was what you said when you were hoping to get laid and your plans had been foiled.

"How was your evening?" he asked.

"It was fine until you showed up and asked me about spreadsheets. So, what is it? What's so urgent that you need to ask me right now?"

"Uh ... I was looking at the payroll ..."

"Yes?"

"And I wondered ..."

"Evan, what?"

"Should Ariel be withholding so much for taxes? I mean, she's single, no dependents. Sure, she'll get a refund, but she'll be missing out on potential interest income."

Candace's jaw went slack as she stared at him.

"I just thought ..."

"Why are you asking me? Why aren't you asking Ariel?"

"Well, she's not here, and you are, so—"

She let out a laugh—not the kind that said you were amused, but the kind that said you couldn't believe someone's idiocy. "I'll ask her tomorrow. Okay?"

"Okay."

"Was that all you wanted?"

"Well ... yeah."

She got up, grabbed her purse from where she'd slung it over the back of her chair, and headed toward the door.

"Candace."

She turned, and only then did he realize he had no idea what to say.

"I just ... I didn't call you in here to talk about Ariel's tax withholding."

"No kidding."

"I thought ... I wanted to make sure you were okay, and that you weren't in any kind of danger with that guy." That was a lie. The only thing she'd been in danger of was making out with some asshole who didn't deserve her. His immediate assumption that the guy didn't deserve her was a surprise to him, but he didn't question it. He just accepted it.

"Well, I wasn't."

"Okay."

She walked toward the door, then stopped with her fingers on the handle and looked back at him. "Is that really what you wanted?"

"Why wouldn't it be?" That wasn't an answer, and they both knew it.

IF EVAN DIDN'T WANT her, why was he so hell-bent on preventing her from being with anyone else?

The question ran through Candace's mind as she left Jitters, climbed the stairs to her apartment, and let herself in.

Twice now, he'd ruined her attempt to have a nice date. Twice now, he'd shown up at exactly the wrong time and had wrecked things for her.

Was he doing it on purpose?

He had to be, but why? It would make sense if he wanted her. It would make sense if he was jealous. But she'd declared her love for him, and he'd never said a word about it. He'd never responded. So, clearly, he didn't want her. He just didn't want her to have a fulfilling romantic life that didn't include him.

Ego, that's what it was. Men and their damned egos.

She put down her purse, took off her coat, and kicked off her shoes. Then she paced around the apartment, keyed up and pissed off.

Okay, so Evan hadn't really ruined her date with Shane. He'd ruined her chance for a kiss, but the date itself had been fine. Better than fine. And Shane had said he wanted to see her again. So, they could pick up where they'd left off. She could go out with him again, and she could kiss him somewhere else—somewhere Evan wouldn't see them.

But why should she have to hide from her boss when she wanted to kiss a man? This was her home. She should be able to enjoy a little tongue-kissing at the front door to her own home after a date. The fact that she couldn't was just ... harassment! It was some kind of labor violation, surely.

She put her shoes back on, stomped down the stairs, and went back into Jitters to find Evan sitting at the same table where she'd left him, his laptop open in front of him.

"What exactly is your problem?" She stood with her fists jammed onto her hips, glaring at him.

"My problem?"

"Yes. You must have one, because you keep ... *showing up* whenever I'm trying to have a normal, healthy life dating people and ... and possibly kissing people. Why do you do that, Evan? Why?"

He snapped his laptop shut and his expression hardened. "I could ask you why you're trying to date people and kiss people after you said you were in love with me."

Oh, crap. So we're finally going to talk about it.

"I said that, and then you never responded. You never responded, Evan! I said that weeks ago, and nothing has changed between us, and that's fine. It's fine! But you can't expect me to just sit at home alone every night waiting for you to have some kind of reaction!"

"You told me not to say anything. You dropped that bomb on me, then you insisted that I keep my mouth shut. Now you're mad that I didn't respond? That doesn't make any sense, Candace."

Okay, fair point.

"I meant that you shouldn't respond right then. But ... I thought you'd say something about it eventually! I didn't mean for you to pretend you'd lost your sense of hearing the moment I said what I said!"

He put his hands up, palms out, to stop her. "Look, Candace. I didn't know what to say. I didn't know how to ... You just dropped that on me, and I needed time to absorb it!"

"You've had time. It should be fully absorbed by now. If you'd felt the same way, you'd have told me. And you didn't. And that's fine. But if you don't want me, Evan, let me find someone else. Please." Her eyes were filling with tears, and she blinked hard to hold them back.

"I don't know how I feel," he admitted.

WHEN CANDACE HAD FIRST SAID she loved him, his initial reaction had been to let her down easy and explain why the two of them being together was a bad idea that would never work.

He'd planned to tell her that at the first reasonable opportunity. But the opportunity came and went, and he didn't tell her. And then he just kept not telling her, and then he realized that he didn't *want* to tell her. He didn't want to cut off the possibility of Candace, because the more time he spent with her, the more he thought, *maybe.*

He had a thousand good reasons not to get involved with her, starting with the fact that he was her boss and ending with his conviction that he did not want to hurt her, and he almost certainly would.

Evan didn't have a single good, rational reason to pursue things with Candace. Except, he was increasingly finding that being rational was overrated.

Still, he wasn't ready to admit that he was maybe beginning to have feelings for her. *I don't know how I feel* was the best he could do.

"You don't know how you feel," she said, her voice quieter now.

"No. I don't."

"Which means you don't know that you don't have feelings for me."

The double negative was confusing him, so he squeezed his eyes shut and rubbed his forehead with his hand.

"Candace ..."

"But you also don't know that you do."

Regardless of any double negative confusion, it seemed like she'd covered all of the possibilities. He nodded. "Yeah. That's about right."

"Well, considering that we met each other when we were five years old, and considering that I've ... Considering all of that, I would think you've had enough time to decide one way or the other."

That was fair, and yet he didn't know. He knew he liked seeing her every day. He knew he liked hearing her voice and listening to whatever she had to say. He knew that his brightest days were the ones with her in them. But he didn't know what he wanted to do with that, if anything.

"It's not that I don't ... I just feel ..." He couldn't seem to finish his thought, so he hadn't managed to clarify anything.

"You know what I think?" Candace said. "I think you want to stay on the fence because having me here every day, feeling all of these ... these *feelings*, gives you a big ego boost that you don't want to give up. You don't want me, but you don't want to *say* you don't want me, because then I might move on and get happy with someone else, and then I wouldn't look at you the way I look at you. And then you'd have to get your ego boost from other things. Like, oh, I don't know. Skills. Or achievements. Something other than your ability to ruin a woman's life."

A fat tear dropped from her eye, and she wiped it away. Then she spun around and stormed out of the coffeehouse before he could say anything else.

CANDACE CLIMBED the stairs to her apartment, threw her purse onto the floor, slammed the door, and said, "Damn it. Damn it!"

Everything she'd said to him was true—or, at least, it felt true—but that didn't mean saying it hurt any less. It was all out there now—all of her conflicting, messy feelings. And if he hadn't taken her into his arms and kissed her by now, he was never going to do it.

He was, however, going to keep preventing her from kissing anyone else.

The situation was untenable, unbearable.

Something had to change if she was ever going to be happy. Clearly, he wasn't going to change. So she had to do it.

CHAPTER 19

"So, I think I need to quit my job. I'm determined to get over Evan. And I can't do that if he's there every day, looking the way he looks and being ... well, being Evan."

Candace and Brittany were having breakfast at the Redwood Cafe on Candace's day off. Brittany didn't have any clients at the salon that morning, so she was available to offer Candace impromptu therapy over pancakes and bacon.

Brittany picked up a slice of bacon between her fingers and bit off a piece. "Still no response to what you said about loving him?" She scrunched her face in sympathy.

"Not really, no. He says he doesn't know how he feels. Which would be better than him rejecting me outright, I guess, if not for the fact that he apparently wants me to live like a nun until he decides." She told Brittany everything that had happened with Shane Brody, including the aborted kiss.

"Jeez. Men." Brittany dropped the remains of the bacon onto her plate in disgust. "If he's not into you, fine. It is what it is. But God forbid you should get your needs met with someone else. That'll never do, because then he wouldn't have you around to endlessly stroke his ego."

"Exactly!" Candace threw her hands into the air. "I mean, I know I can't moon over him forever. I know that. And I don't want to. But he's making it impossible for me to find someone else and have the kind of life I want! I deserve that life, Brittany."

"Hell yes, you do."

Sitting there with a mug of coffee and a half-eaten breakfast in front of her, Candace thought how lucky she was to have Brittany. What would she do without a best friend to cheer her on at a time like this, when she really needed it? How much bleaker would things look without someone to tell her she deserved better? Deserved more?

Having her friend's support helped so much, but it didn't make what she was about to do any less scary.

"I'm not going to have a place to live," she said. "I'll have to move back in with my parents."

"They won't mind."

"And then there's Shane," Candace said.

"Ooh." Brittany wiggled her eyebrows. "Are you going out with him again?"

"He asked."

"And what did you say?"

"I said yes."

"That's great." Brittany cut off a piece of pancake, dipped it into a puddle of maple syrup, and ate it. "So, you like him?"

"I like the idea of him," Candace said. "You know? He's great. He's really great. I should like him."

Brittany tilted her head to the side and regarded her friend. "Saying you should like him isn't the same as saying you like him."

"I could like him, if I could just give it a chance. If I could get away from Evan long enough to make room for me to have feelings for someone else."

"Fair enough," Brittany said. "So, when are you giving your notice?"

~

EVAN HAD THOUGHT things were going okay with Candace. Well, maybe not okay, exactly. But he didn't think there was any kind of crisis.

So, when she handed him a sheet of paper one day at Jitters while he was in the storage room checking the bean supply, he thought it was something related to the shop's bookkeeping.

He was shocked to find that it was her written two-week notice.

"What's this?" He stared at her, the sheet still in his hand, shelves full of coffee filters, flavored syrups, cups, and lids surrounding them.

"It's clear, I thought. I wrote it clearly."

"You're quitting?" Evan felt lost, as though he'd somehow misunderstood her intentions, or as though he might be able to rewind time five minutes by sheer force of will.

"I ... yes. But I'd be happy to stay long enough to train my ... my replacement." She was stammering a little, and surely that meant this was some kind of April Fool's joke. Even though it wasn't April.

"Candace, why?" Was she unhappy here? Was he an asshole to work for? He didn't think so. Maybe she'd gotten a better offer somewhere else. All right, if that was the case, he could give her more money. He could fix this.

"It's ... ah ... personal reasons. That's all."

When she said *personal reasons*, his mind went straight to things like illness, family crisis, tragedy. It didn't occur to him then, even for a moment, that she might be quitting her job to get away from him.

"Are you all right? Is it your family? Did something—"

"I'm fine, Evan. And my family's fine. And I don't want to get into it, okay? I have to go help David. He's training the new barista, and the line's getting long."

She left him standing there with her resignation letter in his hand, the scent of coffee beans wafting through the air.

CANDACE LEFT the storage room feeling sick. He'd looked so flummoxed. So hurt and confused.

She'd had a speech in mind—something about her feelings for him being counterproductive for her, and how it would be a healthy thing for her to get out of his orbit long enough to build a life that didn't include him.

But at the last moment, she couldn't say it, so she'd come up with the vague *personal reasons*. That was true, as far as it went. She had reasons, and they were most definitely personal.

But telling him those reasons would be mortifying when she'd already announced her feelings. When he'd already chosen to ignore them.

She went behind the counter and started taking espresso orders for David.

"IT'S NOT that I want to quit. I really don't," Candace told her mother that evening after closing, when she popped by her parents' house to feel them out on her moving back in.

"Then what's going on, honey?" Melissa was sitting in her favorite chair in the living room, leaning forward with her hands pressed between her knees.

"It's just … Evan."

"What about him? Is he treating you badly at work? Oh, Candace."

"Nope. No. That's not it."

"Then what?"

Candace sighed and slumped down onto the sofa. "You know I've got feelings for him. I already told you that."

"I know. Has he tried to take advantage of you? Did he—"

"No. No! He hasn't done … anything. He hasn't said anything. I put my feelings out there, and I made myself all naked and vulnerable. Metaphorically speaking." She added the last bit before her mother could draw false conclusions. "And he acts like it never happened! Except when I'm with another man. Then he gets all weird and, 'Candace, can I talk to you about the spreadsheets?' But the spreadsheets are fine, Mom. He's just trying to prevent me from being kissed!"

Melissa, whom Candace hadn't told about Shane, looked understandably confused. "Could we maybe back up a bit?"

So they did. Candace told her about Shane and their date, and the way Evan had interrupted the end of it. Then she reminded Melissa of how he'd done essentially the same thing in Seattle at the conference when Candace had been having dinner with another man.

"Okay. About this Shane ..."

Of course Melissa would focus on that. "What about him?"

"Well, tell me about him. Did you have a nice time? You said you wanted to kiss him before Evan interrupted you. That's good! And he's a doctor? Oh, honey. Are you going to see him again?"

Now that Candace thought about it, Melissa was doing exactly what Candace needed to be doing: she was taking the emphasis off of Evan and everything he had or had not done, and she was turning her attention to a lovely man who actually did want to start a relationship with Candace.

Her glass was half-full, romantically speaking, and she needed to try to see it that way instead of perpetually thinking of it as empty of Evan.

"Yes. I'm going to see him again."

"Well, that's wonderful." Melissa patted her thighs with her hands once to emphasize it. "Someday, you and Shane will tell your kids the story of how you almost didn't get together because of your high school crush, but then you did, and everything worked out fine."

Their kids? Now her mother had her married with kids?

Well. Stranger things had happened, she supposed.

SHANE CALLED CANDACE, and they set up their second date. They would be attending an art opening in San Luis Obispo, then they would have dinner at a sushi place down there. Afterward, if Candace felt like kissing Shane, they'd do it somewhere other than outside her front door where Evan might see her.

"Ooh. Doctor Hottie gets a second date!" Brittany was thrilled when Candace told her the news. "Please tell me you're going to figure out some way to get around Evan acting like he's your father trying to protect your chastity."

"I will. I'm already thinking about it."

Brittany had come into Jitters for a cappuccino, and now they were chatting over the counter as David made Brittany's drink.

Candace kept her voice low so the baristas wouldn't hear about her love life.

"You could always go to his place," Brittany suggested.

She could, but that might suggest to Shane that she wanted to go further than a kiss, which she didn't. The idea of the kiss alone—just that—was nearly overwhelming to her because Shane wasn't Evan. She needed to take baby steps. She needed to gradually get used to the idea of being with someone who wasn't Evan Bridges. Jumping into bed with Shane and tearing off the Band-Aid had some appeal, but she wasn't up to it. A kiss was all she could manage.

"Too risky," was all she said.

"Okay, then, you could always do the classic car kiss. Make out in the front seat a little. Just make sure he parks around the corner so Evan can't camp out at Jitters and see you."

"But *why* is he camping out at Jitters? If he doesn't want me, why does he even care who I see? It's not like he stays there late as a matter of routine. He doesn't! But when I'm coming home from a date, there he is! Why?!"

"*Hmm*," Brittany said.

"What does that even mean, Brittany? What does that sound mean?"

"It means, he might not have said he's interested in you. But the way he's acting, he isn't *not* interested."

Candace had considered that possibility. Of course she had. But she was in her thirties now, and she was still alone because she'd never given up on the chance that Evan might want her. She'd waited long enough. She didn't have time to wait anymore.

CHAPTER 20

he thing was, Evan himself didn't know why he'd broken up Candace's date. But he had some theories, and he tried them out on Nix one night at Otter Bluff when they were hanging out, drinking beer, and getting ready to watch a movie on Netflix.

"She's a nice girl, that's all, and I don't want to see her end up with some asshole who's not good enough for her."

They were lounging on the sofa, longneck bottles in their hands, the remains of a takeout dinner from the Main Street Grill strewn across the coffee table.

"Yeah, okay," Nix said.

His words were agreeable enough, but from their delivery, Evan could tell that Nix thought he was full of shit.

"What?" he said.

"Nothing."

"Come on, asshole. What's on your mind? Just say it."

Nix shrugged, unperturbed by the *asshole* comment. "I just think you talk about her a lot for a guy who claims he's not into her. And you think about her a lot. And you worry about who she might be seeing. A lot. You know, for a guy who's absolutely not interested."

Evan shot Nix a middle finger, but there was no heat behind it. The guy was just saying what Evan had been thinking.

"I don't want her to quit," he said. Which danced around the corners of the main point without actually engaging with it.

"Have you told her that?"

"Not in those exact words."

"What words did you use?"

Evan squirmed a little in his seat and took another gulp of beer to steel himself for the conversation they seemed to be having.

"Well ... I didn't tell her in any words, exactly. I was too shocked."

Nix nodded. "So, because you didn't tell her you wanted her to stay, she probably thinks you don't give a shit whether she stays or goes. But if you get lucky maybe she'll have some sort of psychic vision that tells her you want her to stay. That's your best bet, probably." He said all of it as though it were a perfectly reasonable supposition.

"You're an ass, you know that?" Evan said.

Nix pointed his beer bottle at Evan. "I do know that, because you used your words to tell me. See how that works?"

Evan slumped a little in his seat. "Yeah, okay. Point taken. I'm definitely going to tell her I want her to stay."

"That's a start. But why do you want her to stay? If you tell her it's because she's a good manager and it'll be a pain in the ass to replace her, then you're an idiot."

"She *is* a good manager, and it *would* be a pain in the ass to replace her."

"Idiot," Nix observed.

CANDACE'S PARENTS were agreeable to having her move back in. Her mother was especially agreeable to it given the fact that Candace was now dating a doctor.

Now she just had to work her two weeks, pack up the apartment, and get settled into her old room. And she'd have to find a new job at an establishment that wasn't owned by Evan Bridges.

Simple.

She went to work in the mornings and went through her routine, helping to open the shop, doing the bookkeeping, writing the schedules, dealing with payroll and supply ordering and all of the other things for which she was responsible. And she tried to do it while having as little interaction with Evan as possible.

Nothing had changed for her, really. She still felt a current of desire running through her whenever they were in a room together. Her eyes were still drawn to him as though he were the only person there, the only one who mattered. She still felt as though he had an aura of light around him that only she could see. And she still felt complete only in those moments when they were together.

Nothing had changed, and yet everything had, because loving him from a distance wasn't enough for her anymore. She wanted a real relationship, and if it couldn't be with him, then it would just have to be with someone else. Maybe Shane Brody. Maybe not. Either way, she had to move forward instead of standing still or, God forbid, looking back.

Moving forward would be easier if she kept her distance, so she was somewhat dismayed when he asked to have a word with her alone in his office.

She walked in telling herself that whatever he had to say was only business. Logistics. He wanted her to interview candidates to replace her, maybe. Or he had a question about the schedule.

But as soon as she saw his face, she knew it wasn't that. He had a look about him that said he knew he'd fucked up somehow, and because it involved a woman's feelings, he wasn't sure how, but he intended to fix it anyway.

"Have a seat." He motioned to the visitor chair in her office. Normally, she'd have sat behind the desk in her own office, but Evan was sitting there. She supposed she couldn't lay claim to the chair, since it wasn't really her office anymore now that she'd quit.

She settled into the seat he'd indicated.

"Want some coffee?" he asked. "I can get Ariel to make you something."

"No thanks." She laced her fingers together across her middle, her elbows propped on the armrests. "What's up?"

"Candace ..."

The way he said her name made her start spinning possibilities in her mind. Was he going to ask her to leave her job early? She hoped not, because she needed those last two weeks of pay. Had she done something wrong? He was looking at her as though whatever he was about to say pained him, so anything was possible.

"What is it, Evan?"

"Well, I ... It occurred to me that I never actually said I don't want you to leave. And I don't. Want you to leave, that is. I'd really like you to stay. I can give you a raise. A small one, because after buying the business and the remodel and the cost of the conference, I don't—"

"It's not about money," she said, interrupting him.

"Okay, then what can I do? What do I have to do to change your mind?"

Love me.

The answer was so clear in her mind that for a moment she thought she'd said it out loud.

She must not have said anything, though, because he was prompting her for an answer.

"Candace?"

"You can't do anything," she said. "It's not about the pay, and it's not about the job. It's about ... distance. I just need distance."

"From me."

"Well ... yes."

THE IDEA that Candace was so uncomfortable being near Evan that she would quit her job over it bothered him. A lot. Why couldn't things stay the way they were? Why couldn't they just work together, and hang out sometimes, and be friends? They could flirt, even. He liked flirting.

Why did it have to be all or nothing? Why should he be in this position where he had to declare his love for her or lose a highly competent manager?

"This is about that thing you said to me." Of course it was. He felt like an idiot having to have it spelled out for him.

Candace pinched the bridge of her nose between her fingers, her eyes closed. "If I could turn back time and unsay it, believe me, I would."

He didn't want her to unsay it, though. He'd liked it. He liked knowing she had feelings for him. He just wished he weren't expected to respond to those feelings.

"Well, you can't unsay it."

"I'm painfully aware of that."

"Look. If you stay, I'll ... I promise I'll be completely professional. We can pretend you never said what you said. We can just keep it all work-related. Okay? Can we do that?"

"No!" She sprang up out of her chair, her hands clenched at her sides. "No, Evan. I don't want things between us to be professional! I thought I made that clear! I don't ... Being around you every day and having things stay professional is unbearable! It's ... it's impossible, and I won't do it anymore!"

Her eyes were getting shiny and red, and he got up from his chair and went to her.

He put his hands on her shoulders and bent down a little so he could look squarely into her eyes. "Hey. Hey, it's okay. Candace, *shh*."

Nix was right, he was an idiot. She was lovely and warm-hearted and smart and funny, and she loved him. What the hell was he doing? Why was he pushing her away? Maybe if he just let it happen. Maybe if he gave it a chance.

He wanted to make the tears go away. He wanted to make her pain go away. And he had the power to do that, didn't he? If he'd caused it, he could fix it.

He reached out and ran a fingertip down her cheek, and her breath stopped. Everything stopped.

"Evan..."

"You said you love me."

"I did. I..."

Whatever she was going to say next was lost as he kissed her.

CANDACE HAD THOUGHT, once or twice in the past, that if Evan ever kissed her, it might break the spell. Maybe he'd be bad at it. Maybe there wouldn't be a spark. Maybe everything she'd imagined about how it would feel to be close to him would be proven false.

All of that had seemed unlikely but possible.

Now, as he held her in his arms and teased her lips with his, she knew she'd been utterly, completely full of shit to imagine it wouldn't be good.

Her limbs went soft and liquid, her heart sped up, her knees went weak, and a current of electricity started in her toes and shot up through the top of her head. She sagged against him, having lost the ability to stand, and he held her tighter to keep her upright.

She'd kissed other men. She'd done more than kiss them. But it had never felt like this. This was the kiss she'd imagined in her feverish teenage fantasies. This was the kiss she'd dreamed of since Evan had come back into her life. This was the only kiss she'd ever wanted, and the only one she would ever want again.

Evan Bridges was kissing her at last, and it was everything.

By the time he pulled away, she'd lost her awareness of the room, the circumstances, and time itself.

EVAN HAD KISSED Candace just to see what it would be like. He'd been thinking about it for a while now, and given the circumstances, it seemed like a now-or-never situation. So he'd thought, *screw the consequences*, and he'd done it.

He liked kissing women, but kissing Candace was ... a surprise. The way her body had melted in his arms was so unbelievably hot that he'd had to restrain himself from shoving her against the wall and taking her right there.

With another woman, he might have done just that. But with Candace, he had to be careful. He knew there was a lot at stake for her.

The idea that there might be a lot at stake for him, too, didn't occur to him in that moment. At first he felt only the sensations—the heat rushing through his body, the desire to take and devour and possess.

Then, as he gradually became capable of coherent thought, he reminded himself that a kiss with Candace wasn't just a kiss. It was a promise—one he wasn't ready to make.

Letting out a low groan, he forced himself away from her.

"Wow," she said. Her cheeks were pink and her hair was mussed, and her chest was rising and falling with her ragged breath.

"Yeah." Everything in his body was on high alert, and he ran his hands through his hair and willed himself to calm the hell down.

"I don't ... I just ... What does this mean, Evan? What was that?" One hand was pressed against her chest, fingers spread like a starfish.

"I don't know. I don't know what it means."

"Well ... God."

The very fact that her first reaction was to ask what it meant confirmed his worst fears—that kissing Candace would mean committing to her. He'd known that before he did it, and yet he did it anyway. *Shit.* He wasn't ready for a big thing.

And anything with Candace would be big.

"What ... Does that mean ... Do you ..." She was stammering, but her meaning was clear enough.

"What it means, Candace, is that I don't want you to go."

She stared at him, wide-eyed, then blinked a few times, her hand still pressed to her chest. "I should …" She pointed at the door, then left, closing it behind her.

He had the uncomfortable sensation that he'd completely screwed things up.

Well, it wouldn't be the first time.

CANDACE WAS SO RATTLED by the kiss that she was barely able to function. She tried to make an espresso but burned her hand. Then she poured a drip coffee from the air pot and spilled it onto the floor.

"Are you okay?" Ariel peered at her with concern.

"I … Yes. I'm fine. Just … fine."

"Well, you look weird. And you're dropping things. Are you sure you're not sick?"

Candace needed to take the opportunity to go upstairs to her apartment and get herself together. She might not have been sick, but that didn't mean she wouldn't accidentally burn the place down if she tried to keep working.

"I do feel a little … off," Candace said.

"I can tell. David and I have got things here, if you want to take a break."

"I think I will. Thanks." She took off her apron with shaking hands, then went upstairs. She couldn't let anyone else see her like this. It was humiliating.

EVAN TOOK a moment to let certain parts of his body calm down, then left the office, putting on what he thought was a pretty good show of normalcy.

He greeted Ariel and David and asked how everything was going.

"Is Candace okay?" Ariel asked.

"What do you mean?"

"She was in the office with you, and when she came out, she was …

141

weird. Dropping things. She looked super freaked out. You didn't fire her or something, did you?"

"No. Of course not."

If anyone was super freaked out, it was him. That kiss … Jesus.

"Where is she now?" he asked.

"She went upstairs. I sent her up to get her shit together before somebody got third-degree burns."

He didn't answer. He just leaned against the counter, his arms crossed over his chest, his eyes unfocused and his mind back in the office with Candace.

"Now that I think about it, you don't look too great, either," Ariel said.

"Ah … just get back to work before I fire you." It was a running joke between them—Evan said *get back to work before I fire you* to Ariel at least twice a day. Ariel guffawed and went to make a vanilla latte for a customer.

Upstairs, Candace poured a glass of water in her little kitchen and gulped it down. Then she lay on the bed, staring at the ceiling. Her body and her mind wouldn't settle, though, so she jumped up and started pacing the little apartment.

The kiss had been her last hope. A bad, substandard kiss would have freed her from this obsession with Evan. It would have let her loose to date other people and do other things besides thinking of him.

But the kiss had been spectacular, better than any she'd ever had, and, in fact, better than any she'd ever imagined. The idea of being set free was shot to hell.

CHAPTER 21

*W*as it fair for Candace to keep dating Shane when she was in love with Evan? Then again, what choice did she have?

It had been a week since the kiss—a full week of being painfully near Evan at work—and he'd said nothing, had done nothing to indicate it had any meaning for him.

She had two choices, it seemed: date other men until one of them made her forget Evan, or turn gradually into one of those elderly spinsters with too many cats.

If the kiss had been intended to make her reconsider her resignation from Jitters, it had failed spectacularly. She needed to get out of there now, more than ever, or his hold on her was going to become even tighter, until she eventually strangled under the force of it.

So she continued looking for new jobs, she continued packing up her apartment for her move back to her parents' place, and she continued dating Shane Brody.

They'd had a few more dates, and the last one had included an uninterrupted kiss. The kiss was nice. Better than nice. The fact that she kept comparing it to her kiss with Evan was an inconvenient wrinkle.

"Candace? Is everything okay?" Shane asked one evening when they were strolling on the boardwalk at Moonstone Beach. "You seem … distant."

"I'm just enjoying the view." The lie emerged from her with practiced ease. She was used to lying about her thoughts when her thoughts centered on Evan. It had been a necessity from as far back as elementary school, when the truth would have made her the butt of her classmates' jokes.

"Oh. I wondered if maybe you were worried about finding another job."

The evening was cool, and Shane held her hand as they walked.

"Well, I am. But it'll be fine. Something will come up."

"You never really said why you quit Jitters."

That was true. When Shane had asked, she'd come up with vague comments about Jitters not being the right fit, about the coffeehouse's limitations in terms of her future prospects.

Now, she needed to come up with something more specific.

"I've been in food service for a while now, and I just don't think it's for me. That's all. I'd like to … you know. Look into other areas."

That wasn't entirely false. She'd been considering other options even before the Jitters job came up. Something that didn't involve her going home with food and beverage stains on her clothes, her hair smelling like cooking oil or French Roast.

"Have you ever considered working in a medical office?" He stopped walking and turned to face her.

"What?"

"We're going to need a receptionist when we get up and running."

"But … I don't have any medical experience. I've never—"

"You don't need it. You'd be checking in patients, scheduling appointments, filing charts, that kind of thing. With your experience running Jitters, you'd have all of the organizational and customer service skills you'd need."

"That's … wow."

"You'd have to interview, of course. Whoever we hire has to be approved by the rest of my family. But I think you'd be perfect."

To Candace, it would be anything but perfect. She'd be going from one situation where she was emotionally involved with her boss to another. What made it worse was the fact that she didn't know how long this thing with Shane would last. He was her practice man, and dating him was an exercise in not thinking about Evan. If she didn't succeed in the goal of not thinking about Evan, she'd be left working for a man with whom she'd broken up.

There were probably more awkward scenarios, employment-wise, but she couldn't immediately think of one.

And speaking of awkwardness, Shane was beginning to want to move beyond kissing, and Candace just couldn't seem to go there.

At the end of their beach date, when they were back at his car, he turned to her and ran his hands down her arms.

"So."

"So."

"I was wondering …" He looked at her with that secret, sexy smile of his, the one that should have made her melt but didn't. "Any interest in coming back to my place?"

"Shane …"

"If it's no, it's no. But we've been out a few times now …"

"We have."

"And when people have been out with each other a few times, like we have, they sometimes take things to the next level. If both of them are amenable. I've heard tell."

She couldn't help grinning at him. God, he was going to make someone a terrific boyfriend. And, there she went again, thinking of it as *someone* rather than her.

"I'm not ready," she said. "I'm sorry."

"Don't be sorry." He shrugged. "It's fine. How do you feel about kissing, though?"

"Kissing's good."

So they did that for a while, and then he drove her home, walking her to her door but not inviting himself upstairs.

"SHANE'S STARTING to get impatient, I think."

Candace and Brittany were at the gym, power-walking on side-by-side treadmills while a TV screen mounted overhead silently showed a reality show, captions running across the bottom of the screen.

"Well, it's been, what? Four dates?" Brittany's skin glistened with sweat, her arms pumping, as she pounded the treadmill.

"Yeah."

"Well, you know what they say. Four dates is the internationally accepted sex point."

Candace side-eyed her friend. "The internationally accepted sex point? You just made that up."

"Well … technically, yes. I did. But I stand by it. People expect sex on or about the fourth date, or they expect a reason why it's not happening."

"Or else what?"

"Or else they expect to break up so they can both go find someone who's willing to have sex on or about the fourth date."

Candace wanted to argue with Brittany's point, but she couldn't. Brittany might have pulled the term *internationally accepted sex point* right out of her ass, but that didn't mean it wasn't true.

"I just … I can't, Brittany." Candace increased her speed, thinking a little more exertion might release some of the stress she was feeling. "I want to. I really do. But I can't."

"You could try. Maybe he's so magically gifted at sex that you'll have complete amnesia regarding anything Evan-related. It'll be like the last twenty-eight years never happened."

"That might be inconvenient," Candace remarked.

"The point is, you can't know unless you try."

Candace had thought of that. She'd seriously considered it. But Shane deserved better than to be used to induce Evan-related amnesia. To ease her conscience, she'd have to tell him why she was doing it and what she hoped to get out of it before anything happened. Then, she supposed, she could go ahead—if he was still interested.

But he wouldn't be. After four dates, there was a lot she didn't know about him, but one thing she did know was that he was looking for a relationship, not a cheap fling. That was part of what made him attractive. But it was also what was going to doom things between them.

"If Shane is going to make me forget about Evan, it's going to have to happen without sex," Candace said. "Or, it'll have to happen *before* any sex, at least. He's a good guy, Brittany. He's a really good guy. He deserves better than to be with me while I'm thinking of someone else."

"But that's what's happening, isn't it? Just without anyone getting naked."

Breathing hard, Candace slowed her speed and began her cool-down. She took a long drink from her water bottle and used her hand towel to wipe her face and neck.

"Are you saying I should stop seeing him?" she asked after a while.

"No. Not necessarily."

"Then what are you saying?"

"I'm saying, if you're going to use someone to get over Evan, maybe switch to someone who won't mind being used."

"Maybe."

"And if you do that …"

Candace came to a stop and turned to face Brittany. "What?"

"Maybe consider introducing the hot doctor to your best friend, who's all healthy and emotionally available." She wiggled her eyebrows at Candace.

"Really?"

"Just a thought," Brittany said.

CHAPTER 22

Candace was still quitting, and she was still dating that Ken doll doctor, and she was still packing up her apartment, getting ready to leave.

Evan hated every one of those things.

He'd kissed her. What more did she want? He'd kissed her, and now she was fleeing so fast she was leaving skid marks behind her.

Okay, so he hadn't said he loved her back. Was he supposed to declare something he wasn't ready to say? Was he supposed to act like he was in the same place she was, when he wasn't?

He and Anna had been apart for a while now, and he was starting to get lonely, and dating Candace was an appealing idea. But after what she'd said about loving him, it was just too dangerous. What if he never got to be where she was? She'd get hurt, and the whole thing would be a mess.

What he needed was a date with a woman who was more his type. Someone attractive and willing who would be able to walk away from the relationship in a heartbeat if it stopped meeting anyone's needs.

He expressed that opinion to Nix one night at Ted's after work. It seemed reasonable enough, so Evan was surprised when Nix called him a dick.

"Why? Why am I a dick? That doesn't even make any sense."

The two of them were drinking pale ale from longneck bottles at a table near the back, the floor sticky under their feet and the air smelling like spilled beer.

"You're a dick because you actually think being in a relationship with someone you don't care about, and who doesn't care about you, is a viable solution to your life issues." Nix shook his head and took a deep drink of his beer.

"It always worked for me before."

"It never worked for you before." Nix pointed one finger at him with the same hand that was holding the bottle. "If it worked, you'd be happy right now instead of here with me complaining about a woman."

That assessment—true as it may have been—made Evan feel sulky and out of sorts. "You're just smug because you're a newlywed," he said.

Nix's eyebrows shot up, and he looked at Evan in that vague, unfocused way he got when he was starting to get buzzed. "I may be a newlywed. And I may be smug. But that doesn't mean I'm wrong. Your love life has been one disaster after another."

Evan wouldn't have thought of his love life as a disaster, and he was surprised to hear Nix characterize it that way. Evan usually had a girlfriend, and he usually had fun with her. When one or both of them wasn't having fun anymore, they walked away. Simple. Easy. Effective.

"That's bullshit, man," Evan said.

"Which part?"

"Every part. The part where you opened your mouth and said things."

Evan wasn't about to condemn the entirety of his dating life out of hand. He'd dated a lot of extremely sexy women, and how could a person regret that? Okay, yes, the sexy women had mostly come to him after he'd had some financial success, and therefore, they had suspect motives. And yes, they'd showed what one might consider a cursory interest in him as a person. And, yes, a few of them had been high maintenance to the point of absurdity. And, okay, they'd all left him eventually. Or he'd left them.

But it was all a question of what he wanted out of a relationship, wasn't it? If you wanted marriage and kids, as Nix did, then the way Evan lived wasn't conducive to that. But if you wanted fun and sex and to be seen in public with a total knockout on your arm, then he'd done okay for himself.

The problem with Candace wasn't the hotness factor. She wasn't as conventionally attractive as some of the women he'd dated, but she was sexy in a different way than they were. Anna, for instance, had been hot in an obvious, smack-you-in-the-face way. Candace was attractive in a way that made you think of evenings by the fireplace, home-cooked meals, and a cool hand on your forehead when you were sick. Candace was attractive in a way that made you think of kids and retirement and—God forbid—eventual grandchildren.

It wasn't that he didn't want those things. But the idea of walking through that door now, at this point in his life, scared the crap out of him. Because once he walked through the door, he wasn't sure he could walk back out again.

He wasn't sure he'd even want to.

"You're just scared because you know it might be real," Nix said, as though he'd read Evan's mind. "Cowardice. That's the problem."

"The problem, in case you want to know, dickhead, is that I don't want to hurt her. I maybe didn't care so much about hurting the others because they didn't care about hurting me, so it was fine. It was even. But Candace? If we start something and it doesn't work, she's going to get hurt. Just because I'm not ready to get into a big thing doesn't mean I don't care about her. I feel protective of her. Is that so wrong?"

"No. It's not." Nix leaned back in his chair, his long legs stretched out in front of him. "But it's kind of bullshit."

"How? How is it bullshit?"

"It's bullshit because the person you're trying to protect is you."

❧

CANDACE HAD ALREADY STARTED SLEEPING in her old room at her parents' house, but she hadn't yet fully cleared her things out of the apartment above Jitters. She still had another week of work at the coffeehouse, and she spent her breaks up in the apartment, packing her things into cardboard boxes, then carefully labeling and taping them.

On Saturday, Shane came with a pickup truck he'd borrowed from one of his brothers, and together, they loaded the last of her furniture and boxes into the truck.

They were upstairs cleaning the empty apartment, Candace scrubbing the toilet and Shane cleaning the windows with Windex and paper towels, when Evan poked his head in the open front door.

"Hey. What's going on?" he said.

Candace heard his voice and came out into the front room. "I'm all moved out, as you can see," she told him. "Shane and I are cleaning, then you'll be free to rent the apartment to someone else."

Evan crossed his arms over his chest, his hands tucked into his armpits. "So, where will you be living?"

"My parents' place. Until I figure out what I'm going to do next."

Shane looked up briefly, then kept cleaning windowpanes one after another.

"What's he doing here?" Evan gestured toward Shane with his chin.

"Helping. Obviously," Candace said.

Evan grunted in acknowledgment.

"Well, I'd better get back to it." Candace waved a hand toward the bathroom, where she still needed to scrub the shower and mop the floor.

"I really wish you'd reconsider," he said.

"It's a little late for that." Shane spoke up for the first time since Evan had come in. "We've already moved everything out. As you can see." His tone was neutral, and his smile didn't reach his eyes.

"Yeah, well, a stupid misunderstanding is no reason to quit your job or move, or—"

"It wasn't a stupid misunderstanding," Candace said, "and I think you know that."

"The windows are done," Shane said in an upbeat tone. "What's next? You need me to take out the trash?"

ONCE EVAN WAS GONE, Shane brought up the question of the misunderstanding that may or may not have been stupid. So far, all Candace had told him was that she'd wanted to pursue a different type of work. She hadn't said anything about a conflict between herself and Evan, so she'd known he would ask.

"What did he do that made you decide to quit?" Shane's tone was neutral, and he kept his eyes on the trash bag that he was tying closed. But no matter how casual he was trying to be, Candace knew it was an act.

"Nothing. He didn't do anything."

"Then what did you do?"

Candace was holding the mop she intended to use on the bathroom floor. She gestured with it, her hands encased in rubber gloves. "Why does anyone have to have done anything? Why can't a person just quit a job because they don't want to work there anymore?"

"A person could do that." Shane let go of the trash bag and straightened to face her. "But a person usually doesn't quit one job without finding another first, and they certainly don't move back into their parents' house if they don't have to. Unless their boss did something that made staying at their job impossible."

His jaw flexed in a way that made Candace think he was moments from charging downstairs and punching Evan in the face if circumstances called upon him to do so.

Candace sighed and closed her eyes. "It's not what he did. It's what I did," she said.

"Okay. What did you do?"

"I ... I told him a thing that ... Let's just say the thing I told him doesn't reflect well on me. And now, staying here is too mortifying."

"So, he was a dick about whatever you told him?"

"No. Not exactly."

"Then what?"

Candace was getting backed further and further into a metaphorical corner, and she didn't know what to do. She couldn't tell Shane that the thing she'd done—the big, bad thing that had forced her to quit—was that she'd told Evan she loved him. If she did, it would end her relationship with Shane, and she wasn't ready to do that. Even though she felt no spark when they kissed. Even though her feelings for Shane felt more like friendship than love. Even though being with him felt like playing a role for which she was distinctly unqualified.

"I don't want to talk about this," she said. That much, at least, was true.

"All right."

"Really?"

"I accept that you don't want to talk about it right now. So we won't. But I want to talk about it at some point, Candace. Something significant happened, obviously, and if I want to know you—which I do—then I want to know what it was. I can wait, but I'm going to want to revisit it. Soon."

She nodded. "That's fair."

"Well. I'll just get this trash downstairs." Shane took the bag and went out the front door with it.

When he was gone, Candace leaned against the wall in the living room and blew out a breath. She didn't have Evan. She also didn't have her job or her apartment. And soon, after a conversation she would not be able to avoid, she wouldn't have Shane, either.

She knew she'd done the right thing quitting Jitters, though. She needed to put the idea of Evan firmly behind her, and she couldn't do that if she was seeing him every day.

It had occurred to her more than once that she might need to leave Cambria if she really wanted to move on without him. Cambria was a small town, and people in small towns had a way of running into each other over and over, day after day.

Everything would have been so much easier if Evan had simply told her he didn't want her. If he'd shut her down firmly and completely. It would have hurt like hell, but it would have provided closure.

Instead, he'd been vague in his response, and then he'd kissed her. Which kept hope alive when, in fact, there was none.

By the time Shane came back into the apartment, she knew she had to start looking for work somewhere other than Cambria—somewhere Evan wouldn't keep popping into her life. Which meant she wouldn't be applying for the job at Shane's medical practice.

It also meant that, once she found a job and a place to live, possibly many miles from here, this thing with Shane—whatever it was—would be over.

A shame, since he was such a great guy. But it was probably for the best.

CHAPTER 23

*E*van couldn't help thinking that the whole thing was epically unfair.

Candace had come to work for him, had proven herself to be exactly the manager he needed for his business, and now was abandoning him.

And what for? Because he hadn't been prepared to say he loved her the moment she'd told him how she felt about him?

It was ridiculous. It was absurd. It was, quite frankly, bullshit.

The only thing to do, he decided, was to tell her exactly that.

She still had one day left at Jitters, so he could tell her at the coffeehouse. But that would be awkward, because he didn't want the baristas to hear their conversation—for the sake of his privacy and hers.

Okay, so he'd just march upstairs to her apartment and have it out with her.

Then he remembered she didn't live there anymore.

He checked the new address she'd given him—the one for her parents' place. Then he waited until Jitters closed, gave her enough time to get home and get settled in, then got into his car and drove to Happy Hill, where the Weaver family lived.

If he had to say what he needed to say in front of her mother, her father, and the family dog, then so be it.

CANDACE CAME HOME from work exhausted.

She'd never found her job particularly taxing before, but now that the tension between herself and Evan was adding pressure to every exchange, every encounter, she was ending each workday feeling as though she'd just finished a triathlon.

At least now, with her job done for the day, she could relax. She could take a hot bath, unwind, and forget about Evan, if only until tomorrow.

She was upstairs in her room and had just changed into a fuzzy terrycloth robe in preparation for the bath when her father called to her. "Candace? There's someone here for you."

"What? Who?"

Her father didn't answer.

She tried to remember if she'd had plans with Brittany, but she was sure she didn't. Was someone here to try to sell her solar energy? Girl Scout cookies?

She tied her robe, a big, white, ankle-length number her mother had bought her for Christmas, and headed down the stairs. She froze halfway down when she saw Evan standing in the doorway.

CANDACE STOOD ON THE STAIRS, halfway down, wearing a robe that made her look like a polar bear. An adorable, huggable polar bear.

"Hi, Candace. Can we talk?" Evan's heart was hammering, but he wasn't sure why he was so worked up. He'd had confrontational conversations before. None of them had rattled him like this.

"I don't think we have anything to talk about."

"Well, I think we do."

"I just ... I have to go put some clothes on first." She started to turn to go back upstairs.

"It'll only take a minute." He didn't want to wait for her to go back up and get dressed, because he was afraid he might lose his nerve. And who knew what he might say to her if that happened? He would make up some bullshit story for why he was here instead of saying what he'd come to say.

"All right."

Candace's father had retreated somewhere into the house, but it was always possible he'd stayed close enough to overhear them, and Evan wanted this conversation to remain private.

"Can we maybe go out on the porch?" he said.

"I guess so."

The evening was mild and the waning light of day was thin and pale as they stepped outside.

Candace's parents' house had a wide, covered front porch with a seating arrangement of wicker furniture and a porch swing that hinted at summer evenings spent outside with lemonade and good conversation.

He wondered if she'd kissed boys out here during high school, when Evan had been so stupidly unaware of her. He wondered if she'd kissed Shane out here.

"You want to sit down?" she asked.

"I'd rather stand."

"Okay. Evan ... what is this about?"

He took a deep breath and plunged ahead. "It's about you treating me like shit and how I don't like it, Candace."

CANDACE HADN'T KNOWN what she'd expected him to say, but it wasn't that.

"What?"

"As your employer, I've never been anything but good to you. You have to admit that. I paid you a fair wage, I gave you an apartment at a rent that's ridiculously below market price. I gave you a health plan. More than that, I treated you like an equal, like a partner in the business. And this is how you treat me? You just quit?"

"Evan, it's not about that. It's—"

"I know. I know it's not about that. It's about the fact that when you said you had feelings for me, I didn't immediately say I felt the same way. I was blindsided, Candace! I just … I needed a minute! But, no. I wasn't right there where you were, so you bailed. You just decided to abandon me."

She closed her eyes and pinched the bridge of her nose between her fingers. "You just … you ignored it! You ignored what I said! Do you know how humiliating that was? How mortifying?"

He lowered his voice, made it more gentle. "Candace …"

"And then you kissed me, but nothing changed. Nothing changed! And I couldn't … There was no way I could stay after that kiss, knowing it was never going to be anything more, knowing how it felt to kiss you but still being so far away …" Her voice was thick with emotion, and she turned her back to him so he wouldn't see the tears in her eyes.

"Candace. Turn around and look at me."

"I don't want to look at you. I can't think when I look at you. Don't you get that yet? When I look at you, I can't think, and I can't breathe, and I can't … I can't live like this! So I need to quit, and I need you to let me. I need you to let me go."

Letting her go was the last thing he wanted.

He couldn't have put a name to what he was feeling, but his heart was beating too fast and his palms were sweating, and his entire body was tingling with the need to touch her.

"Candace. Turn around. Please."

She did, slowly, and in the pale glow of dusk, he saw the raw need on her face. Need for him.

His control broke. He grabbed her, pulled her into his arms, and kissed her, and she let out a low moan that made his legs shake.

He devoured her mouth with his, caressing her tongue with his, feeling her breath on him and the warmth of her body in his arms.

"What are you wearing under that thing?" he murmured, his voice rough.

"Uh … I … Nothing."

He shoved her back against the wall and slipped his hand into the seam of her robe, sliding it around her bare waist, feeling his entire body ignite at the sensation of her skin under his palm.

He was sliding the hand downward toward the curve of her ass when the front door opened and Mr. Weaver's voice said, "Candace? Is everything okay?"

Evan jumped back as though he'd been burned, and Candace pulled the robe closed around her.

"Fine, Dad! Everything's fine."

The tremor in her voice gave her away.

CANDACE HAD BEEN SO CAUGHT up in what was happening, so caught up in Evan, that she'd forgotten where she was. At the sound of her father's voice, she snapped back into awareness, the sensation of re-entry giving her an unpleasant jolt.

Fortunately, her dad hadn't seen anything. The way he'd opened the door just a crack, calling out to her without actually looking at her, told her he'd had his suspicions about what might have been going on out there on the porch.

"I … ah … You should go," she said, wrapping the robe so tightly around her that she might have been huddling for warmth in below-freezing temperatures.

In fact, her body felt like it was on fire.

"Right. I'll just … Right." Evan walked down the porch steps and toward his car.

～

OKAY, Evan thought as he drove back to Otter Bluff from Candace's house. *Okay.*

He'd had a lot of good, valid reasons for his reluctance to get into a relationship with Candace. But now, he had a better reason to go forward with it: the searing, blinding passion he'd felt when he'd kissed her and touched her bare skin.

It was still true that she'd be at risk if her feelings for him were as strong as she said they were. But life was risk. And it seemed like she wanted to take this one.

If they tried it and things didn't work out, it would affect more than Candace's heart. It would make working together—if he could get her to take her job back—difficult or impossible and would throw his business into disarray.

But, hell. If they didn't give it a try, she'd go ahead with her plan to quit, and that was disarray, wasn't it? At least this way, their professional relationship would have a chance.

And it was utter bullshit that he was focusing on their business relationship at all. That wasn't what he'd been thinking about on the front porch with his hand inside Candace's robe. He'd be willing to bet it wasn't what she'd been thinking about, either.

He could admit that the idea of being with Candace scared him. She wasn't a woman from whom he could casually walk away. And walking away had been his Plan B for every relationship in his life.

Until now.

CHAPTER 24

*C*andace didn't sleep well that night because she had too much on her mind.

Evan wanted her. He actually wanted her. No matter what he might say, that much was obvious after what had happened on the porch.

But wanting her wasn't the same as wanting a relationship with her. She wasn't naïve enough to believe otherwise. So, what now? What came next?

One thing was certain: she had to break up with Shane. Things with Evan might progress or they might not, but either way, she couldn't be with one man while having these kinds of explosive feelings for someone else. To do that would be wrong, and it would be unkind.

She had to tell Shane, and it had to be soon.

It weighed on her mind, along with the questions of where things with Evan might go, whether she should go through with quitting her job, and what might happen if she didn't. Having a relationship with him would be so much simpler if it weren't complicated by them working together. But she loved Jitters—loved the baristas, the customers, the ambiance. She didn't want to leave.

Amid all of the questions, all of the uncertainty, she lay in bed thinking about the kiss, about the taste of Evan, the feel of his hand on her bare waist. She thought about what might have happened if her father hadn't come out, and it made her weak with need.

What if Evan wanted her but could never love her? What if he used her for his pleasure, then moved on to someone else?

She knew she would take the risk. She'd loved him too long to walk away now.

CANDACE'S TWO-WEEK notice at Jitters was almost fulfilled.

She wanted to talk to Evan, to figure all of this out. But first, she had to come clean with Shane.

She got up in the morning feeling bleary-eyed and unsettled, took a hot shower, and dressed. At the breakfast table, her father carefully broached the topic of Evan Bridges.

"So." Ed was sitting at the table with the newspaper open in front of him and a mug of coffee in his hands. His reading glasses were perched on the tip of his nose, and he peered through them at the paper as he spoke. "That was Evan Bridges."

It wasn't a question, so Candace felt no need to answer.

"What did he want?" Now Ed slid his gaze over to Candace without turning his head to face her.

"He wanted ... He wants me to stay. At Jitters. He wants me to keep my job." Candace went to the counter and poured a mug of coffee, then added sugar from the bowl next to the pot.

"Seems like that's not all he wanted." His voice stayed mild, as though he were discussing something of interest he'd read in the paper.

"Dad." Her voice held a futile plea that maybe, just possibly, they could opt not to talk about this.

He carefully folded the paper, took off his glasses, and looked at her. "I don't usually talk about this kind of thing with you. About your ... activities. With men. I usually leave that to your mother."

"Which I appreciate. So much."

"But."

Here it came. Candace steeled herself for whatever fatherly admonishment was about to come her way.

"You've been dating that doctor. That Shane Brody," he said. "So your mother tells me. And he's a good guy, she also tells me."

"He is."

"So, whatever was happening last night out on the porch with Evan Bridges ... well. It just doesn't seem right."

"Nothing happened on the porch with Evan."

Ed twisted his face into the expression he'd used for as long as she could remember, whenever he knew his daughter was lying to him but didn't want to say so outright.

"Okay, fine," she said. "Something did happen. But you don't have to worry about Shane. I'm going to break up with him today."

Ed looked pained.

"Dad, what?"

"Nothing."

"Dad!"

He folded his arms on the table and sighed. "Well, honey. let's look at the facts. This Shane is clearly interested, and he's been a gentleman. Has always treated you with respect. Am I right?"

"Yes. You're right."

"While this Evan has brushed you off for years. Decades. And even though he's likely to keep doing just that, he doesn't mind feeling you up on my front porch the minute he has the opportunity."

The fact that her father was talking about someone feeling her up made Candace cringe with embarrassment.

"He didn't—"

"I'm just saying," he went on. "Is Shane Brody really the one you should be breaking things off with? Seems to me you might be betting on the wrong horse."

~

CANDACE TEXTED Shane later that day to ask if they could meet. A neutral location was always best for a breakup, so she arranged to meet him for coffee on the patio at Linn's Easy as Pie Cafe at ten a.m.

When he arrived, he looked so good that she began to doubt her decision. But despite how handsome he was, how kind, how smart and funny and fun to be with, she didn't feel the same things for him that she felt for Evan.

They ordered their drinks and found a seat under a shade tree, the sounds of activity on Bridge Street filtering through to them.

"I was so glad when you texted me." Shane flashed her a smile that should have made her knees weak. "Though, since we're meeting for coffee, I'm kind of surprised we're not at Jitters."

"I wanted to talk, and I didn't want Evan to hear it." She toyed with her cup, rotating it on the table.

"Oh." The way he said it told her he knew what was coming.

"It's just …" Her voice sounded small and miserable, even to her.

"You want him instead of me," Shane finished for her.

Her first impulse was to correct him, to frame it in a way that sounded better, less hurtful. But there was no better way to frame it. No way to say it that would change what she meant.

"I'm sorry."

"Yeah. I am, too."

She expected him to storm off, angry, but he didn't. Instead, he leaned back in his chair and laid an ankle on the opposite knee, like a man who was fully at ease. He picked up his cup and took a sip.

"You're not angry?" she asked.

He shrugged. "We gave it a try, and it didn't work. It happens."

"I guess it does."

"But if you don't mind my saying so, you're making a mistake."

Her eyebrows rose. "Shane, it isn't that you're not—"

"Stop." He put up a hand, palm out. "You don't have to do that. My self-esteem is pretty strong—probably stronger than it should be. I don't need you to shore it up. And anyway, I didn't mean you were making a mistake by breaking it off with me. If you don't feel it, then you don't."

"Then what?"

"You're making a mistake with that Evan guy."

She sighed and looked at the table instead of at him. He certainly wasn't the first to tell her this, but that didn't mean she wanted to hear it.

"I don't know much about what's going on there," he went on, "but what I'm gathering is that you have feelings for him, and he's playing you like a cat with a wounded bird."

Her eyes snapped up. "That's not fair."

"Isn't it? It was pretty clear to me that he was trying to come between us, but has he ever said anything about wanting a long-term relationship with you? If he has, tell me, and I'll apologize."

"I ... no."

"That's what I thought. I might not know him, but I know his kind. I know his kind quite well. My brother is one of them."

"Shane ..."

"Look. If he's what you want, then I wish you well. I really do. But don't be surprised when he uses you and then hurts you. Because I won't be."

CANDACE LEFT LINN'S feeling awful. Shane had claimed not to be hurt, but he had been. The bitterness in his voice when he talked about Evan told her that.

She hadn't meant for that to happen, but it couldn't be helped.

She had no idea what might happen with Evan. Just because they'd had a moment of passion on her front porch didn't mean he was ready to embark on a relationship with her—or that he ever would be. But if there was the slightest chance, she wanted it. She wanted him.

At home that evening, she called Brittany to discuss everything that had happened.

"Wait. You broke up with Shane? Hot doctor Shane? I swear to God, Candace, if you weren't my best friend—"

"Evan kissed me," she said, interrupting Brittany. "On the front

porch at my parents' house. Actually, it was more than a kiss. It was …
If my father hadn't come out right when he did …"

"That's why you dumped Shane? Over a kiss?"

"No!" Candace had raised her voice, and she lowered it again when she realized her parents might hear. "No. I broke up with Shane because when he kisses me, I don't feel anything. But with Evan … it was like my whole body burst into flames. That has to mean something. It just has to."

"Okay, point taken," Brittany said. "But that exploding into flames thing won't get you very far if you're looking for a long-term, loving relationship and all he wants is to grope you on your parents' front porch."

"I know, Brit. I know."

Candace didn't want to be that weak woman who was willing to take whatever a man was willing to give her on whatever terms he was willing to give it. She wanted to have more self-respect than that. She wanted to be strong enough to demand more.

But she worried that she was exactly that weak woman, and that the promise of another kiss like the one they'd shared would be enough to make her endure anything, sacrifice anything.

CHAPTER 25

The next day, Evan planned out what he was going to say to Candace.

If she still worked at Jitters, he'd have found time to talk to her on her break, but she didn't, so he would have to call her.

He would tell her how much he'd enjoyed kissing her—this last time, and the time before.

He would ask her out on a date. A proper one this time, and not just a casual work-related dinner.

He would tell her he didn't know where things might go between them, but he wanted to give it a chance and find out.

Then, he would ask her to come back to her job. He would tell her how much he valued her, how essential she was to his business, and how much he'd come to rely on her.

If none of that worked, he would say please.

But as he got ready to call her, he became more and more worked up about the whole thing. He hadn't done anything wrong here. Why should he have to say please? Why should he have to beg?

He dialed before he could second-guess himself and bail on the whole thing.

"Hi, Candace. Do you have a minute? Is this a good time?"

He was in the office that had been Candace's and was now his. The baristas had opened Jitters a few hours before, and the place was full of customers seeking their morning caffeine.

"Sure. What's up?" she said.

He'd had it all worked out. When he opened his mouth, he was supposed to say how he couldn't stop thinking about that night on her parents' porch. Instead, what came out was, "You know what? This is stupid."

Candace hesitated. "I ... Excuse me? What's stupid?"

"This. All of this. It's stupid." Evan gestured around him, as though she could see him through the phone. "You leaving your job. You leaving your apartment. It's ... I don't want any of that. It's dumb."

"It's not stupid to me," she said softly.

"Yeah, well."

This wasn't going as he'd hoped. In his imagination, he'd have hung up the phone after a minute or two having secured her promise to stay at Jitters, to move back into the apartment—and to date him.

He'd achieved none of those goals, and they were already a good ninety seconds into things.

It was time to get back to his original strategy.

"Candace ... I can't stop thinking about the porch. Well, not the porch itself, obviously—it's just a porch—but about what happened on it. With you." And, hell. He used to be so good with women. Or, if not good, then at least he'd been smooth and effective with them. For some reason, that didn't seem to apply to Candace.

"I can't either." Her tone was soft and a little rough, emotion taking the usual gloss off of her voice.

"Okay. Okay, then. I think ... I have a plan, and I just want to lay it out for you and see what you think."

"All right."

"It's a three-part plan," he went on.

"A three-part plan."

"Yes. Part one: You stay on at Jitters as manager. Part two: You move back into the apartment. And part three." He took a deep breath. "We date."

"You want us to ... to date."

"Yeah. It's right there in the plan."

She didn't say anything, and he wasn't sure how to interpret the silence.

"So, what do you think?" he asked.

IN ALL OF the scenarios Candace had imagined regarding Evan and the beginnings of a romantic relationship with him, never had she thought it might involve a three-part plan. Roses, maybe. Champagne wasn't out of the question. But bullet points?

She told herself to stay focused. Evan wanted to date her. He wasn't saying he wanted to sleep with her or use her for his momentary pleasure. He wanted to begin seeing her publicly and socially. Maybe even in a way that might lead to something long-term.

The moment she'd always waited for was here, but it wasn't happening the way she'd thought it would.

She wanted to say yes, drive over to Jitters, jump into his arms, kiss him, and agree to everything in the three-part plan and more. But she had to be smart about this. She'd waited for this chance for so long, and if she wasn't careful, she might not get another one.

"I ... have to think about it."

Evan sputtered, "But you said ... I thought ..."

"I want to," she told him. "I really, really want to. But ... this is too important for me to make some snap decision and get it wrong. I just ... I need to think."

The fact that he'd presented it as an organized list of agenda items wasn't necessarily working in his favor.

As though he'd heard her thoughts, he said, "I'm not very good with women."

She let out a quick bark of laughter. "That's not the impression I got."

But he sounded so miserable that she struggled to understand. Then her eyebrows rose, her eyes widened, and she got it. "Oh. You don't mean that you're not good with women. You mean you're not good with relationships."

"Isn't it the same thing?"

"No. It's really not."

The revelation made Candace so happy she wanted to dance. Evan wasn't inept with women—not usually. But he was inept now because he didn't want a fling. He didn't want a temporary solution for his empty bed. He wanted to give this thing a real chance.

He was inept with Candace because she mattered, and that scared him.

It scared her, too, but it also excited her—especially knowing that he'd had to leave his comfort zone in order to attempt it.

"I'll think about it," she said again, then hung up before she could say something stupid and impulsive.

"I SWEAR TO GOD, Brittany, it was like he'd made a PowerPoint."

Candace was at Brittany's place, the two of them eating pizza and sharing a bottle of wine as Candace brought her friend up to date on the events of her love life.

"At least a three-point plan is clear," Brittany responded, a slice of pepperoni pizza in her hand. "Usually, it's impossible to tell what the hell a man wants. You remember Scott? The guy I was seeing for a while about five years back? The Realtor?"

"Yeah."

"I thought he was breaking up with me, and it turned out he was proposing." Brittany rolled her eyes. "I was ready to throw a glass of water in his face and storm out of the restaurant until he brought out the ring. Clarity is a virtue. Of course, we broke up anyway when I said no, so …"

"Evan was so awkward, I almost felt sorry for him. And awkwardness hasn't been a problem for him with women before. Not if Anna was any indication. So, I think he's just awkward with me."

Brittany looked carefully at her friend. "You seem weirdly happy about that."

"I am! Because it means I'm different to him, Brittany. It means I'm special."

"Okay, maybe it does. But it doesn't mean he's capable of having a real relationship with anyone, let alone you."

"I know."

"Which means you need to temper your expectations, Candace. I mean it. If you go into this expecting a lifetime commitment ..."

"I won't. I don't."

"I just don't want to see you get hurt."

"I get it." Candace picked up her wineglass and took a sip. "I really do. And I'll be careful. I'm not expecting anything."

Brittany's words played over and over again in Candace's mind that night as she tried to sleep.

Don't expect anything. Don't get your hopes up.

Her hopes were up, though. They were sky high. After a lifetime of wanting Evan, she finally had some indication that he wanted her, too. Why shouldn't her hopes be up? Why shouldn't her expectations be high?

She knew Brittany had a point, though, and she forced herself to take that into consideration as she thought about Evan's three-point plan.

Surely a compromise between hope and realism was possible.

Point one: He wanted her to stay at Jitters. She could do that. She wanted to do that.

Point two: He wanted her to move back into the apartment. That one, she wasn't so sure about. It was one thing to be dependent on him for her paycheck. It was quite another to be dependent on him for shelter, too. In the event of a nasty breakup, she didn't want to have him as her landlord. She would say no to that one.

And point three: He wanted to date her.

Abso-freaking-lutely.

She was so excited at that prospect that she could barely close her eyes. She'd talk to him tomorrow. She would tell him what she'd decided.

But a voice inside her said, *Tell him now.*

She grabbed her phone from her bedside table, opened the texting app, and sent him a message.

Regarding your three-part plan: yes to parts one and three, no to part two.

She sent the text.

She waited a few minutes for his response, worrying the whole time. Was he thinking about how to answer? Or was he away from his phone? Had he changed his mind about the whole thing? Was he already ghosting her? Oh, God. Was he?

When the answer came, it was a considerable relief.

So, yes to Jitters and yes to me.

That's right. But I'm going to hold off on the apartment for now.

Works for me, he wrote.

EVAN HADN'T REALIZED how tense he'd been about Candace's response until he received it and every muscle in his body seemed to sigh.

He'd thought it didn't matter. If she said yes, she said yes. If she didn't, there would always be other women. There would always be other opportunities.

But he'd really wanted her to say yes. He hadn't known how much until it happened.

And that realization scared the crap out of him.

He'd been tense waiting for her response. Then he'd relaxed when he'd gotten it. And now he was tense again, thinking about what that profound and deep relief had meant.

Shit, he was a mess.

Evan knew *works for me* was a lame response and he could have done better. He was off his game.

The thing was, this didn't seem like a game.

Where should I take Candace? he texted Nix, his phone still in his hand from his exchange with Candace. *She said she'd go out with me on a real date, and now I don't know what to plan.*

What are you talking about? Nix answered. *You've been on, what, about ten thousand dates? Give or take? How can you not know how to do it?*

Fuck off, Evan answered.

Okay, okay. Take her to a restaurant and then for a walk on the beach. It's a classic for a reason. Madeline's is good.

Nix wasn't wrong. Evan had been on a lot of dates with a lot of women, starting with his first date at age fifteen—Cindy Meyers—and running right up to his ill-fated relationship with Anna.

But all of those relationships with all of those girls and women had one thing in common: they'd ended.

Something different was required this time.

The fact that he was thinking about how he could make this one not end meant something that he was too frightened to look at very closely. He told himself it was just that Candace was a nice girl and he didn't want to hurt her.

It was more than that, though.

He didn't want to hurt himself, either.

"I'M NOT QUITTING JITTERS," Candace announced to her parents the next morning at breakfast. "I'm going to stay."

"Oh. Sweetheart, that's great, if you're sure." Melissa was sitting at the table with a mug of coffee and the paper, and she looked up from the article she'd been reading to regard her daughter.

"I am sure. And also? Um … Evan wants to go out with me. On a date. He wants us to see each other." Candace tried to keep the giddy giggle out of her voice, but it was pointless. Her joy was bubbling to the surface.

"Really?" Melissa gave her daughter a hopeful smile.

"Really."

"That's wonderful, sweetie." Candace's mother got up from the table and went to hug her. "But, are you sure about this?"

"I've never been more sure of anything," Candace said.

CHAPTER 26

They took Nix's advice and had dinner at Madeline's, with a walk at Moonstone Beach planned for afterward. Evan would have worn a jacket and tie in San Francisco, but here in Cambria, that would have seemed glaringly out of place. Instead, he wore a pair of pressed khakis, a V-neck cashmere sweater with a hint of white T-shirt peeking out at the neckline, and polished leather loafers.

He'd pondered whether to wear cologne, since some women liked it and others didn't. In the end, he opted to wear just a little.

He picked up Candace at her house at six p.m. and held the car door for her. As they drove to the restaurant, he felt a much different vibe between them than what they'd had when they'd been just friends and coworkers.

Now, the air was thick with expectation.

Evan let his hand rest on the small of Candace's back as they walked into the restaurant and as the hostess led them to their table. He held out her chair, and she smoothed her skirt over the backs of her thighs as she sat.

"You look beautiful," he told her.

She was wearing a white silk button-down shirt with the top two buttons undone, showing him a hint of cleavage. Her skirt was short enough to be flirty but not so short as to be suggestive, and her high-heeled sandals made him wonder how she'd navigate a walk on the sand or on the uneven wooden boardwalk.

He ordered the duck and she ordered the lamb, and they shared a bottle of pinot noir by the light of the candle in the center of the table.

It was the kind of date he usually chose when he was seeing someone new. Romantic, elegant, and expensive enough to show he was making an effort without it being too much.

Normally, he'd have thought everything was just right.

The problem was, Candace wasn't his usual woman, so it felt wrong that they were on his usual date.

Not that she seemed to mind—or even know—that she was getting his standard first-date treatment. She smiled at him in a way that said she meant it, a smile that reached right into the center of her and lit her from within.

Nobody else had ever smiled at him in quite that way. Nobody else had ever lit up for him the way Candace did.

They talked about her for a while—he knew about her childhood, because he'd been there, but there were still the years between high school graduation and today that they had to account for. She told him about her parents, her friends, the reasons she'd decided to stay in Cambria instead of moving to LA or the Bay Area, and the reasons she wanted to continue to live here.

She was open, relaxed, and engaging.

Then she asked about him.

CANDACE THOUGHT she knew everything about Evan. So why was he stiffening up over the subject of himself and his life?

"I'm sorry." She dabbed her mouth with her napkin and placed the cloth back into her lap. "I didn't mean to make you uncomfortable."

"It's fine. You didn't."

But she clearly had. There was something he didn't want to talk about.

The first date was not the time to push it. If things worked out between them the way she hoped, there would be time. There would be the rest of their lives. She didn't need to know everything about him now. She wanted to take the next forty years to learn every part of him.

And that, in itself, was not the healthiest attitude, she reminded herself. The fact that he was thinking first date and she was thinking about their lifetime together indicated that she needed to slow her roll. She needed to slow it to a crawl if she wanted to meet him where he was.

Instead of pushing him, instead of asking again the questions he was avoiding, she sipped the last of her wine and smiled. "Should we look at the dessert menu?"

ON MOONSTONE BEACH, Candace dealt with the issue of her shoes by taking them off and holding them in her hand while she walked barefoot on the sand. They held hands and strolled at the waterline as the sun sank toward the horizon.

Evan felt like an idiot.

He'd been distant and reticent during dinner, and he knew it. What he didn't know was why. It wasn't like he had a lot to hide. She knew the highlights. She knew about his mother, his work, his ex-girlfriend. What else was there?

Except, there was much more, and something about telling it to her worried the hell out of him.

So he'd deflected. He'd given her minimal answers to perfectly reasonable questions about himself and his life. He'd acted like she was just some acquaintance who'd been prying when she asked about the things that mattered most to him. Now, thinking back on it, he was tense as they walked side by side.

"Is everything all right?" She stopped and looked up at him in the glow of the sunset.

"Yeah, I'm good." He rubbed at the stubble on his chin. "This is just … It's a little weird, that's all. *Good* weird. But weird."

"You've been tense all night."

"I'm sorry. I don't mean to be."

She could have been annoyed, she could have been angry. She could have asked him to take her home. Instead, she smiled—that smile that reached every part of her face and, hell, probably every part of her soul—took both of his hands in hers, and said, "I have an idea of something that might relax you." Then she went up on her toes and kissed him.

The kiss started slowly, tentatively. It started with a brush of lips, a gentle hum of breath. But then he sank into it, pulling her into his arms, molding his body to hers, his mouth exploring hers with greater and greater urgency.

She was right, it was relaxing him. He felt a rush of bright liquid happiness running through his veins.

He'd never felt that with Anna. He'd never felt that with anyone. Until now.

He pushed his fingers into her hair and deepened the kiss, and at this moment, he didn't want to be anywhere else, with anyone else. For this moment, he felt complete. He felt pure, simple joy.

And that feeling terrified him.

He pulled away from her and looked down at her face, still upturned toward him, her lips still gently parted.

"Let's walk," he said.

HE TOOK her home and left her at the front door with a brief good-night kiss.

Candace had expected and hoped for more.

She shouldn't have, she supposed. For one thing, he probably didn't want her father to catch them making out on the front porch again. For another, it was their first official date, and he was being a gentleman.

But she'd hoped they might go back to his place, that they might end up together in his bed.

She could wait for that, though. She'd been waiting a long time, and she could continue waiting.

She had no doubt that he often ended first dates in someone's bed, and she told herself to take heart from the fact that he didn't do that with her. She was different, and he was treating her that way. As though she was not just one of the many. As though she was special.

She went to bed that night remembering the kiss on the beach and wondering when it might lead to more.

THE NEXT DAY, Evan waited for Candace to arrive at work.

The baristas had already opened the place, but Candace wasn't scheduled to start her shift for another hour. Evan normally wouldn't even be here—he didn't work at Jitters every day, because that's what he had a manager for—but the promise of seeing her had brought him to work.

He made up things to do in the office, pushing papers around and answering emails, creating busy work for himself until she got here.

Every time he heard the front door open, he craned his neck from where he sat in his desk chair, office door open, to see if it was her.

The simple fact was, he didn't feel right when she wasn't nearby.

The bell above the door rang, he looked, and he felt a distinct pang of disappointment to see one of their regular customers—a busboy from the restaurant across the street—instead of Candace.

What kind of business owner was disappointed to see a regular customer walk into his shop?

Finally, five minutes before her shift was scheduled to begin, Candace walked in, her purse slung over her shoulder, her cheeks pink from a nip of cold in the morning air.

It was so good just to see her—just to know she was here—that he

179

felt like a kid who'd finally heard reindeer hooves on the roof on Christmas Eve.

He was losing his shit, and he knew it, so he focused on the screen of his laptop instead of on her.

If someone had told him in high school that he would someday lose his shit over Candace Weaver, he wouldn't have believed it. Yet here he was.

She came into the office, hung her purse and jacket on the coat rack, and smiled at him, that smile that made his chest warm and his legs weak.

"Hi." She gave him a little two-fingered wave that was cute as hell.

"Oh. Hi." He said it as though he'd just noticed her there—as though he hadn't been waiting for her, hadn't been holding his figurative breath until she'd arrived.

"I had a really good time last night," she said, grinning.

He nodded, not looking at her. "Hey, could you please teach the new barista to clean the air pots tonight? I ran her through the rest of the routine, but we didn't get to that."

Candace's smile collapsed, as though the foundations beneath it had crumbled. "Uh .. sure. I'll do that."

"Thanks."

CANDACE WENT BEHIND THE COUNTER, greeted the baristas, and tied an apron around her waist. She chatted with one of the regulars, and she checked the pastry case to make sure they didn't need more of anything.

While she did all of that, she thought she was doing a good job of pretending everything was fine. Clearly she wasn't, because Ariel came over with a concerned look on her face and put her hand on Candace's shoulder.

"Are you okay?"

"Yes. Fine. I'm good. How are you?"

"I'm a little worried that you're going to step out in front of traffic. What happened, Candace?"

Oh, God. Was she that transparent? Was it that obvious that her feelings had been hurt?

"Nothing. Really. I just ... I got into it with my mother a little bit this morning, that's all. It's hard to be living at home again." The lie came out smoothly, even though Candace was not an accomplished or experienced liar.

"Oh, jeez. I can imagine." Ariel rolled her eyes in sympathy. "I lived with my parents all through college. I seriously considered sleeping in my car."

Ariel got to work on a vanilla latte, and Candace told herself that she had to do a better job of faking happiness.

CHAPTER 27

"The air pots. That's what he said. I said I had a great time, and he asked me about the air pots."

Candace and Brittany were on their usual treadmills at the gym, pounding the treads side by side as they moved over simulated hills and through computer-generated valleys.

"I swear to God, men are idiots." Brittany pumped her arms, her face glistening with sweat. "Would it have been so hard for him to say he had a good time, too? Would it have been so hard for him to have bent you over the desk and had his way with you?"

"That's ..." Candace had been about to say something, but the mental image Brittany had created for her was too distracting. Candace blew out a breath and gave her head a quick shake to clear her mind. "Maybe he didn't say he had a good time because, you know, he didn't have a good time. Maybe he's regretting having gone out with me. Maybe he thinks the whole thing was a mistake." She felt the sting of tears in her eyes, and she wiped her face with her towel, passing it off as sweat.

"Or maybe he thinks he's being professional. You know, keeping his work life and his personal life in separate boxes."

"Maybe."

That was possible, she supposed. But if so, he needed to be more clear, because Candace was miserable trying to interpret his behavior.

"At least you're dating someone," Brittany went on. "I haven't been on a date in months. Which sucks. You've got so many prospects that you threw away a doctor. A doctor! And here I am, spending every night watching rom-coms on Netflix."

"Speaking of that." Candace decreased her speed to a slow jog. "If you still want me to set you up with Shane, we could do that."

"Really?" Brittany's eyebrows rose.

"Sure. I mean, I know a lot of people hate being set up on blind dates, so I get it if—"

"Set me up! I'm not one of those people! Blind date, online dating, reality show—whatever! If it means I can go out with a hot doctor, I'm on board."

Candace grinned at her friend. Setting up Shane and Brittany would ease Candace's guilt over breaking up with Shane, and it would also get her mind off Evan. Well, it might not do that. It was a matchmaking project, not a miracle. But it seemed worth a try.

"Do you think he'll go for it?" Brittany asked.

"I don't know. I'll have to ask him. But he might. He's clearly looking."

"Oh, shit. If I'm going to date a hot doctor, I'm going to have to step up my workout routine." Brittany increased both her speed and her incline. "After this, I'd better do my abs."

"So? How are things going with Candace?"

Nix was holding the heavy bag for Evan at the gym down in San Luis Obispo. Nix himself didn't box, but he did enjoy racquetball, and the deal was that they would spend a half hour on Evan's boxing workout followed by a half hour of Nix's chosen sport.

"Things are good." Evan hit the bag with a steady combination: jab-jab-cross, jab-jab-hook. Every time he hit the bag, Nix let out a soft "Oof."

"You sure you don't want to spar with me?" Evan asked, feeling the welcome burn in his muscles and the light sheen of sweat on his body and his face.

"You'd kill me," Nix said.

"Lightweight," Evan remarked.

"Exactly. And also, I'm wondering why you changed the subject."

"I didn't."

"Like hell you didn't. What's going on with you and Candace?"

Evan stepped back from the bag, grabbed his towel from the bench where he'd put it, and wiped his face. Then he took a long drink from his water bottle.

"We went out," he said.

"I knew that. What I'm asking is, what happened?"

"I could tell you it's none of your damned business."

"You could," Nix agreed. "Or, you could tell me what the problem is so I can solve everything with my superior wisdom."

"Superior wisdom, my ass."

"Really?" Nix raised his eyebrows. "Which one of us is in a happy, committed relationship, and which one of us is beating the crap out of an inanimate object in a futile effort to tame his inner rage?"

Evan put down the bottle, sighed, and rested his hands on his hips. "Fair point."

"You can either tell me, or I can ask her. And I don't think you want me to ask her."

They still had a twenty-minute wait until their racquetball room was free, so they went to the gym's juice bar, ordered something weirdly green, and sat at the bar while Evan told Nix about his date with Candace.

"The thing is, it went fine. Better than fine. I had a good time, and I think she did, too. But at the end of the evening ... I froze up."

"Ah, man." Nix shook his head sadly. "Equipment failure? That sucks. It happens, though. So I'm told. Not that I have any personal experience with that particular problem."

"No, asshole. It never got that far. I mean, I froze up before I could even ask her to my place, or go to hers, or anything. I dropped her off at her door like we were dating in a goddamned 1950s sitcom. The only thing missing was Pa on the front porch with a glass of lemonade."

"Oh. Well, that's not so bad. She probably thought you were just being gentlemanly."

"Sure. Except."

"Except what?"

"Except, yesterday when she came to work, she told me she had a good time, and I asked her about the air pots."

"I assume that's not a euphemism," Nix said.

"It's not."

"All right. So now, she probably thinks you're not really into her. Which is fine if that's how you feel."

"It isn't!" Evan threw his hands up in frustration, the revolting juice concoction on the bar in front of him. "It's … I am. Into her, I mean."

"Okay. You like her, but your immediate impulse was to act like you don't. Which is new for you."

"Yeah."

"I mean, I get the impression you never acted that way with Anna or any of the others."

"No. I was smooth. Or, at least, I think I was. Based on the results, I definitely was."

"Now we're getting somewhere." Nix sipped his juice, looking smug.

"Where? Where are we getting?"

"She's different. Your reaction to her is different. Now we just have to figure out why that is."

"I know why." Evan fiddled with his plastic cup, rotating it counterclockwise on the bar. "I don't want to hurt her. You know? She's had a thing for me for … well, forever, I guess. And so it's going to be a big thing if it doesn't work out. And I don't … I'm just afraid of hurting her."

"So, what makes you think you'll hurt her? What makes you think it won't work out?"

"Nothing has ever worked out before, has it? With women, I mean. Every relationship I've ever had has ended, so ..."

"It only takes one."

Evan side-eyed his friend. "So, what? Just because you're married now, you're suddenly Dr. Phil? Did you get a psychology degree I'm not aware of?"

"No, shithead. But I'm an objective observer. And as an objective observer, it seems to me that she's not the one you're worried about."

"Fuck off." He said it conversationally, without heat.

"Mature." Nix checked his watch. "You ready to get your ass handed to you? I think our room's open."

CANDACE WAS ALMOST CONVINCED that Evan wasn't going to ask her out again, and that made her glad she hadn't moved back into the apartment. He didn't want her, that was all. She could accept that. She could move on. She'd gotten her hopes up, and that was a dangerous thing to do. Now she just had to tamp her hopes back down again.

She worked at Jitters, being friendly but professional with him. She tried to ignore the sting every time he asked her about the schedule, or their suppliers, or something that didn't have to do with the two of them.

And she told herself she would have to start looking for another job. It hurt too much to be around him knowing he didn't want to be with her.

But just when she'd given up hope—just when she'd resigned herself to job interviews and Craigslist and nights crying in bed—he did ask her out again. The way he did it, though, made her wonder if she was misinterpreting everything.

"I've got a gift card," he said one day out of nowhere while she was in the back room getting a stack of cardboard cups to restock the baristas.

She wasn't entirely sure how she was supposed to respond.

"You do?" she said.

"Yeah. For Neptune. Somebody gave it to me a while back, and I never got around to using it."

She'd been up on a step stool getting the cups, and she stepped down, the cups in her hands, and faced him. "Well, I don't think they expire, so you should be good."

Candace started to walk toward the front of the shop, and he stopped her.

"I just thought … maybe. The two of us. Ah … I thought you might want to use the gift card with me. At Neptune. For dinner."

By now she was so thoroughly convinced that he didn't want to date her that the suggestion took her by surprise.

"You want to have dinner with me?"

"Yeah. Yes. I thought … I mean, we said we were dating."

"That was before you went all weird on me."

"I didn't go all weird."

"Yes. You did."

"Okay, maybe I did. But … I thought we could try again. If you're willing."

And, damn it, she went all soft inside the way she did whenever he was near, whenever he talked to her or looked at her or … or breathed. She went all squishy and stupid and dreamy-eyed. Why couldn't she use her brain when he was with her? Why did she have to think with her idiot, love-addled heart?

"Oh, Evan." It was more a gentle, exhaled breath than words.

"What?"

Please don't do this to me. If you don't want me, let me go. Please don't play with me like this, because it hurts too much.

"That sounds nice," she said.

CHAPTER 28

*C*andace needed to get her mind off her impending second date and the many ways in which it might go wrong. Applying herself to the Shane-Brittany pairing seemed like a productive way to go about it.

She texted Shane one afternoon on her break while she was sipping a latte in her office.

I know this is an awkward question, given the circumstances, but would you be interested in going out with my friend Brittany? I think you two would hit it off.

He didn't answer for a while, and she decided he probably wasn't going to. Well, fair enough. A lot of people objected to being set up, and being set up by someone who'd dumped you was probably even more objectionable.

She was just getting ready to go back to work when her phone pinged with a text.

I don't think so. Thanks for thinking of me, though.

Well, that was the expected response, wasn't it? But Candace wasn't ready to give up that easily. She found a picture of Brittany in her phone—one that was particularly flattering. Candace had taken it on Moonstone Beach, when Brittany was glowing with happiness. The sun shone in her hair, and her smile made her radiant.

She sent the photo to Shane.

A moment later, he responded: *On the other hand, I might be willing to give it a go.*

SHANE WANTED to ask a few questions about Brittany before he decided whether to go out with her, so Candace agreed to meet him for coffee.

He initially balked at going to Jitters because of Evan—he didn't relish the idea of running into him—but Candace persuaded him to come on a day when Evan was scheduled to be off.

They met during Candace's morning break time. The day was bright and warm, so they ordered lattes and scones and sat at a cafe table on the sidewalk.

Shane, in jeans and a sweater, looked more casual than usual. His hair was still damp from the shower, and his face was shadowed with a day or two of stubble.

Looking at him, she lamented the fact that she hadn't been able to want him the way she wished she could. Things would be so much easier if she'd just been able to react to Shane the way any normal woman would.

Any normal woman who wasn't obsessed with someone else.

Brittany would love him, though, she was sure of it.

"So, how are things going with ... you know." Shane tilted his head toward Jitters, and it was clear he meant Evan.

Candace shrugged. "Oh ... I don't know. Not as well as I'd hoped."

Shane's eyebrows rose. "Don't tell me it's already over."

"No. It's not. It's just ... things are a little one-sided, that's all."

Shane gave her a look of sympathy that embarrassed her. "You deserve to be with someone who's all in."

She felt a heat behind her eyes, and she blinked a few times to clear it.

"Yeah, well. I'm not here to talk about that. Let's talk about you and Brittany."

They chatted for a while, and Candace told him all of the basic facts about Brittany: what she did for a living, how Candace knew her, Brittany's interests and hobbies, and a little bit about her dating history—enough to give Shane the big picture but not enough to violate Brittany's privacy.

"She's my best friend in the world. She's great. I really think you'll like her," Candace said.

From there, they talked a little about Shane's medical practice, the renovations on the office, and the Brody family's efforts to hire a receptionist.

"You still haven't found anyone?" Candace took a sip of her latte, enjoying the sunshine and the foot traffic past the shop.

"I'm afraid not. I guess you're not interested anymore, then?"

Candace gaped at him. "You mean you'd still consider me?"

"Sure. Why not? Just because things didn't work out between us doesn't mean you wouldn't make a great receptionist."

Candace had told Evan she would stay at Jitters, and for the moment, that was her plan. But that was when she thought things might go well between them. Now, she wasn't so sure they would. And if they didn't, she would need a change. She would need to go to work every day somewhere she wouldn't see him, wouldn't want him. Somewhere separate from the endless, gnawing desire she felt for him.

"I'm good here for now," she said.

"Well, if things change—and I'm thinking they might—give me a call."

They talked some more about his practice and his family, her parents and her job. She was relaxed and comfortable.

All of that relaxation and comfort ended when she looked up, latte cup in her hand, and saw Evan on the sidewalk staring at her.

In an instant, she could see how it looked. Here she was, sitting with Shane, laughing and talking and, to all appearances, enjoying a casual date with a man she clearly liked.

"Evan." The way she said his name, she sounded guilty.

He didn't say anything. He just leveled a hard look at her, then at Shane, and then walked past them into the shop, his lips pressed into a hard line, his fists clenched.

"Oh, God." Candace put down her drink and watched him go.

"If you want, I can talk to him," Shane said. "Tell him this was all about you fixing me up with your friend."

Her first impulse was to agree to that. Surely if Evan knew the reason she was here with Shane, he'd drop his attitude.

On the other hand, she didn't want Shane to have to deal with Evan. He hadn't done anything wrong, and he shouldn't have to defend himself.

"That's okay. I'll talk to him," she said.

"Are you sure?"

"Yes. I'm sure."

The fact that she felt a cold dread at the prospect probably didn't say anything good.

EVAN WASN'T EVEN SUPPOSED to be at work. This was supposed to be his day off—a day of lounging around or going to the beach or hanging out with a friend. He'd come here to be near Candace—and here she was with that Shane asshole. At Evan's own business. So, not only was she cheating on him, she was doing it right in his own bed.

So to speak.

He went inside, said hello to the baristas, and locked himself in the office as though he had work to do in there, as though he wasn't just brooding.

He opened his laptop, looked at the screen without seeing it, then closed it again.

Shit.

Shit, shit, shit.

He should have known better than to get emotionally attached. He hadn't made that mistake with the other women in his life, and he shouldn't be making it now. How had he been so stupid?

When he heard a gentle knock on the door, he knew it was Candace.

"What?" he barked.

"Evan? Can I come in?"

He didn't say anything.

The doorknob turned, but the door didn't open.

"Evan? It's locked. Could you let me in, please?"

The thing to do was to act as though he didn't care. Actually not caring had worked for him in the past, but that didn't seem to be an option this time. Pretending not to care would be the next best thing.

He got up, unlocked the door, then went back to his seat behind the desk, feigning a casual attitude that he didn't feel.

"Hi." Candace stood in the doorway looking at him with a worried expression, her brows drawn together.

"Oh. Hey. How's it going?" He sounded like an idiot—he knew that. Talking as though he didn't even know she was at Jitters that day, as though he were mildly surprised to see her.

Had he ever thought he was smooth with women? He'd clearly been deluded.

CANDACE WALKED into the room fully expecting to smooth things over between them.

But Evan was acting like such a child—brooding over what he'd seen and now pretending it hadn't happened—that she changed her mind, pivoting out of pure spite.

Why couldn't men just be honest? Why did this have to be so hard?

He could just stew, then. He could think whatever he wanted to think and feel whatever he wanted to feel, and she had no obligation to make things easier for him.

"Fine. It's going fine," she said, her voice artificially perky. "I didn't think you were working today."

"Obviously."

"What's that supposed to mean?"

He scowled at her. "It means, if you thought I was going to work today, you probably would have taken your side piece somewhere else."

Her mouth fell open.

"My *side piece?*"

"Well, assuming I'm not the side piece. Which I guess I could be, now that I think about it."

"You are ... just ... What a ..." She couldn't seem to finish her thought.

"That's fine. That's ... whatever. I obviously never meant as much to you as you said I did."

And that was it. That was the last straw. After all of the pining, all of the wanting, all of the unconditional adoration, this was what she got? No. She didn't owe him reassurances. She didn't owe him anything.

"Maybe you didn't," she said. She turned and left the room, ignoring the look of shock on his face.

EVAN HADN'T EXPECTED things to go the way they'd gone.

For one thing, he'd planned to play it cool, like he didn't care what she did with Shane Brody. That had all been shot to hell as soon as he opened his mouth.

He hadn't intended to act like a petulant child. It was undignified.

And once he had acted that way—once he'd spouted off about his jealousy—he'd expected Candace to reassure him that nothing was going on with Shane.

She hadn't done that.

Now he had a couple of choices. He could walk away from this thing, pretend his relationship with Candace had never happened, and go find someone who would present less of an emotional challenge to him.

His other choice was to fight for her.

Okay, he could acknowledge that he'd been a bit distant with Candace lately. He could admit he hadn't exactly swept her off her feet. And yes, maybe he'd broadcast a sense of ... well, disregard. He wasn't sure why he'd done that, but he had.

So, yeah. Maybe if she'd turned to Shane Brody, Evan wasn't entirely blameless in the matter. Maybe it was even more or less reasonable.

Well, shit.

They had a date scheduled for Thursday night. He could cancel it, reasoning that he didn't want to compete with another guy, or he could double down on it and use the date to show Candace that he was twice the man Shane Brody was.

He stood up, walked around the room, then sat down again. Then he stood up.

Okay. Okay, then.

He went to the office door, opened it, and called out, "Candace? Could you come in here for a second?"

"Sure, Evan. I'll be right there." He heard a hint of annoyance in her voice, but he would take care of that.

CANDACE DIDN'T PARTICULARLY WANT to fight with Evan, but if that's what he had in mind, she could hardly refuse. It wasn't like she could decline to speak to her boss when summoned.

She finished the cappuccino she was making, gave it to the customer, then wiped her hands on a dish towel and went into the office to confront Evan.

The things he'd said about her and her side piece. For God's sake. She was gathering up a head of steam as she went back to the office, ready to tell him about treating women with respect, ready to insist that he stop acting like a child.

She walked into the office, closed the door behind her, turned to confront Evan—and found herself pushed against the wall, Evan kissing her senseless.

When his lips met hers, when he pressed his body against her, grabbed her by the wrists, and pinned her hands above her head against the wall, all thoughts fled her mind and she was only a mass of delicious sensation.

She let out a moan as he ravaged her mouth with his. Her body felt like it was on fire. Her heart pounded and her legs shook. She felt lightheaded with desire.

Then he released her, and she almost collapsed to the floor.

"I'm looking forward to Thursday night," he said, looking pleased with himself. Then he grabbed his laptop bag and walked out of the office, out of the shop, and toward his car.

A few minutes later, when Shane texted her offering to straighten things out with Evan, she responded, *Don't you dare.*

This jealousy thing had a lot going for it.

CHAPTER 29

*C*andace planned Shane's date with Brittany for Wednesday night, the evening before her own date with Evan.

The idea was that Shane and Brittany would meet at Robin's, and Candace wasn't supposed to be directly involved. Instead, Candace changed the plan at the last minute. The three of them would meet for a drink, and then, if things went smoothly, she would leave Shane and Brittany alone to continue the date, having dinner together and maybe extending things from there.

And she suggested they do it at Madeline's—which was directly across the street from Jitters.

"Why Madeline's?" Brittany asked when Candace told her about the change in plans. "Why not Robin's? I like Robin's."

"You also like Madeline's."

"I do. But if they're both good, why the switch?"

Candace had considered making up a story, but why? Brittany was her best friend. Candace could tell her anything.

Candace took in a deep breath, let it out, then spilled everything in one long sentence. "I'm suggesting the change because the other day after Evan saw me sitting at Jitters with Shane, he got jealous and kissed the crap out of me, and I wouldn't mind that happening again, and Madeline's is across the street from Jitters, and there are outdoor tables—tables where, say, someone at Jitters might clearly see me and Shane sitting and having a drink before you get there, whereas Robin's is set up so someone at Jitters would likely never see who might be there having a drink with a handsome doctor."

"I see," Brittany said.

"So, can we make the change?" Candace asked.

"Of course. You get a little something, and I get a little something. It's perfect."

ON THE EVENING of Shane and Brittany's date, Candace dressed carefully and took time with her hair and makeup. She wanted to look like someone who was on a date without actually being someone on a date.

She told Shane to show up at six thirty, but she told Brittany not to arrive until twenty minutes later. Considering the fact that Evan usually left Jitters between six thirty and seven, Candace figured that would provide ample time for him to spot her having a glass of wine with Shane.

When she arrived, she was pleased to see that a sidewalk table was available, and she asked the hostess to seat her there. Shane arrived a few minutes later, and she waved him over.

She stood and gave him a kiss on the cheek, then he got settled into his chair.

"You look great," she told him.

"So do you." He gave her an appraising look. "Come to think of it, *why* do you look so great? You're ducking out after a glass of wine. Looks like you went to some trouble."

Candace winced apologetically. "Okay, don't get mad." She told him her plan, including the fact that it would just be the two of them until a bit later.

She'd worried that he might be upset with her—that he might lecture her for using him to chase a man who didn't deserve her—but instead, he laughed, a big, booming guffaw that came from deep in his belly.

"You're not upset?" she asked.

"Oh, I guess I should be. But … I have to give you credit for creativity and imagination." He wiped at the tears of mirth that sprang from his eyes. "I can't be mad at someone who's so damned determined."

"I'm glad you feel that way. Let me buy you a glass of wine for your trouble."

"Sounds good." Shane settled into his seat, stretching out his long legs under the table. "Wait, though. Am I going to get hit? That Evan guy looks like he can throw a punch."

"He can. He's a boxer."

"Terrific."

"But he won't. I promise." Candace wasn't entirely sure she could keep that promise, but it didn't seem wise to say so.

They ordered wine, then they sipped and talked while the bustle of Main Street went on around them. The evening was mild, and the sun was still well above the horizon. An outdoor heater cast warmth on them, and the waitress brought a candle for the table, creating a romantic atmosphere that was sure to improve the effect she was hoping for should Evan see them.

About ten minutes later, he did.

Candace caught movement out of the corner of her eye, and she looked up to see Evan across the street, locking the front door of Jitters. He turned the key, tested the door, then turned—and froze when he saw Candace and Shane.

"Here we go," Shane muttered, taking a sip of his wine, maybe for fortification.

Evan seemed to be rooted to the sidewalk. He couldn't move, couldn't think, couldn't seem to do anything but stand there and stare at Candace, who was happily having a drink with that Shane asshole.

After the kiss, too. And after he'd made it clear that the two of them were still dating—tomorrow night, in fact.

Part of him wanted to storm across the street, pull that Shane guy out of his chair, and pound him into oblivion. But one couldn't really do that without police interference, and he suspected it wouldn't endear him to Candace.

He reflected that when this thing between himself and Candace had started, Evan had thought it would be easy. Why wouldn't it be, when she'd already made it known that she had feelings for him? Surely the hard part was done, and all he'd have to do was enjoy being with her.

What an idiot he'd been.

But just because things were proving to be a little more complicated than he'd imagined they would be, that didn't mean he was going to concede defeat.

Screw defeat.

He'd thought maybe he would be able to walk away without Candace seeing him, without him having to say or do something or make some kind of gesture. But she'd looked up and locked eyes with him, and now here he was, being called upon to react in some way.

Well, he could be a grownup about this. He could be mature, even if what he really wanted was to break the bones of a certain stupidly handsome doctor.

Hell, if he did that, at least the guy would have good medical care.

Instead of assaulting anyone, Evan pasted a smile on his face, raised his hand, and gave Candace a jaunty wave.

Candace waved back tentatively.

Should he approach, or just leave it at the wave? The wave seemed like a safe bet, as it had already been well-received and he'd managed not to clench his teeth while he was doing it. But somehow, he couldn't seem to keep himself from going over there.

He walked across the street toward Madeline's, his laptop bag slung over his shoulder, and kept a smile on his face—the kind of smile he regularly gave customers who were a pain in the ass but who were, after all, paying to keep his business afloat.

"Hey. How're you guys doing?" he asked. It felt strained as hell, but he thought it sounded okay.

"Fine, Evan. You heading home for the day?" Candace asked.

"Yep." He bobbed his head up and down, his eyebrows raised in a pantomime of good-natured friendliness. "Nice night to be having dinner outdoors," he remarked.

"It is, isn't it?" Shane looked to the sky, as though he had to check to confirm what he'd just agreed to about the weather, in case a stray storm cloud might appear overhead and make him a liar.

"So." Evan was still standing there, even though he knew he should leave. Even though he knew the longer he stayed, the more likely he was to screw things up.

"So," Candace repeated, smiling at him in a friendly way, as though she hadn't just been caught on a date with some other guy.

"I guess I better get going," he said. "I have to ..." *Oh, shit.* He couldn't think of one damned thing he had to do that he could insert into the conversation to make it seem like he was too busy to worry about what Candace was doing.

I have to go home, get drunk off my ass, and brood.

I have to sort my socks.

I have to hurry home to get ready for a date with a fictional woman I'm inventing right this second just to spite you.

"I ... have to get to the gym," he said finally, settling on something that, at least, might intimidate Shane Brody. "I'm meeting my new sparring partner. The last one quit because I broke his nose."

That last part, at least, was true.

Shane blanched, just as Evan had hoped he might.

AFTER THAT PAINFUL EXCHANGE, Evan turned and walked toward his car. Candace grabbed her wineglass and took a hefty gulp.

"Oh, shit. Did he really break some guy's nose?" Shane asked.

"I don't know. Maybe. Probably. I mean, he's a big guy, and he's been boxing for a while, so ..."

"Why did I go along with this? Why didn't I just turn around and go home?"

"Because Brittany is great, and she'll be here any minute."

"Right. Brittany. Does she know about this whole ... scheme?"

"Yes," Candace admitted, "but none of it was her idea. I just sort of sprang it on her at the last minute."

"Like you did with me."

"Well, at least I told her before she left her house."

Shane laughed, though maybe a little less heartily than he had before. He picked up his wineglass. "I'm glad I ordered an expensive cabernet. You owe me, in case that guy jumps me in a back alley and pounds my face in."

"I could get you an appetizer, too," Candace suggested. "Maybe the crab cakes?"

EVAN DIDN'T MENTION anything about Candace's drink with Shane the next day at work. Of course, he didn't stay at Jitters long. He popped in just after opening, stayed for an hour or so, making small talk and checking on things, then said his goodbyes and left in the middle of the morning rush.

He was polite to Candace, but he didn't mention anything personal. He kept all conversation centered firmly on Jitters.

She'd almost wondered if he'd changed his mind about their date that night, but he threw out a casual "See you tonight" before he headed out the door.

So, they were still on.

Candace was distracted all day as she went through her duties at the coffeehouse. By the time she'd helped the baristas with the closing routine and was on her way home, she was wired with nerves.

She went into the house, said a quick hello to her parents, went up to her room, and called Brittany.

"So, how was your date with Shane?" she asked.

"Oh, my God. He's great. I'm so glad you dumped him. At dinner we—"

"That's awesome. Let's talk about me."

Candace really did want to know about Brittany's evening, but right now, she was in the middle of a crisis, and she needed her best friend to help her navigate it.

"Crap. What happened?" Brittany asked.

"Nothing, it's just … ever since the thing last night, when Evan saw me and Shane together, he's been … distant. Polite. As though he might, at some point, try to sell me some car insurance."

"Oh, no. That's not good."

"But we're still on for tonight, so I guess we'll see. What do I do, Brittany? Should I tell him the thing with Shane wasn't real, or—"

"No! Don't do that. I mean, the jealousy thing worked before, right? He went from being all cool and standoffish to making out with you against a wall. That's got to indicate it's a winning strategy."

"I guess so."

Still, Candace didn't feel one hundred percent right about it. She'd never been a dishonest person, and continuing to use deception to win Evan's affections wasn't something she felt comfortable with. Still, if it led to more making out against walls, she could find a way to live with herself.

"Wear your good underwear," Brittany suggested. "If the wall thing was any indication, Evan just might go caveman on you tonight. And I mean that in the best possible way."

Candace shuddered happily at the thought.

CHAPTER 30

On Thursday, the day of his date with Candace, Evan went to the gym because he felt the intense need to hit things—or people.

This urge to hit and to hurt had started when he was a teenager, and it wasn't a result of anger, despite what many people thought. It was simply the best way he knew to relieve stress. When he'd been a young teenager—about fourteen or fifteen—he'd gotten into a lot of fights at school until his stepfather had encouraged him to channel his aggressions into sports.

Football had worked well, but he wasn't nearly good enough to go pro, so he'd needed a new outlet once he graduated from college. Boxing had filled the void nicely.

He didn't have anyone to spar with this time, so he hit the heavy bag, happily pounding it and making it dance despite the sweat in his eyes, the burning of his muscles, and the hard, heavy beat of his heart.

Hitting the bag was a meditation of sorts. As he worked, he thought about Candace, and that Shane guy, and what might happen that night.

Let her go. This is stupid.

That thought kept coming back to him over and over. If she

wanted Shane, she could have him. Competing for her affections was just too damned hard.

Then again, Evan had never shied away from a challenge. Hard was something he could handle. He just had to figure out if he wanted her enough.

Yeah. Yeah, I do.

The answer came quickly, with no hesitation.

How had he gotten here? When he'd hired Candace, he'd remembered her, but he'd thought of her as a nice, smart woman who might make a good coffeehouse manager. He'd seen her as someone trustworthy and resourceful, someone who'd always done well in school.

When he'd learned that she'd had a thing for him all this time, he'd thought it was sweet, but he hadn't seen it as something he'd want to pursue.

But she'd worked her way into him, and now the idea of giving her up to someone else was impossible. Unbearable.

And yet he felt distinctly uncomfortable with the idea of committing to a relationship with her.

Why? What was he afraid of?

Everything.

Nix was right—every woman Evan had ever been involved with was someone he could easily walk away from with no emotional muss or fuss. They'd occasionally loved him—he knew that—but he'd never loved them. He'd never even wanted to. He'd found their companionship pleasant, certainly. He'd loved the sex, the sensation of having someone in his life. He'd liked having someone beautiful on his arm, and he'd liked not having to be alone.

But love? With all of his previous relationships, he'd felt lonely even when he was in them. He'd felt ... empty.

But Candace was different. When he was with her, he felt complete in a way he never had.

And that shook him.

He didn't need a therapist to tell him the root of his problem. His parents had broken up when Evan was just a kid. His mother had cheated on his father, and his father had cheated on his mother, and then his mother had left his dad for someone else.

After that, there'd been more weddings, more divorces, more cheating, more men coming in and out of his mother's life.

As a result, Evan thought of marriage as a hellscape of agony and betrayal.

None of that mattered, though, if you didn't fall in love. None of it mattered if you didn't really care.

He thought about it as he hit the bag, feeling the sweat trickle down between his shoulder blades, feeling the burn in his arms, the reverberation of each impact traveling up through his muscles.

He knew all of this. None of it was a revelation.

But for the first time, he was beginning to think he had to find a way to move past it. For the first time, going from one loveless relationship to another seemed like an untenable situation.

What would happen if he tried to have more?

She's already seeing somebody else. She's already cheating, just like Mom cheated on Dad.

That was bullshit, though. He'd been pushing Candace away from the minute she'd stepped into his office for her job interview. He'd kissed her a few times, then he'd deliberately frozen her out.

He'd sent the message that he was unavailable, unattainable. So he didn't really blame her if she was keeping her options open. They'd never said they were exclusive.

Hell, they weren't even in a relationship—not really. A couple of dates, a few kisses, and a lot of subtext from Evan that it wasn't going any further than that.

Candace wouldn't cheat on him if he gave her a reason not to. If she thought he was in this thing between the two of them, she'd be in it, too.

He wasn't sure how he knew that for sure, but he did.

This is crap. Get out while you can.

He told his inner voice to shut the hell up. His inner voice didn't know shit.

CANDACE WOULD BE GOING to Otter Bluff for tonight's date. Evan would be cooking for her.

Generally, when a guy offered to cook for you, it was understood that sex would be the main course. It occurred to Candace that she should be apprehensive, but she wasn't. She'd wanted him for so long that she couldn't be anything but eager and hopeful.

Of course, the whole charade she'd orchestrated with Shane outside Madeline's could ruin everything. Or it could force Evan to finally decide whether he wanted her. The ploy had been a big gamble, and she was hoping it would pay off.

As Brittany had suggested, Candace wore her best underwear—a white, lacy bra and panty set that was so delicate it was transparent, leaving little to the imagination.

She just hoped she'd get to show it to Evan.

She drove to his house just as the summer sun was beginning its descent toward the ocean. As she knocked on the door, every nerve in her body hummed with anticipation. She'd wanted to look casual but sexy, so she'd worn a knee-length wrap dress—one pull of the tie on the side, and he'd be able to open her like a present.

He opened the door and smiled at her, and the smile was a little too predatory to be warm or friendly. She felt a thrill of desire tingle up her spine.

EVAN HAD BEEN WANTING Candace for a while now, and the wanting wasn't going away. The only way he could quiet it, he figured, was to satisfy it. Maybe then he could get the whole thing out of his system. Then, if she wanted to keep seeing that Shane guy, Evan could deal with it and move on.

That was his theory, anyway.

But now, seeing her walk into his house with that dress and that hair and those legs, the idea of her with Shane made him want to establish the issue of possession once and for all.

That wasn't an enlightened way to look at things, though, and Evan liked to think of himself as an enlightened guy.

There was another, better way to look at it: he would show Candace everything she'd be missing if she didn't choose him.

He let her in, poured her a glass of Chardonnay, and led her out to the back patio to enjoy the panoramic view of the ocean his house provided. He was sure Shane Brody couldn't offer her a view like this. If you couldn't use your beachfront house to seduce women, then what good was it?

"This is beautiful," she said. She settled into an Adirondack chair with her glass of wine, sighing and looking out at the pounding surf.

"You're beautiful," he said.

It was a line, but, hell. It was true.

"Evan. About Shane—"

"Could we not talk about him? I mean, I get that you're free to see other people. We never said we wouldn't. But ... could we just not talk about him?"

"All right."

"I'd better ... I've got to check on dinner." He went inside and closed the sliding glass door behind him.

SHIT. Shit.

He'd had it together, had his plan for the evening, had even given her a smooth-as-hell compliment, and then she'd brought up Shane.

Now he was rattled, and he didn't like being rattled. He'd come into the house on the pretense of checking on dinner, but the dinner was fine. The salad was in the refrigerator waiting to be dressed, and the baked pasta dish he'd made was in the oven with another twenty minutes to go.

He opened the oven and peeked in so he wouldn't be a liar, then he stood in the kitchen for a moment just gathering himself.

The door to the patio slid open and Candace peeked in. "Do you need any help? Is there anything I can do?"

He raked his hands through his hair. "Yeah. Yeah, there's something you can do." He covered the ground between them in a few long, fast strides, pulled her into his arms, and kissed her.

CANDACE HAD THOUGHT things weren't going well. After a good start —Evan telling her she was beautiful—she'd made the mistake of mentioning Shane, and Evan had fled.

She'd been wondering how to back up, erase what she'd said, and get things on track again. But now, with Evan holding her and kissing her, it seemed there was no need to regroup. Whatever she'd done to bring this moment about, she wouldn't change a thing.

One of his hands pressed against her back, holding her to him, and the other was entwined in her hair. Her breath came in a ragged gasp as he ran his mouth down her neck and to her shoulder.

"Oh ... God," she said.

He brought her body to vivid, glorious life. No other man had been able to do that with just a kiss, just a touch. What was the chemistry of it? Or was it just magic?

She took his face in her hands and brought him back up to her mouth, parting her lips for him, willing him to devour her.

"Evan," she murmured.

"This isn't ... I didn't ..."

He didn't get out a full sentence, but she knew what he was trying to say. He hadn't brought her here for this. He hadn't intended to entice her with dinner and then take advantage of her. He was trying to offer an apology.

But right now, she didn't want his apology or his explanation. She just wanted him to take off his clothes.

"Let's go to your bedroom," she said.

EVAN MEANT TO STOP. He meant to control himself, to tell her he wasn't in the same place she was and so this was a bad idea.

But somehow, all of his good intentions were buried in an avalanche of lust and need.

He'd always liked sex—hell, he'd loved it—but he'd never needed it the way he needed it now, with Candace. He'd never felt this kind of all-consuming hunger. After Anna, he hadn't been with anyone for a while—surely it was nothing more than that.

Even though he knew he should make himself stop, he couldn't bring himself to do it. He led Candace to his bedroom, undid the tie that held her dress together—and nearly reached the finish line way too soon when he saw what she was wearing underneath.

I'm going to hell for this.

The thought popped into his mind, and he didn't think it was wrong. Because of his own lust, he was being careless with a woman whose heart was on the line.

Right now, though, it seemed to him that eternal damnation might be a reasonable price to pay.

CANDACE DIDN'T MEAN to say the words. She thought them every day. She'd felt them for years. But she knew better than to say them when things between them were so precious and fragile.

But she'd waited for this moment so long that she couldn't keep all of those feelings inside even a minute longer.

"God, I love you," she murmured on a sigh when she was lying beneath him and all of her senses were filled with Evan.

She couldn't not say it any more than she could just stop feeling it.

The words grew and grew inside her until they simply had to come out.

He froze for just a moment when she said it, and he didn't say it back.

She kissed him hard and deeply to cover for his silence.

THE DINNER BURNED, but neither of them cared.

Evan made sandwiches from ingredients he had on hand, and they ate them with the salad he'd made to go with the pasta that was, even now, smoking and black in its pan on the counter.

When they were finished eating, Candace didn't know what to do next. Should she leave? They might make love again if she stayed—an appealing prospect—but if he didn't want her to stay, things would get more and more awkward the longer she lingered.

The question of what she wanted was an easy one to answer. She wanted to climb back into his bed, worship his body, and hold him until morning, or, even better, until she grew old and eventually died in his arms. But she'd said she loved him and he hadn't said it back. Maybe he didn't want her to spend the night. Maybe he'd gotten what he wanted, and now he was waiting for her to go.

Unsure, she felt him out on it.

"This was ... God, this was wonderful. But I guess I should ..."

He was supposed to tell her to stay. He was supposed to hold her and kiss her and take her back into his bed.

But he didn't.

"Yeah." He bobbed his head. "Early morning tomorrow."

She put herself back together and gathered her things, and he walked her to her car.

She drove home with the sting of tears in her eyes.

CHAPTER 31

"*A*n early morning? An *early morning?*" Nix stared at Evan in disbelief. "Given your ineptitude with women, it's a wonder you ever persuaded one to sleep with you."

"What do you mean, one? I hate to tell you this, but I have a pretty impressive track record."

"That's what I mean. I'm surprised you managed to get even one, let alone the multitudes you've managed to attract."

"It's not multitudes." Evan's voice carried a sulkiness that made him feel like an angsty teenager.

"Dude. The women you've slept with could start their own soccer team." Nix paused in thought. "Actually, they could start their own league."

Nix and Evan were having a beer at Ted's. It was still early, not yet eight p.m. on the evening after Evan's date with Candace, and most of the tables and barstools were empty. At the other end of the room, two guys played pool while the jukebox blasted something by Aerosmith.

"I just ... I don't know. I didn't want her to go. She was the one who said she'd better leave, and I was just being agreeable."

"You were being agreeable."

"Yeah."

Nix looked at Evan as though he were about to scold a wayward toddler. "She said the thing about how she'd better get going because she was trying to feel you out on whether she should stay. She was waiting for you to invite her to sleep over."

"She was?"

"Yes, dipshit. And you dropped the ball."

Damn it, Nix was right. That was why Candace had been so cool and distant with him at work. That's why she'd avoided eye contact. He'd wondered if maybe she'd regretted sleeping with him, but that wasn't it. She'd been waiting for his cue—his verdict on whether he saw her as a relationship or a sex buddy. And he'd chosen sex buddy.

Except, he hadn't. Not really. The reason he'd held back was precisely because this thing with her felt more like a relationship than any he'd ever had. Was it so wrong that he'd been a little hesitant? Was it such a crime that he'd opted to take things slowly?

He told all of that to Nix, who gazed at him with pity.

"Evan, taking things slowly means you don't sleep together until you're sure. It doesn't mean you sleep together and then tell her to get the hell out."

"That's not how I said it."

"Well, it's how she heard it. I guarantee it."

Shit. He'd panicked, and he'd said the wrong thing, and now Candace was angry and hurt, and he'd never intended any of it.

"It's not supposed to be this hard," he said, murmuring it as though he were talking to his beer instead of Nix.

"What isn't?"

"The whole thing. Women. Relationships. All of it. I never used to make these kinds of rookie mistakes. But now, with Candace … you'd think I'd never dated anyone before."

Nix leaned back in his seat and his eyebrows rose. "There's probably a reason for that."

"Yeah." Evan bobbed his head and took a swallow of beer. "Yeah, I can see that. There's definitely a reason."

Nix looked at him skeptically. "I'm thinking that the reason I've got in mind is different than the reason you've got in mind."

Evan shrugged. "It's hard because it's not right. That's all."

Nix scoffed. "Asshole. It's hard because it's the first time in your entire, miserable life that it actually *is* right, and that means the stakes are high, and you're not used to that."

Evan wanted to protest, but he couldn't. Not when he had the sneaking suspicion Nix was right.

"So, what do I do now?"

"Now, you've got to find a way to stop screwing it up."

"HE'S AN IDIOT. That's what he is."

Candace and Brittany were in Candace's car on their way to San Luis Obispo to buy Brittany something new to wear for her next date with Shane. The clothing boutiques in Cambria were high-priced and geared more toward an older demographic, and Brittany needed something younger and more budget-friendly.

Candace had told Brittany about her date with Evan, and the sex, and how he'd ushered her to the door before the afterglow had fully faded.

"I mean, here I am, offering him ... well, everything! All of me! Offering him my body and my heart and my love. And he said he had an early morning!" Candace gestured wildly with one hand while she drove. "What is that? What am I doing? What even is the point of this?"

"The point is, you love him, and you've always loved him, and you're never going to stop loving him, and he's finally maybe thinking about you the way you want him to. That's the point. Even if he is proving to be stupidly inept." Brittany said all of that with a calm patience that she used whenever Candace ranted about Evan. But surely she had to be sick of hearing about it. Surely it had to be getting old.

"I'm sorry," Candace said. "I'm self-absorbed and tiresome, and I'm really sorry. Let's talk about you and Shane."

The way Brittany bounced in her seat, Candace knew she'd been waiting for just this opening. "He's great. He's just … he's so great."

Candace smiled at her friend. "He is, isn't he?"

"I can't believe you gave him up. I mean, I know there's the whole in-love-with-Evan thing, but seriously. Shane is pretty close to the perfect man."

"So, does that mean you … you know."

Brittany's eyes widened. "What? No! Of course not! It was our first date!"

"I wouldn't have judged."

"I know you wouldn't, but first-date sex is for some guy you meet at a bar and don't care if you ever see again. Shane is relationship material, and I want to do this right."

"He really is," Candace agreed. "And you might not understand why I walked away, but it's a good thing I did, right? I haven't seen you this happy in a long time."

"I haven't been this happy in a long time."

Candace was glad for Brittany—really, she was. But was it so wrong that she also felt a stab of jealousy? Not over Shane, but over the fact that Brittany was, by all appearances, heading into what might become a fully functional, healthy relationship. That was all Candace wanted, but she wasn't sure Evan was capable of it.

And if he wasn't, she still might have to force herself to walk away.

At the thought of that, her vision blurred as tears filled her eyes. She blinked them away, but not before Brittany noticed.

"Hey, hey. Are you all right?"

Candace took in a ragged breath and nodded. "Yes. I'm fine."

"You don't seem fine. If you don't want to do this, we can—"

"We're buying you a dress," Candace said with finality. "We need a win. And if it's going to be you instead of me, I'll still take it."

Now that Candace wasn't seeing Shane anymore, and given the fact that Evan hadn't wanted her in his bed overnight, Candace was rethinking the idea of applying for the receptionist job at the new Brody medical practice.

Maybe things would work out with Evan, and maybe they wouldn't. More likely, they wouldn't. Either way, there would be so much less at stake if Candace didn't work for him while whatever was going to happen was happening.

Seeing him—being near him—was wonderful when he seemed to want her. It was torturous and impossible when he didn't.

If she was going to have to learn to live without him—which was looking more and more likely—it would be so much easier if she didn't have to see his face at her place of employment every day.

One morning on her break at Jitters, she texted Shane and asked if he'd filled the job yet, and if he'd be willing to put aside their ill-fated relationship in order to consider her for it.

His answer was a welcome one. No, they hadn't filled it yet, and yes, he'd be happy to interview her. No hard feelings about her dumping him, he assured her; if she hadn't, he never would have met Brittany.

All right, then.

He texted that he would check with his brothers, with whom he shared the practice, and let her know what day and time worked for them.

She already felt a little bit lighter as she went about her work, making drinks, ordering supplies, and chatting with the regulars.

She would miss them, she thought. But maybe not. Maybe she'd be seeing them again at Bridge Street Wellness.

Candace heard back from him later that day while she was sitting in her office working on the schedule for the following week.

How's Tuesday at ten a.m.? he texted.

This was real. This was happening. She was taking an important step toward moving on and leaving Evan behind.

Tuesday at ten is perfect.

She was to meet Shane and his brothers on the patio at a Bridge Street cafe because they were still working on renovations to their office.

Candace felt nervous, but it was the right thing.

If Evan couldn't stop playing with her heart, she had no choice but to do this.

She jotted down the information on a notepad on her desk: *Shane, Tuesday, ten a.m.* Then she focused on the job she still had.

CHAPTER 32

Okay, so Evan hadn't asked Candace to sleep over. And, okay, he hadn't asked her out again since that night. And yes, maybe he was acting a little distant when they were at work. None of that meant anything. Their relationship was still in its early days. Why would either of them assume that she'd sleep over? And why would either of them assume they'd be seeing each other every free moment?

He'd convinced himself everything was fine. They were taking it slowly, that was all. That was good. Healthy, even.

He would ask her out again at a time that worked for him, and until then, they would act like the colleagues they were.

Simple. There was no problem, and it made no sense that Nix thought there was.

And if Candace seemed a little standoffish since they'd slept together, well, there was no accounting for the thoughts and behaviors of women.

He was actually starting to believe his own bullshit—starting to feel good about it, even—when he went into the office at Jitters, sat down at Candace's computer to check something on the payroll spreadsheet—and saw what she'd written on the notepad next to her keyboard.

Shane. Tuesday. And the time and location where they would meet. His mouth dropped open.

Was it possible she was still seeing that guy, even after she and Evan had slept together? What kind of game was she playing?

His first impulse was to confront her, but it was after five, and she'd gone home for the day. He could go to her house and do it there, but her parents might be home, which would make the whole thing even more awkward than it otherwise had to be. Plus, if he went over there, he'd have to admit he'd looked at the note on her desk—a conversation that might not go his way.

Damn it. Damn it.

All right, fine. He knew exactly what to do—nothing. He'd pretend he hadn't seen the note, and he simply wouldn't ask her out again. This thing with her was over. It didn't require a big, uncomfortable talk, because things between them hadn't gone that far in the first place.

They'd tried it, and it hadn't worked out.

If she wanted some Ken doll doctor, then so be it. Who was he to stand in her way?

IN EVAN'S MIND, the matter was settled.

So why couldn't he sleep?

He lay in bed at Otter Bluff, looking at the moonlight on the ceiling and willing himself to drift off.

It wasn't working.

He didn't want to think about Candace, but he couldn't seem to stop it.

She was always in his thoughts, always messing with his head. It had been days since they'd slept together, yet he could still smell her skin when he closed his eyes. He could still feel her.

What the hell was happening to him?

He'd always been able to walk away from women. Always. But this was different. He didn't just want to sleep with her, he wanted to *be* with her. He wanted to talk to her. He wanted to share his thoughts about random things, and when he was upset, like he was now, he wanted her to comfort him.

He was breaking, coming apart, and it was all her fault.

He got out of bed, paced around, then went into the kitchen, took a bottle of whiskey out of the cupboard over the sink, poured himself a couple of fingers, and downed it to calm his racing mind. Then he went back to bed and stared at the ceiling some more.

All of this—all of these feelings, all of this unrest—was evidence that he needed to walk away, find someone else to sleep with, and get Candace Weaver out of his system.

He convinced himself that was exactly what he was going to do.

ON TUESDAY, it turned out he was full of shit.

Candace wasn't working that day, so Evan should have been able to focus on his business without thinking about her.

But he kept looking at the clock as her date with that Shane asshole drew near.

Ignore it, he told himself. *Ignore it.*

None of it mattered. *She* didn't matter.

It just so happened that he had an appointment on Bridge Street— that was the only reason he was nearby at ten a.m. just as Candace was getting out of her car and walking into the patio area of the cafe where she was meeting Shane.

No reason other than that.

CANDACE SHOWED up for the interview five minutes early. When she got there, looking as professional as possible in a navy pant suit with a sky blue blouse, Shane was sitting by himself on the patio at a table shaded by an umbrella. He stood when he saw her.

"Candace. Thanks for coming. My brothers got held up, but they'll be along in a few minutes," he told her.

She gave him a sisterly hug. "Thanks for setting this up. Especially after everything."

He waved her off. "I'm thrilled that we might be able to fill the job. Can I get you a coffee?"

"That would be nice."

She got settled into her seat while Shane went to get her drink. She was reaching into her bag for the copies of her resume she'd made for Shane and his brothers when she became aware of someone approaching her table. One of the Brody brothers, probably. She looked up, a professional, pleasant look affixed to her face—and saw Evan, his expression ablaze with anger, storming toward her.

HE'D BEEN okay until he saw her hug that Shane asshole. Yeah, it was just a hug—it wasn't like they'd been making out—but as far as he was concerned, she might as well have been screwing him right there on the cafe table.

The guy's hands had been on her. He'd *touched* her. Evan hadn't heard what they'd said to each other; he'd been too far away. Even if he hadn't been, the blood pounding in his ears was too loud for him to have heard anything.

Before he could stop himself, think about what he was doing, or formulate any kind of plan, he was marching over to where Candace was sitting. The shock on her face when she saw him told him everything he needed to know. She looked like a woman who'd been caught.

He opened his mouth to say something to her—and stopped, frozen, when Shane came out of the building with two paper cups of coffee in his hands.

"Evan," Shane said. "What are you doing here?"

"What am I doing here?" Evan said. "What am *I* doing here? The question is, why the fuck were you hugging my girlfriend?"

"Since when do you care what I do?" Candace broke in. "And since when are you suddenly acting like I'm your girlfriend?"

Candace didn't know why Evan was here or why he was suddenly acting possessive, as though she belonged to him, as though she were territory he could pee on.

What she did know was that he'd misunderstood the situation. Obviously, he thought she was still seeing Shane. She was about to open her mouth to correct him when Shane gave Evan a cocky grin.

"Dude, you waited too long. You had your chance, and you let her go. Stupid. Now move along so I can spend some time with your *ex*-girlfriend." He pronounced the *ex* with a particular edge.

"Shane—"

Candace tried to butt in, to impose some kind of order on everything that was happening, but neither man was paying attention to her anymore. They were focused on each other, Shane eyeing Evan with a grim challenge, the cups of coffee still in his hands. Evan's face clouded with rage, and Candace worried that someone might throw a punch.

Evan nearly did.

Instead of hitting Shane in the face, the way Candace had worried he might, he reached out and slapped one of the cups of coffee out of Shane's hand, and it splatted to the patio floor.

Shane looked down at the mess impassively. "Looks like you owe me two dollars and twenty-five cents."

"I'm going to give you more than that, asshole." Evan moved forward, crowding Shane, but Shane held his ground.

"Both of you, stop it." Candace's voice was shrill, and she looked around for someone who might intervene.

"She wanted you, and you didn't want her, so she's moved on," Shane went on, his voice a low growl. "Your loss, my gain. Now back the fuck off."

Evan slapped the other coffee out of Shane's hand, creating a twin splat to the one that had come before.

"I said stop it!" Candace stepped in between the two of them and put her hands on Evan's chest, trying but failing to push him back. "This isn't what you think it is."

But then, she wondered why she had to explain anything. She didn't owe Evan an explanation. She didn't owe him an apology. True, it wasn't what he thought. But even if it had been, he had no right to come barging in, acting like an angry caveman.

"Candace, step back. I don't want you to get hurt." Shane's voice was deadly calm.

"The asshole's right. Step back," Evan said.

"Stop it. Just stop it!" Candace shrieked.

"I don't know what she ever saw in you, to be honest," Shane said. "Candace, you dodged a bullet."

Evan reached around Candace and shoved Shane in one shoulder, pushing him back a couple of paces. Shane charged forward, and Candace jumped out of the way, deciding that as small as she was, if she got in between the two of them, she was going to get flattened like a squirrel on Highway 1.

EVAN DIDN'T HAVE A PLAN. He didn't have an ideal scenario for how this thing might go. He was operating on instinct, and his instinct told him to pound the hell out of this smug, grinning fuckhead who'd put his hands on Candace.

Candace. Pushing past her to shove Shane had been a bad move—Evan knew that—but she was out of the way now, she'd stepped aside, so there was nothing stopping him from throwing a punch, a punch that was going to feel so damned good when his fist hit this dickhead's face.

He couldn't hear anything beyond the roar in his ears. He couldn't see anything beyond his target. He couldn't think of anything beyond the need to hit, to hurt, to shed some blood.

He pulled back his arm, feeling the rush of adrenaline, ready to let go. Ready to do some damage.

He turned into the punch, felt the glorious forward momentum of his arm—and then found that, for some reason, he was frozen in place.

"Hey, hey, hey," a voice said from behind him. Arms grabbed him and hands held him still. "Let's just calm the hell down. I can't let you hit my brother, no matter what stupid thing he did."

Two guys were grabbing Evan while two more stood by as reinforcements, and Candace didn't know whether to be relieved or alarmed at the appearance of the other Brodys. None of them was as big as Evan, and none of them looked like they knew how to fight as well as he did, but there were five of them and only one of Evan.

Okay, she thought. *Okay. It's over. It ends here.*

She was still thinking that when Evan snapped his head back into the face of the Brody brother directly behind him, which caused a geyser of blood to shoot from the man's nose. He let go of Evan.

One still had him, but Evan's sudden counterattack had surprised him, so he loosened his grip. Evan twisted around, pulling himself out of one Brody's grasp and throwing a punch at another one, who ducked and missed most of the impact.

Shane, who was now positioned behind Evan, grabbed his shoulders in an attempt to pull him away from the other Brodys. That was when Evan's shoe slid in a puddle of spilled coffee, his legs flew out from under him, and he fell in a heap onto the cement, his head hitting the ground with a sickening thump.

"Evan!" Candace screamed and went down onto her knees next to him. His head was bleeding, but he was still conscious.

"Shit. That took a turn," one of the Brodys said.

Candace looked up from Evan's side to see a uniformed police officer standing over them.

"Someone want to tell me what the hell's going on?" the cop asked.

CHAPTER 33

*I*t was bad enough that he'd lost the fight. Anybody could lose a fight when it was five against one. But Evan hadn't even been beaten properly by a worthy opponent—he'd been defeated by a puddle of coffee and a patch of slippery concrete. Now, adding to his embarrassment, he was in the house of one of the guys he'd been fighting, getting the cut on his head stitched up.

Could have been worse. He could have been arrested, but the Brodys had insisted that Evan had just slipped and that nothing else had happened. An unlikely story, given the fact that one of the Brodys had a bloody nose, but the cop had chosen to accept it.

The fact that they'd been so decent about the whole thing—going so far as to tend to his wounds—made him feel like a jerk for going up against them in the first place.

"This isn't bad," Rowan Brody said as he sutured the cut on the back of Evan's head. "And you're not showing signs of a concussion. Unless idiocy is one of the symptoms."

They were in Rowan's kitchen in a little farmhouse on Main Street with a medical kit laid out on the kitchen table. Evan sat in a straight-backed chair at the table while Rowan worked on him. The back of

Evan's shirt was stained with blood. Evan couldn't see it, but he could feel the sticky wetness.

The other Brodys stood around in the kitchen watching and looking smug.

"Dude, it wasn't even a date," Shane said. He leaned his butt against the kitchen counter, his arms crossed over his chest. "I just said that because you were pissing me off."

Candace had wanted to stay to make sure Evan was okay, but he and the Brodys had all urged her to go home. Evan didn't want her to see him like this—bloody and steeped in humiliation. She'd gone, reluctantly.

"If it wasn't a date, what was it?"

"A job interview."

"What?" Evan winced—not at the pain in his head so much as the fact that he'd misread things so badly.

"She's in love with you, but you were being a dick to her, so she thought it might be best to get another job. We're going to need a receptionist when we open our medical practice, so ..." Shane spread his arms to indicate the logic of the situation.

"She's going to quit? Again?" Evan felt bewildered. Yes, he'd been taking things slowly, but was that cause for Candace to abandon him? And did it qualify as dick behavior the way Shane said it did?

"She's thinking about it," Shane said.

"But ..." Evan turned his head to look at Shane, and Rowan used his hands to move it back where it had been. "You might want to hold still unless you want me accidentally putting a stitch in your eye," he commented.

"I wasn't being a dick," Evan said, his voice sullen.

"You slept with her, then you asked her to leave your house and you neglected to invite her out again. Dick," Shane said, as though that were simply the only logical conclusion.

"Sorry, yeah. I have to agree," said Nolan, another brother, from where he sat on a nearby kitchen chair. "Sleeping with someone and then freezing them out? That's prime douche behavior."

"I just … I wasn't sure. I wanted to be sure."

Evan was embarrassed by his words even as he said them. If someone had treated his sister—if he had a sister—the way he'd treated Candace, he'd kick the guy's ass.

"Seems like you're pretty sure if you were willing to take on five guys over her." Finn Brody, who was standing in the kitchen drinking from a bottle of lemonade, raised his eyebrows pointedly.

"I didn't know I was taking on five guys when it started," Evan said. "I thought I was taking on one guy. The rest of you showed up later."

Aidan, the final Brody brother, was still nursing his nose, which was bruised and bloody but not broken. "We should have let the cop arrest you, if you ask me."

"Thank you for not doing that, by the way," Evan said.

"Okay, we're done here." Rowan applied a bandage to the area he'd just stitched and gave Evan a friendly smack on the shoulder. "Keep it clean and dry for the first couple of days, and see me in a week so I can take the stitches out. I think you'll live."

"He might not want to once Candace gets hold of him," Shane remarked.

Candace. How was he going to explain himself to her? What was he supposed to say?

CANDACE COULDN'T GO HOME—NOT with Evan inside Rowan Brody's house bleeding like he'd been shot. But he'd been adamant that he hadn't wanted her in there, so she was outside at the curb, pacing and cursing the unfathomable nonsense of men.

What the hell had he been doing? Why had he shown up in the first place? What had he been thinking, threatening Shane? And, God, had he broken Aidan's nose?

And why, oh why, had Shane pretended Candace had met him for a date? He'd intentionally made the situation worse, and for what?

Because he didn't like Evan's behavior? His own behavior left a lot to be desired.

She stomped back and forth in front of Rowan's house, muttering four-letter words under her breath and worrying about Evan. The sound when his head hit the pavement had been awful. Did he have a concussion? Head injuries were nothing to mess with. Oh, God. Should he have gone to a hospital? Should she go in there and demand to take him to an emergency room?

She was still pondering that when the door opened and Evan came out, bloody and sheepish.

"Oh, my God. Are you all right?" She ran up to him but didn't touch him—she worried that he was hurt and fragile, and she kept her distance.

Rowan stood in the doorway, leaning against the jamb, his arms crossed over his chest. "He's fine. He needed some stitches, but he'll live."

"There was so much blood," Candace said.

"Yeah, scalp wounds are like that. Looks worse than it is, though."

"Thank you. Thank you so much. And … thank you for not letting the police take him."

"No sweat. Just give us a call when you want to reschedule the interview."

Candace's eyes widened. "You still want to interview me?"

He shrugged. "Why not? You're not the one who pounded the crap out of Aidan's nose."

All this time, Evan hadn't said anything. She turned to him, ready to tell him what an ass he'd been, but the humiliation in his eyes made her decide to go easy on him.

"Come on. I'll take you home," she said.

"I can drive."

"Shut up. My car's just down the street."

~

EVAN WAS silent on the drive to Otter Bluff. What could he say? How was he supposed to explain himself?

He expected to feel Candace's rage radiating from her every pore, but he didn't. She seemed more concerned and confused than anything, and that made him feel even worse.

She parked in the driveway at Otter Bluff, then walked him inside, either because she felt she was owed some kind of explanation or because she wanted to make sure he wouldn't pass out on the front doorstep.

She was the one to break the silence.

"Are you okay?"

"Yeah. Yes. I'm fine."

"Are you sure?"

"I'm sure. Candace ... I'm sorry."

Her expression softened. "Thank you. But ... why did you ..." She shrugged, leaving the rest unsaid.

There was no way to play it cool on this one. All he could do was come out with it. With everything.

"I was in the office at Jitters, and I saw the note you left on the desk about meeting Shane. I thought you were still seeing him. I thought ... I didn't mean to follow you. I just ... found myself there somehow. And then when I saw you hug him ... I lost it. And I acted like an idiot. I'd understand if you never want to see me again."

He slumped down onto the sofa, his hands dangling limply between his knees.

"You were jealous."

"Yeah. Hell, yes. I thought ... I thought I was too late. I thought you'd given up on me."

CANDACE LOWERED herself onto the sofa next to him. Part of her thought he was right—he was too late. But another, bigger part of her knew he could never be too late. Whenever he got there, to where she was, he'd be right on time.

She laid a hand on his knee. "You're not too late, Evan."

"No?"

"No. But I can't keep doing this. I can't keep dealing with you being hot and cold. First you want me, then you don't. You sleep with me, then you ignore me. Do you know how long I've loved you? How long I've wanted you?" A tear slipped from her eye, and she wiped it away with her hand. "Every time you give me hope and then tear it away, you break my heart. And I can't do it anymore. I deserve better."

"I know. I know you do."

EVAN TOLD himself to just do it, just say it. Just tell her he loved her. Because he did love her. More and more, he was sure of that.

But loving her didn't mean he was capable of treating her the way she deserved to be treated. It didn't mean he could stay in a long-term relationship. It didn't mean he wouldn't keep breaking her heart, over and over.

"I don't want you to move on. I don't want you to be with anyone else," he said. "But ..."

Her eyes were red and wet with tears, her face full of the misery he'd caused her.

"But?" she asked.

"But, you're right. You do deserve better. You deserve ... hell, one of those Brodys, probably."

"I don't want one of the Brodys, Evan. I want—"

"Just listen." He reached out and took her hand, squeezing it to quiet her. "I've screwed up every relationship I've ever had. I did that. Me. I made the same mistakes again and again, and I hurt people, then I walked away. It's what I do. And I'll do it to you. You know I will, because I already have."

Tears spilled down Candace's cheeks, and he'd caused them. Knowing he'd caused them made him feel like shit.

"I get into relationships because I'm lonely and sad, and then when I don't need them anymore because the loneliness and the sadness have receded a little bit, I either hit the door at a run or I make the other person so miserable that she does. Is that really what you want? Because that's what I have to offer, Candace. That's all I've got."

He was still holding Candace's hand, and he focused on that—that point of connection between them—as he went on.

"I think you should take that job with the Brodys if they offer it. And I think … I think you should go out with Shane, or somebody else who isn't me. I've already hurt you enough, don't you think?"

Candace didn't say anything. She pulled her hand away from his, wiped her face with her hands, took in a shaky breath, and stood up. Then she picked up her purse and walked toward the door.

When she was there, she stopped and looked back at him.

"You know, just because you've always done that, it doesn't mean you have to keep doing it. For what it's worth." Then she left him alone with his self-loathing and regret.

So, that was it.

Evan didn't want her. Or, he did, but he wasn't willing to do what it would take to make things work with her.

Well, she might have loved him since the moment she'd learned the meaning of the word, but at this point, even she could see it was time to walk away.

She went home, sneaked upstairs before her parents could notice her, and had a good cry. Then she called Brittany.

"Candace, what's wrong?" Brittany asked, alarmed, when she heard the tone of her friend's voice.

"It's over. The thing with Evan—it's really over. I know it's for the best, but … I just …" And here came the tears again.

"Oh, no. Sit tight. I'll be right there."

THE THING about a best friend was, she would come running at a moment's notice with Ben & Jerry's and a bottle of Chardonnay and sit with you until you were full and drunk and you couldn't cry anymore.

Candace and Brittany lay side by side on Candace's bed the way they had when they were teenagers and agonized over a boy, just as they had then.

The wine hadn't been part of the equation back then, but everything else was shockingly similar. They were even agonizing over the same boy as when they were seventeen.

" … And then he told me I should date Shane instead of him. Which I'm not going to do, by the way, because Shane is really into you."

"Thank you for that." Brittany sipped from her wineglass, her shoes off and her legs crossed at the ankles atop Candace's duvet. "But the rest of it? He's right, Candace. You really should find someone else."

"I know. I kn-kn-know …" She'd thought she was done crying, but emotion clogged her throat and made it hard to get the words out.

"This is about his mom, you know," Brittany added.

"What about his mom?"

"Don't you remember? Back in senior year, when he was out for a few days because his mom was getting married? That was her third husband."

Candace hadn't remembered that, but now it was beginning to come back. "Oh. I … You're right. Jeez, I'd forgotten that."

"And now? I think she's on husband number four. It's not like he had a good role model for long-term relationships."

Candace knew Evan's mother a little—a person didn't live in a town this small for this length of time without knowing just about everyone, at least a bit—and she didn't seem dysfunctional. She was pleasant, warm, and always seemed upbeat and happy. But a person's outward persona wasn't the true measure of them, and it didn't mean Evan had enjoyed a happy home life when he was growing up.

"Well … if that's the problem, then I'm sorry," Candace said. "I'm sorry he can't get past his childhood in order to love someone. But I can't keep putting my life on hold just hoping that he'll manage to work it out someday."

"Of course you can't. And you shouldn't."

So she'd move on, finally. She would get another job. She would date someone else.

And she would hope like hell that one day, sometime in the future, if she tried very hard, she might figure out how to stop loving him.

CHAPTER 34

*C*andace gave her notice at Jitters—again—and worked her last two weeks, trying not to pay attention to the way Evan looked at her whenever they were together in the shop.

She considered going through with the job interview with the Brodys, then rejected that idea, reasoning that she would never get past the humiliation of the circumstances under which she'd met four-fifths of them.

For her parents, she made up an excuse for why she'd quit her job.

"I just don't think it's the right line of work for me," she said vaguely when she broke the news to her mother. "My experience is in restaurants, not coffeehouses."

"But that's not true anymore, is it?" her mother asked. "You do have coffeehouse experience now. You went through all of that training, what with the conference and everything."

"I guess," Candace said, then changed the subject.

Once she was finished at Jitters and was officially unemployed, she didn't have anything to keep her busy, so there were no distractions to keep her from thinking about Evan.

The more she thought about him, the more she missed him and the more miserable she became. But she was also more and more certain she'd done the right thing. She needed to move forward with her life, and continuing to love Evan meant she would just keep standing still.

She wanted things. She wanted marriage, a family … and Evan wasn't going to give her any of that. She needed to close off the part of her heart that held him in it and find someone who wanted the same things she did.

"I think I'm going to go back to restaurant work," she told Brittany a couple of weeks after her last day at the coffeehouse. "I hear Neptune is looking for a kitchen manager."

"You could do that," Brittany agreed. They were having coffee at Cambria Coffee Roasting Company during Brittany's morning break from the salon. "Or …"

"Or?"

"Or, you could think about going somewhere else. San Luis Obispo, maybe, or even the Bay Area. I'd hate to lose you, Candace, but as long as you live in Cambria, and as long as Evan lives here, you're going to run into him. And you're going to get that moony-eyed look whenever you do, and afterward, there'll be three days of me trying to put you back together. And God forbid he starts dating someone. Can you really handle that?"

Brittany had a point.

"Thank you, by the way," Candace said. "For all of the times you've put me back together. I don't know if I've ever said how much I appreciate it."

Brittany reached across the table and took Candace's hand. "Hey, I'll keep doing it as long as I have to. That's what best friends are for. It just hurts me to see you in pain over him again and again."

"I know," Candace said, her voice shaky. "I know."

SOMEHOW, she'd imagined that when she and Evan stopped seeing each other, and when she left Jitters, Evan would exist in some state of suspended animation, living but not doing anything of consequence that didn't involve her.

That fantasy had allowed her to table the question of how she might react if he started seeing someone else, and if she had to witness it as she ran into him and his new woman around town.

A few weeks after she'd parted ways with Jitters, when she was still weighing her options about what she wanted to do next, the question stopped being theoretical and became real.

Candace was running an errand for her mother, picking up some milk and laundry detergent at Soto's True Earth on Main Street, when she saw Evan across the street, walking with a tall, shapely brunette, his hand resting on the small of her back.

He didn't see her, thank God.

Candace froze in the doorway to the market, the milk and detergent in her hands, unable to move, think, or speak.

"Hey, lady. I need to get by," someone said from behind her, and she moved aside to let him pass.

She tried to tell herself the woman was just a friend or maybe a customer—but then the brunette turned to Evan, said something Candace couldn't hear from this far away, and laid her head on his shoulder, just for a moment.

Okay, so she wasn't a friend or a customer.

Candace lowered her head, held tight to her purchases, and rushed to her car before he could see her.

Evan had told himself it would be good to date other people now that he and Candace weren't together anymore.

It had seemed like a good idea. He'd welcomed the concept, reasoning that it would make him feel like himself again and not like some hollow shell who was only full and complete when Candace was with him.

But now that he was actually doing it, nothing felt as good as he'd hoped. He felt like he was playing a part—one he was poorly qualified for.

He'd gone out with Erica a couple of times, and she was exactly the kind of woman he used to go for before Candace. Tall, gorgeous, built —and clearly attracted to him. But last night, when they'd gotten to the moment of truth, he hadn't been able to go through with taking her into his bed.

They'd kissed, and it had felt all wrong. Then she'd taken his hand and led him toward his bedroom, and he'd made some excuse about needing to get up early and having a lot on his mind.

Erica had looked doubtful, but he'd ushered her out the door with the promise of meeting her this morning for coffee.

Now here she was, and all he could think was that he looked forward to her leaving.

Candace had broken him, apparently. Now he couldn't function the way he used to before he'd reunited with her. He couldn't do simple things like enjoying a little harmless sexual fun. Which really sucked.

Inside Jitters, he got their drinks—a black coffee for him, a flavored latte for her—and took them to a table in back where Erica was waiting.

He didn't say anything as he got settled into his seat.

"Is everything okay?" She peered at him through thick eyelashes, her doe-brown eyes questioning.

"Sure. Of course." He sipped his coffee, avoiding her gaze.

"It's just … You seem a little distant. A little preoccupied. And last night …" She left it out there, all of the things he'd failed to do, all of the ways in which he'd failed to perform.

He shrugged. "The thing last night? It's just a little soon for me, that's all. I guess I'm kind of an old-fashioned guy."

That was as big a lie as he'd ever told. It wasn't too soon, and he wasn't old-fashioned. One of his greatest pleasures in life had always been jumping into bed with a hot woman as soon as she'd have him. But then Candace had come back into his life and had ruined everything.

"That's sweet." Erica grinned and reached across the table to put her hand on his. "I guess we'll just have to keep seeing each other so we can get there that much sooner."

It should have been the right response. Anyone would have said so. But right now, all he felt at the prospect was dread.

Before he knew what he was doing, he made a stupid tactical blunder: he told the truth.

"Look, Erica. It's not that you aren't ... I mean, you're great. Really. But I recently broke up with someone, and I guess I'm not past it yet. I'm kind of messed up about it, honestly."

"I see." She retrieved her hand, her voice suddenly chilly.

"We could keep doing this and see if things change," he said. "But I don't think they will. Not yet, anyway."

She stood, gathering her purse and picking up her coffee in its takeout cup. "You know, you don't have to make up some bullshit story to get rid of me." She looked down at him with a scowl.

"What are you talking about?"

"The *I just broke up with someone* line is old and tired, Evan. If you're not into me, just say so. It's a lot less embarrassing for both of us." She walked out without waiting for his response.

After all of the lines he'd given to all of the women in his life over the years, he found it ironic that he was being accused of lying the one time he was being painfully honest.

THE BRODYS still hadn't found a receptionist, and Shane called Candace to ask her to reconsider taking the job.

"You haven't found anything else yet," he said. "It's a small town. I hear things."

"Right. I know, but—"

"The pay is competitive. We offer health benefits. If the problem is that thing that happened with Evan, I think you should get past it. We have. Aidan's nose is barely even bruised anymore."

"I appreciate that, but ..." Candace hesitated. The problem was, in fact, Evan, but not in the way Shane thought. She wasn't worried about her embarrassment—at least, that wasn't her main concern anymore. She was worried that if she stayed in Cambria, she'd have her heart torn out over and over again every time she saw Evan with another woman. "I'm looking for work out of town," she said. "I'm thinking about Los Angeles."

She hadn't been thinking of Los Angeles—not specifically—but now that she'd said it, she was. She didn't want to leave her family or the town where she'd lived her entire life, the town she loved like a member of her own family. But she couldn't keep doing this. She couldn't keep living with her feelings exposed and raw for Evan Bridges to abuse.

"Really," Shane said. "I didn't know you were planning to leave. And, incidentally, Brittany doesn't seem to know that, either."

"It was Brittany's suggestion." Candace simply hadn't told her friend that she was going to take it.

BRITTANY CALLED her later that day, probably after hearing from her boyfriend that Candace was planning her big escape from Cambria.

"Oh, jeez. I know I said you should think about it, but it's going to suck not having you here."

"I'll miss you, too." Candace could already feel the tears springing to her eyes at the thought. "But I need a new start somewhere else. Somewhere far from Evan's flavor of the week." It came out more bitter than she'd intended.

"Why should you be the one to leave? He's the asshole, not you. Why shouldn't he leave?"

"Because he owns a business here. I kind of doubt he's going to abandon it at this point."

"I know. I just hate this, that's all."

Candace hated it, too. She hated all of it. And her parents were going to hate it when she told them.

" ... And there are so many more opportunities in LA. I might even go to grad school."

Candace knew that argument would be persuasive to her parents; they'd always encouraged her to continue her education, though she'd mostly brushed them off until now.

Candace and her parents were sitting in their living room, Melissa and Ed on the sofa, Candace across from them in a chair. Candace sat perched on the edge of the cushion, her hands pressed together between her knees.

"Well, honey, I like the idea of you getting a master's degree. But Los Angeles? It's so far away and so expensive. And the traffic ..."

"I know." She nodded agreeably. "But it's full of world-class restaurants. With my experience, I can get a good job, somewhere with potential for advancement."

"I do like the sound of that," Ed admitted.

So far, Candace had kept Evan's name out of it. She wanted her parents to think her decision was smart and rational, not impulsive and emotional. She wanted them to think she was moving toward something, not away from her heartbreak.

Melissa wasn't fooled.

"Honey, are you sure this isn't about Evan Bridges? I know it was hard for you, what with the breakup ..."

"It's not about Evan Bridges," she lied.

Candace didn't like being dishonest with her parents, but the truth was just too humiliating.

"Well, when are you planning to leave?" her father asked.

"I don't know. At this point, I'm just sending out resumes. I'll have to wait to see what happens."

In the meantime, she was staying home as much as possible to avoid sightings of Evan and the brunette. She might have decided to move on, but her heart hadn't yet gotten the message.

ABOUT A WEEK after the incident with Erica, Evan started to wonder why he hadn't seen Candace around town lately.

Sure, they could be just missing each other due to chance. But he'd been giving chance a nudge—showing up in places he knew she frequented, like her gym and her favorite cafe—and he still hadn't seen her.

Where was she? Was she okay?

It wasn't like he was stalking her—that would be creepy and wrong—but he didn't like the way they'd left things, and he wanted a chance to make it right. He didn't know how he might do that, but it wasn't going to happen if he didn't see her.

Not that he felt he'd done the wrong thing in letting her go. He was bad for her—any idiot could see that. He was bad for anyone. He killed relationships—it was what he did—and he didn't want her getting flattened under the steamroller of his emotional failings. No more than she already had, anyway.

And yet, he couldn't seem to stop thinking about her.

"Can you maybe check around?" he asked Nix one day when the two of them were doing a trail run at Fiscalini Ranch. They'd done a few miles, and now they were sitting on a bench, drinking from water bottles and toweling off.

"You want me to spy on your ex-girlfriend for you? And nothing about that sentence sounds wrong?" Nix side-eyed his friend.

"I don't want you to spy on her. Just ... you know. Ask around. Find out if she's okay. See what she's doing. That's all."

"So, spying."

"It's not spying," Evan said, irritated. "Spying would be if you staked out her house with a pair of binoculars and a camera. I just want you to find out if she's okay."

"Who am I supposed to ask?" Nix ran a hand through his shoulder-length hair, which was damp with sweat. "It's not like she and I are besties."

"Oh, for God's sake." Evan turned on the bench to face Nix more fully, the ocean wind on his skin and the blue Pacific Ocean stretching out to the horizon. "Use your imagination. Your wife knows Brittany a little, right?"

Nix shrugged. "I guess. Yeah, maybe she does."

"And Candace's mother comes into the market now and then, doesn't she?"

Nix worked at an organic market on Main Street, and Evan remembered Candace mentioning that her mother liked the produce and the locally produced milk.

"Yeah, shithead. She does. Fine. I'll ask."

"That's all I'm saying."

With that settled, Evan smacked Nix companionably on the back. "You ready to do another two miles? Or are your little girl legs too tired?"

"Bite me," Nix said.

EVAN DIDN'T KNOW what he'd expected Nix to find out. That Candace was seeing that Shane guy, maybe, or that she was staying home at night pining away for Evan. Best-case scenario, she was pining and she'd told Shane Brody to shove his receptionist job up his ass.

Whatever it was, he'd thought he was prepared. But when Nix called him at Jitters a couple of days later and reported what he'd learned, Evan had to sit down to absorb the news.

"She's gone, man. She's in LA."

"What? What do you mean, she's gone?"

"Her mom says she's moving down there."

"She moved? What the hell? She's lived here forever. And now she's just ... gone?"

"It's not a done deal yet, I guess. She's down there now for a few days interviewing for restaurant jobs. Apparently, she's interested in a change of scenery."

Evan knew what Nix meant by *a change of scenery*. Candace was looking for the kind of scenery that didn't have Evan in it.

How had he not seen this coming? Candace had always been a part of Cambria, so he'd assumed she always would be. Just like he'd assumed she would always want him, whenever he was ready to accept what she was so ready to give. Yes, she'd said she was going to move on, and yes, he'd encouraged her to do it. But somehow he'd never imagined she actually would.

"So she's coming back, then." Evan seized on the one hopeful thing in the entire scenario.

"Yeah, in a few days. She hasn't gotten a job offer yet, but she thinks she will. Her mom said she's doing a second interview for a kitchen manager job at this place in Santa Monica."

Evan felt cold dread in the pit of his stomach. His first impulse was to meet her the moment she came back into town and beg her never to leave again. But did he have any right to do that? A job at a restaurant in Santa Monica would provide more opportunities than anything she might get here. Los Angeles was a world away from Cambria—living there would open things up to Candace in a way she'd likely find thrilling. Who was he to take all of that away from her?

"I hope she gets the job," he said, trying to be big about it. "She deserves it."

"You are so full of shit it's coming out your goddamned ears," Nix said.

Evan stood up from his chair in the office at Jitters, then sat down again, not knowing what to do with all of his energy and anxiety. "Dude. What are you talking about? I just want her to do well, that's all."

"You want her to get the job in LA so you won't have to find your balls and take the risk of having a real relationship. You're scared shitless that if she stays and you two decide to be together, you'll get hurt, so you push and push and push at her until she's got no choice but to leave. You're not afraid to take a punch to the face, but love? Oh, hell no. You're not man enough for that. Jesus, the least you can do is admit it."

"Shut up," Evan said.

CHAPTER 35

*C*andace knew it was a coup to get a second interview at Amour et Joie, a French restaurant in Santa Monica that had recently gotten rave reviews in *Food & Wine* magazine. She was qualified, but she had no reputation in LA, and that had made it unlikely she would get a first interview, let alone a second.

But here she was, in her hotel room touching up her makeup, in a skirt, blazer, and heels that she rarely had occasion to wear in Cambria.

She knew what to say, how to act, which accomplishments to play up and which weaknesses in her resume to explain away.

She just didn't know how to actually want the job.

She should want it. She knew that. It would be more money than she earned at Jitters, more prestige, more interesting challenges, more glamor—more everything.

But the only thing she wanted more of was Evan, and Amour et Joie couldn't offer her that.

Get it together, Candace, she coached herself as she fluffed up her hair, straightened her blazer, and got ready to head out to the interview. *Just get your shit together.*

Just because she didn't want the job now didn't mean she wouldn't like it if she got it. She was certain she would love it—eventually.

As she was on her way out the door, her phone pinged with a text from her mother.

Good luck, sweetie! Love, Mom.

And that was another thing: If she took this job, she would be living four hours away from her parents. All her life, they'd been either in the next room or just a short drive away. She relied on them. She felt comforted by her emotional and geographical closeness to them. She didn't want to leave them, and she knew her mother didn't want her to go, despite Melissa's unfailing support of her job search.

Candace told herself it was time she got more independence. She was an adult now, not a child. She didn't need to check in with her mother every day. Even if she really wanted to.

She sent a text thanking her mother, slung her purse strap over her shoulder, and headed to her interview.

HAVING HEARD what Nix had to say about Candace, Evan did the only logical thing.

He Googled Brittany, got her cell phone number from the online White Pages, and called her to get the real story.

"There's nothing to tell, Evan," she said, sounding exasperated. In the background, he heard noises and voices. He'd caught her at work, likely while she was doing someone's hair. "She got an incredible job opportunity—worlds better than her job at Jitters, by the way—and she's in LA checking it out."

"But ... I mean ... Is she committed to moving down there, or is she just, you know ... testing the waters?"

"She's committed to not seeing you prancing around town with every D-cupped bimbo who's dumb enough to be charmed by you," Brittany said. "So there's that."

He pinched the bridge of his nose between his fingers and squeezed his eyes shut. "What are you talking about?"

"Are you telling me you're not seeing other women?"

"Well ... I'm not saying that, but—"

"Did you think she wouldn't *see* you? Or, when she did, that it wouldn't hurt? Or, wait. You just didn't care, did you?" Brittany's voice seethed with scorn.

"Oh," he said.

"Yeah, oh. And now I'm losing my best friend because she's too hurt and heartbroken to live in the same town with you. Nice job, asshole."

Then she hung up on him.

Two things happened to Evan during the phone call with Brittany.

The first was that he went from thinking he had time to change his mind about Candace to being certain it was too late.

He'd fucked it up—irreparably, this time.

The other thing that happened was that he suddenly and with certainty realized Candace had been his one shot at true, pure happiness.

God, the universe, fate—whatever you wanted to call it—had laid everything he'd ever wanted at his feet, and he'd been too stubborn, stupid, and scared to pick it up and take it.

"Shit. Shit. Shit!" He paced the living room at Otter Bluff, his hands entwined in his hair at the top of his head, as though he were trying to keep his skull from flying off of his body.

God, he was a fuckup. He was too much of an idiot to deserve love, especially from someone as perfect as Candace.

If he was miserable for the rest of his damned life, he would deserve it.

He felt as though the light of understanding had finally shone down on him, but he'd dug himself into too deep a hole for the illumination to reach him.

"Fuck. Shit. Goddamn it."

What if it wasn't really too late? What if he could still salvage the situation through sheer force of will? Maybe all of these feelings he was having were his subconscious telling him to get off his ass and do something.

Muttering words of encouragement to himself, he went into his bedroom and began throwing a change of clothes and some toiletries into a bag.

～

"So, I really need to get hold of her, Mrs. Weaver. If you could just tell me where she's staying …"

Evan was on the phone with Candace's mother, and even over the phone line, he could imagine the look of irritation and skepticism on her face.

"Well, Evan, I suggest you call her on her cell phone and ask, and if she wants you to know, she'll tell you."

It was a reasonable enough answer, but he'd tried that, and she hadn't picked up. He'd tried texting, too, and she'd ignored his message.

"I can't seem to get her, ma'am. I really need to ask her something about … about the payroll at Jitters. I need to clear something up from when she was here. It's important, and it'll only take a minute. I thought if I'm not getting through to her cell, I can call the hotel, or the Airbnb or whatever. She'd want you to help me get through to her so I can take care of this. I'm sure she would."

He'd made up the story so easily that it had rolled off his tongue seemingly without conscious thought. The fact that he could fabricate a lie that easily probably bore introspection, but not today.

"Well …"

He could hear her weakening, so he pushed a little bit more.

"Candace told me when she left Jitters that I could call her anytime about the books if I needed her help. She did say that, ma'am." She hadn't said anything of the sort, but he was certain she would have, if pressed.

"All right," Mrs. Weaver said, defeated.

She gave him the name and number of the hotel.

~

HE DIDN'T CALL HER.

He didn't call the hotel, either.

Instead, he got up early the next morning, grabbed the bag he'd packed, got into his car, and headed south on Highway 1 toward Los Angeles.

He couldn't be sure he'd find her. He couldn't be sure she wasn't already on her way back. But what he had to say should be said in person, not over the phone, and certainly not via text message. If he didn't try to find her right now so he could say what he needed to say, he'd regret it the rest of his life.

He might regret it anyway if she shot him down, but he had to at least throw himself into the effort.

~

THE TRUTH WAS, Candace hated Los Angeles.

She hated the traffic, hated the crowds, hated the way all traces of nature had been covered over by concrete. Hell, she even hated the beaches—flat stretches of sand leading to featureless, endless water. Where were the bluffs? Where were the dramatic, rocky shorelines? When you turned your back to the water to look at the hills, where were the trees?

Oh, she knew there was a lot to love about LA, but she wasn't in the mood to feel anything positive about it. She was here for the express purpose of running away from a man, and that covered everything in a pall of gloom and defeat.

Her interview was done, and they'd offered her the job. She knew she should have accepted it enthusiastically, but instead, she'd said she needed to think about it. Relocating and leaving her family was a big step, and she needed to weigh the pros and cons before committing.

She should have been over the moon with excitement. She should have been planning all of the wonders of her new life.

Instead, she felt like crying.

The interview had taken place in the morning, and she got back to her hotel before check-out time. She considered staying an extra night to explore what could be her new neighborhood, look at apartments, and gather more data that would help her make her decision.

Maybe.

She went to her room and changed into casual clothes. Leaving her options open, she packed her things, loaded them into her car, checked out, and confirmed that there were other rooms available should she decide to extend her stay.

Then she went to the hotel restaurant to have an early lunch and consider her next move.

Evan had left home early in the morning, and he'd driven straight through without even stopping for gas or a cup of coffee.

Traffic had been favorable, so he arrived at Candace's hotel at around 11:20 a.m., just after checkout time.

He let the valet park his car and got to the front desk with his heart pounding, knowing that what he was about to do would change his life.

"I need to speak to one of your guests, please. Candace Weaver," he told the woman behind the front desk.

"Do you have a room number?" she asked.

He didn't.

"I'm sorry, sir. I can't do anything without a room number."

"That's ... all right. Wait a minute." He stood aside while the woman helped someone else, and he texted Candace's mother to ask about the room number. She got back to him right away. She didn't know—she hadn't needed it. She'd been in touch with Candace via cell phone, so it hadn't come up.

Well, he hadn't planned to call Candace because he hadn't wanted to warn her he was coming. He hadn't wanted to give her the chance to avoid him. But now it seemed he had no choice.

He tried calling her, but she didn't pick up. Then he tried texting:

Candace, I'm at your hotel and I need to talk to you.

No response.

God, he'd really screwed things up if he couldn't even get her to answer a text like that.

~

CANDACE SAT in a booth at the hotel restaurant and pulled out her phone to check her email. That was when she realized she'd let the battery run down, and the thing was dead.

Oh, well. She had a charger in her car, and she could revive the phone while she drove to wherever she was going next.

The waitress brought Candace her club sandwich, and Candace dug in. She hadn't eaten breakfast because she was too nervous about the interview, and she was starving.

~

EVAN TRIED to figure out what to do.

There was a good chance Candace wasn't even here anymore. Melissa told him the interview had been early—Candace might have checked out. She might already be gone.

If she wasn't gone, she might be anywhere in LA doing God knew what. But he couldn't scour everywhere in the city, so he decided to focus on the hotel. What did they have here? A gym. A pool. A restaurant. A business center. The lobby.

He took them one by one. He followed the signs to the gym and found one guy on a treadmill and a woman who wasn't Candace working the elliptical. The pool contained a couple and two kids. The kids were splashing and screaming with excitement in the water, colorful pool noodles in their grasp.

Business center? He checked, and the place was empty, the printers and computer monitors silent and alone.

That left the restaurant.

Candace was halfway through her sandwich when she got up, told the waitress she'd be right back, and went to use the ladies' room.

She peed, washed her hands, and checked her face in the mirror. She was still wearing her makeup from the interview, and some of her mascara had smudged. She dug a makeup removing wipe from her purse and went to work on fixing it. When she was done with that, she pulled a hair tie out of her bag and started putting her hair up to get it out of her way.

She was in there a while, but so what? She had nowhere to be, and her sandwich wasn't going anywhere.

Evan walked into the restaurant, bypassing the hostess stand as though he knew exactly where he was going and what he would do once he got there.

He tried to come off as though he was just going to his table, maybe to meet a friend who was already seated. Nothing to see here.

He made a circuit of the place: it was mostly empty, but a few tables were occupied. A youngish couple with a toddler. Two older men with cups of coffee. A middle-aged woman working at her laptop. And a table with half of a club sandwich and nobody there to eat it.

Damn it.

He left the restaurant feeling defeated. She wasn't here. He'd come all this way, and he'd missed her.

Then it occurred to him to check the parking lot and see if her car was there. Obvious. Why hadn't he thought of it before?

He went to the front desk and asked about parking, and a guy with a name tag that said CHAD directed him to the visitor parking lot. When Evan corrected him and said he wanted guest parking, Chad asked for his room number. When he didn't have one, Chad said he couldn't give Evan access to the guest parking lot, since it was—as its name implied—for guests only.

His first impulse was to grab Chad by the collar, haul him over the desk, and hold him upside down by his ankles until he let Evan check for Candace's car. Instead, he decided to check in. Why not? He had money to throw at this situation. He might as well throw it.

That seemed like a perfect solution until Chad pointed out that check-in time wasn't for another three hours.

The ankle thing was looking better and better.

CANDACE DECIDED NOT to finish her sandwich, which was enormous, full of bacon, and more calories than she usually ate during breakfast and lunch combined. She paid the check, then headed out the door that led directly to the street instead of using the one that connected to the hotel lobby.

She was keyed up and had so much on her mind that she felt the nervous energy of it coming out her pores.

She wasn't sure whether to take the job, and that meant she wasn't sure whether to stay another night and look at neighborhoods, apartment buildings, rental houses, and other elements essential to relocating to Los Angeles.

What she needed was a good walk.

She strolled along the Third Street Promenade for a while, people-watching and browsing in some of the upscale boutiques. The prices of everything reminded her how expensive it would be to live in LA. Of course, Cambria was expensive, too, and the salary the restaurant was offering her was much higher than what she earned at home.

Santa Monica was bustling with activity; Cambria couldn't offer that kind of excitement and energy. And there were so many attractive men here. If Candace managed to get over her feelings for Evan

—*when, not if,* she reminded herself—she would have more prospects for meeting someone new here.

Damn it, she didn't know what to do.

What she needed was a little bit of fun to get her mind off the weighty decisions she needed to make.

She walked down toward Ocean Avenue, and from there, she went toward the pier.

She'd always wanted to visit the Santa Monica Pier, and now seemed like an opportune time.

EVAN RAISED hell until someone agreed to let him check in early. They found him a room that he didn't even want, and he handed over his credit card. Then he used his key card to access the underground parking garage.

The hotel was big, and there were a lot of cars in the lot. He trotted up one aisle and down another, looking for Candace's gray Prius. If she'd already left, or if she was simply out for the day, seeing the sights or interviewing for another job, all of this would be for nothing. But if he did find the car, he'd know to stick around until she eventually showed up.

By the time he found the car, he'd been about ready to give up. He'd gone up and down every aisle and had been given false hope when he'd spotted not one, not two, but three cars that looked just like Candace's. But hers had a Cambria license plate frame—he'd noticed it when she'd visited Otter Bluff and he'd walked her to her car. None of these had the frame, and he'd looked everywhere.

Then he realized the parking garage had another level below this one.

He jogged down the ramp and began again, going up and down the aisles, scanning for the car.

When he found it, he restrained himself from doing a little victory dance. She was here, either in the hotel or nearby.

He asked himself where she might go if she was in the neighborhood on foot.

The pier was one possibility, the Third Street Promenade the other.

It was a flip of the coin—six of one, half a dozen of the other.

Choose, asshole. Choose.

He dug around in his pocket, found a quarter—and flipped.

CHAPTER 36

*C*andace didn't know why she decided to ride the Ferris wheel. Ferris wheels were for kids, and she wasn't a kid. Still, the idea appealed to her. The view from the top, the rush of wind in her hair, the soaring, weightless feeling as the wheel spun—all of it might get her mind off her troubles. At the very least, it was worth a try.

She bought a ticket, got in line, and felt a little silly going on the ride alone, among the families, couples, and friend groups surrounding her.

When it was her turn, she got seated on the ride while the attendant lowered the safety rail. Then she rose, stopped, and waited while the next rider got on. Rose, stopped, and waited.

EVAN'S COIN-FLIP said he should go to the Third Street Promenade. He headed that way ... and then a gut feeling told him to go to the pier instead. He hadn't always had the best luck following his gut feelings, but in this case, one choice wasn't any better than the other. Chances were that he wasn't going to find Candace, anyway, so it probably didn't matter which way he went.

He began walking toward the pier. Then, he started running.

If she was there, if he was destined to find her, he wanted it soon. He wanted it now. Walking wasn't fast enough to match everything he was feeling.

～

CANDACE ROSE, stopped, and waited again.

She was about halfway up, facing the inside of the wheel, two pairs of feet dangling above her and a flirty, giggling couple across the way, when the ride stopped again to let one set of riders off and another on.

Candace breathed in the ocean air and looked down toward the crowd on the pier. Everyone looked so small from up here. They were all so carefree, so relaxed beneath the clear, bright sky.

Except that one, she thought.

One man amid the crowd was in a hell of a hurry, rushing through the masses of people, his head pivoting this way and that as though he were looking for something or someone.

His size, coloring, and body language reminded her of Evan. Of course, everyone and everything seemed to remind her of Evan. That's how it was when you were heartbroken over someone.

Then he looked up toward the wheel—and a jolt of electricity ran through her.

Oh my God, it's really him.

～

EVAN RAN through the groups of people on the pier, heading toward the end, looking among the faces, searching for the only face he wanted to see.

He'd looked everywhere, and she wasn't here. Inside one of the shops, maybe. Unlikely, but possible. He trotted past the Ferris wheel and looked up to take in the towering height of the thing.

When he spotted her, he thought he might be seeing things, hallucinating because he wanted so badly to find her.

But if he was imagining her, why was she staring at him in shock?

"Candace!" He yelled her name, and just as she opened her mouth to answer him, the wheel started moving again.

Oh, my God.

He was here, and he'd seen her, and he was calling to her. Was it possible that when he'd been running around looking for something, the thing he'd been searching for was her?

The wheel was moving in earnest now, with all of the passengers boarded. She rose higher, higher, looking down at Evan, who was staring up at her. He was yelling something, but she couldn't hear what it was amid the wind and the noises of the pier and the sounds of the ride.

She crested the top and started her descent. At the bottom, she yelled, "Evan!"

And now, closer to him, she could hear what he was saying to her: "Candace, I love you!"

Did I really hear that? Did he really say that?

Upward again, and she was too far away from him to be sure. He was still calling to her, gesturing to her, but his voice was buried under the din.

She swept past the lowest part of the wheel and heard a part of what he was yelling: "Candace, I want—"

But the rest was lost.

As she rode, she watched him run into a shop. A moment later he came out holding something, intently focused on it. Then she saw what it was: a large piece of paper, and he was writing on it.

When she was at the bottom, he held it up, his neat block letters written in thick black marker.

I LOVE YOU. PLEASE COME HOME.

EVAN KNEW he should just wait for the ride to end, then he could talk to her, and she could hear him, and they could work all of this out and then kiss as though they were breathing life into souls that had been, until this moment, mere hollow shells.

But he couldn't wait that long. Now that he finally knew what he wanted, now that he finally had solved the puzzle of where his happiness lay, he didn't want to wait even one more second.

So he'd borrowed the paper and the marker and he'd written a plea to her.

If he had to, once she was off the ride, he would get on his knees and beg.

I LOVE YOU. PLEASE COME HOME.

Six words that contained everything he knew about himself and his heart. Six words that were too long in coming, but hopefully not too late.

CANDACE'S HEART pounded as she waited for the ride to end. When she'd been a kid and had ridden a Ferris wheel at the county fair, the ride had felt impossibly short. Now, it seemed interminable.

Some of her fellow riders had noticed Evan and his note, and they were pointing and talking excitedly, a few peering at Candace from their own seats.

"He loves you!" a guy in the seat above her yelled down.

"What are you going to say?" someone else shouted to her.

She had wanted Evan forever. She couldn't remember a time when she hadn't. But he'd hurt her, and the hurt had been deep and searing, a pain that felt like it might never end.

Much like this ride.

Good God, is this thing ever going to stop spinning?

Evan tried to be patient, but he couldn't. He needed Candace in his arms and in his life right now, not five minutes from now.

He held his sign, prayed, and hoped that he hadn't already screwed up too deeply and irreparably for Candace to change her mind about him. His nerves were rattling him so badly he thought he might throw up.

If he did, that would pretty much scuttle the romantic moment he was hoping for once that damned wheel stopped turning.

After what seemed like forever, the Ferris wheel came to a stop to let its first passengers exit the ride. That left Candace high atop the wheel, waiting for her turn to get off.

Damn it, why couldn't she have been first? Why couldn't that one thing have worked out for her?

At least, now that the wheel wasn't in motion anymore, she could hear what Evan was yelling to her.

"Candace! I love you!" He thrust the sign at her for emphasis.

"What are you doing here?" she yelled back at him.

"I came to find you! When I heard you were gone, I … I knew I'd ruined my chance to really be happy for the first time in my life. So I came for you!"

"Oh, wow. That's really romantic," the woman in the seat below her called up to her.

The wheel lurched forward as another seat moved into place for its exchange of passengers.

"I can't risk you changing your mind and hurting me again!" Candace yelled down.

"Jeez, lady. Give him a chance!" the guy above her, who was sitting with his wife or girlfriend, chimed in.

The wheel moved again, stopped again. With each stop, she was a little closer to Evan and could hear him a little better. He still had to raise his voice for her to hear him, but now he didn't have to yell.

"I'll do anything to prove I'm in it this time. I'm ready," he said.

"But you were seeing someone else."

"That's over. It's over. It never really got started."

"Why?" Candace threw her arms into the air. "What was your excuse for running this time? Why wasn't this one good enough?"

The wheel moved, and now, finally, it was her turn to get off. The attendant lifted the safety bar, and Candace scrambled off of the ride, hurried down the ramp, and emerged to face Evan, the man she'd loved all of her life, the man she'd wanted as much as she wanted to go on living. He was right in front of her, and she wanted to take him into her arms and never let go. But she had to know it was real this time. She had to know he meant it.

"So?" she asked. "What terrible failing did this one have that made you dump her like a pile of trash on the side of the road?"

"I didn't—"

"Just tell me. What didn't she have?"

"She wasn't you." He put his hands on her arms and looked down at her with such adoration that her knees almost gave way. "That's all. She just wasn't you."

A crowd had gathered around them—everyone who'd watched things play out so far and who couldn't leave until the story was done. When Evan pulled her into his embrace and kissed her, they broke into applause and cheers.

Now that Evan had declared himself here in front of God and the crowd at the Santa Monica Pier, he couldn't imagine why he'd been so scared. Everything about this felt right. Everything about it seemed inevitable.

Kissing her, holding her in his arms, Evan forgot anything else existed. Candace was all that mattered. He put everything he had and everything he was into the kiss, hoping she'd know all he was feeling and that she would, at last, trust him. That he would, at last, deserve her trust.

Finally, after what felt like a lifetime, he pulled away, just a little, and touched her face with his fingertips. She was crying and laughing all at once, and he brushed the tears off her cheeks.

"I want to be with you, Candace. Forever. I don't know what took me so long to realize that, but I know it now. Will you give me another chance?"

"Of course I will, you idiot. I love you. I've always loved you."

The crowd erupted into shouts and hoots and applause. Candace, her face flushed with emotion and the ocean breeze, looked more beautiful than she ever had. And she'd always been beautiful, even if he'd once been too stupid to realize it.

"Dude. Can I put this on YouTube?" some guy called out from the group surrounding them.

Evan looked up and saw a guy holding up his phone questioningly.

"Why the hell not?" Evan said.

He was so happy in this moment. If recorded documentation of his joy could bring some of it to someone else, then why shouldn't he allow it?

CANDACE DIDN'T HAVE any way of knowing that Evan wouldn't get cold feet and throw her over for some stacked brunette. She didn't have any guarantee that while he was saying *forever,* what he meant was, *for now.* He might break her heart again. He might crush her, leaving her a broken ruin.

But she was his to ruin. She was his to hurt and break—and to love. She always had been, and she always would be. And if he did break her, she would never regret loving him. She would never regret taking the leap and trusting that the net would appear.

Gazing up into his face, she took one of his hands in hers. "Let's go home," she said.

"Yes," he said. "But ..."

Candace felt a brief moment of panic. "But what?"

He shrugged. "It's just ... I've got a hotel room I don't need. If you're not in a hurry ... you want to try it out?"

She went up onto her toes, entwined her fingers in his hair, and kissed him, pressing her body against his.

It was all the answer either of them needed.

CHAPTER 37

*B*y the time Candace and Evan got back to Cambria, the news was out. Evan had found the video on YouTube, and he'd posted it to his Facebook page, and now all of their friends and acquaintances—and those people's friends and acquaintances—knew about the incident at the pier.

"Why didn't you call me?" Brittany wailed into the phone as soon as she saw the video. "Why didn't you tell me right away?"

"I was too busy having sex," Candace answered.

"You know, smugness isn't a good look on you."

"I can't help it. I have the only thing I've ever wanted, Brit. It's like my teenage fantasies are all coming true."

"As well as your adult fantasies, for that matter," Brittany said.

"Those, too."

Just talking about it, Candace was smiling so hard her face hurt. She'd have to work on that to avoid annoying those who weren't as happy as she was. Which meant pretty much everyone.

"So, what now?" Brittany wanted to know. "I didn't see him get down on one knee and propose in that video."

"No, he didn't. We talked about it, though."

"Oh my God. You did?"

"We did. He asked if I wanted to make a detour on the way home. To Vegas."

"Holy shit. If you got married without me there, I swear to God—"

"I didn't. And I won't. I want to wait. I might be crazy in love, but that doesn't make me stupid. At least, it doesn't make me completely stupid."

Candace had wanted to take him up on the offer—she'd wanted it more than anything. But all she had were his assurances and her own foolishly optimistic heart. What if he got scared again, but this time, it was too late for him to do anything about it? She wanted to be his wife, but she needed him to want it, too. Really want it, in a way that would last the rest of their lives. For the first time, she believed he would get there. But she didn't want to rush him. She needed him to get there on his own.

"Well ... how long do you need to wait?" Brittany asked.

"Six months," Candace said. "If he still wants it in six months, I'll move in with him. And if he still wants it six months after that, we'll get married." They'd talked about it, and that was what Candace had come up with: a one-year escape clause for Evan, should he want it. He swore he wouldn't need it.

"And I get to be your maid of honor, of course," Brittany said.

"Of course."

～

THEY STILL HAD SO much to do.

Candace had met Evan's mother on many occasions, given that they both lived in the same small town where everyone knew everyone else. But she hadn't Met His Mother in the formal sense, as one did when one was heading toward a lifetime with someone's son.

Evan still had to find someone to replace Candace at Jitters, and Candace still had to find a new job.

She'd considered staying at Jitters, but it didn't seem like a good idea. People in a relationship needed space from each other sometimes, and they couldn't have that if Candace was with Evan all day at work and then all night at home.

She was trying so hard to be sensible, and being sensible meant she'd have to keep her work life separate from her home life.

"Evan? I have to ask you something," she said one night when they were in bed at Otter Bluff, naked and covered in a light sheen of sweat from the evening's exertions.

"Yeah?" He turned onto his side to face her.

"Would it bother you if I go to work for the Brodys? Brittany says they hired someone and it didn't work out. So I called, and they're willing to give me another interview. Hopefully, this one won't lead to bloodshed."

"No, it won't bother me."

Her eyes widened. "Are you sure?"

"I'm sure that it *shouldn't* bother me, and I'm trying to be a bigger, more mature man than I've been in the past, so you should do it if that's what you want. And if the interview leads to bloodshed, I promise it won't be because of me."

She leaned forward and kissed him, and the kiss led to other things, and the talking trailed off until they were communicating in other ways that were more direct and infinitely more pleasant.

"DUDE. That YouTube thing? It ruined everything for the rest of us guys," Nix said. "You've raised the romance bar too damned high. We should all kick the crap out of you."

The two of them were at Otter Bluff, drinking beer and watching a movie on a night when Candace was doing some kind of girls' night with Brittany.

"You're just jealous," Evan said.

"I'm not, because I'm in a committed, loving relationship with the woman of my dreams."

"Hey. Me, too."

"Welcome to the club," Nix said. "The entry fee is high but the perks are worth it."

"So ..."

"So?"

Evan shifted uncomfortably on the sofa. "You'll be my best man, right?"

Nix sat up straighter. "Oh, crap. You proposed?"

"Not yet, but I'm going to."

"When?"

He shrugged. "Candace says she'll marry me if I still want to a year from now. I'm supposed to wait until then to propose. But ... man, I can't wait that long. Now that I know what I want ... I'm ready to just start having that, you know?"

"Yeah." Nix nodded. "I get it. But one of the things about Candace that makes her good for you? She's no fool. She wants you to be sure. Because you haven't always been sure in the past, and if you're not now ..."

"I'm sure."

He'd never been this sure about anything.

They settled in and watched the movie a little bit, and then Evan said, "So you think I need to wait?"

"I think she told you what she needed, and you should respect that."

"Yeah. Yeah, okay."

Evan wasn't big on waiting, but Candace had been waiting since kindergarten. She'd waited for him, and she'd loved him, and he'd let her down again and again. He wasn't going to let her down this time, and if she needed him to show her that for a year before she would be his wife, then he'd show her.

If she needed him to wait, he would wait.

He would be here for her in six months, in a year, in twenty years and beyond.

He finally knew his place in the world, and that place was beside Candace. Knowing it gave him a sense of peace he'd never known. And so, he would wait forever if he had to.

"You think I should take her back to the Ferris wheel when it's time to pop the question?" Evan asked.

Nix looked at him like he was stupid. "Well, obviously."

Evan could already see it in his mind. He could already hear Candace saying yes as the Ferris wheel turned above them. He could see their children on the ride one day, soaring above the ground and crying out in glee. He could see them all as a family visiting that same spot for anniversaries, birthdays, for decades into the future, their lives together bound by the moment in time when Evan had let go of his fear and had reached out to Candace.

That moment when he'd said, I LOVE YOU. PLEASE COME HOME.

And, miraculously, she had.

www.ingramcontent.com/pod-product-compliance
Lightning Source LLC
Chambersburg PA
CBHW030103260626
47156CB00008B/2500